Annja looked Bryant ... *said, "I'm going to kill you."*

Bryant was obviously taken aback. "You're welcome to try," he said after a moment, laughing it off.

Jones scowled at the other man and then turned his attention back to her. "Dr. Crane told us about the clues my father left to the location of the Lost City. Be a good girl and turn them over now, why don't you?"

Annja stared at him without saying another word.

"Uncooperative to the end. I expected no less," Jones said with a smile. "So be it." He extended a hand toward Bryant, who was already in the process of passing him something.

Realizing what it was, Annja charged—but she was far too late. She made it three steps before the dart took her high in the chest, near her neck.

She managed another step before darkness closed in and she crashed to the ground.

Titles in this series:

ROGUE AngEl™

Alex Archer

THE VANISHING TRIBE

A GOLD EAGLE BOOK FROM

WORLDWIDE®

TORONTO • NEW YORK • LONDON
AMSTERDAM • PARIS • SYDNEY • HAMBURG
STOCKHOLM • ATHENS • TOKYO • MILAN
MADRID • WARSAW • BUDAPEST • AUCKLAND

Recycling programs
for this product may
not exist in your area.

First edition May 2013

ISBN-13: 978-0-373-62162-0

THE VANISHING TRIBE

Special thanks and acknowledgment to
Joe Nassise for his contribution to this work.

Printed in U.S.A.

The
LEGEND

...THE ENGLISH COMMANDER TOOK
JOAN'S SWORD AND RAISED IT HIGH.

The broadsword, plain and unadorned,
gleamed in the firelight. He put the tip against
the ground and his foot at the center of the blade.
The broadsword shattered, fragments falling
into the mud. The crowd surged forward,
peasant and soldier, and snatched the shards
from the trampled mud. The commander tossed
the hilt deep into the crowd.
Smoke almost obscured Joan, but she continued
praying till the end, until finally the flames climbed
her body and she sagged against the restraints.

Joan of Arc died that fateful day in France,
but her legend and sword are reborn....

PROLOGUE

Humphrey stumbled forward.

It took everything he had to put one foot in front of the other, but he persisted despite the immense effort it required, knowing that if he did not, if he stopped and let himself rest, the likelihood of getting up again was practically nonexistent.

The knife wound in his shoulder had become infected two days ago. *Or was it three?* He was no longer certain. The days began to blur together as the pain spread and his fever grew. To make matters worse, he couldn't trust his ability to recognize the passage of time. Twice now he'd come to his senses to find himself stumbling through unfamiliar territory, his body powering him onward while his brain had been on hiatus. He had no way of knowing how long he'd been disoriented. He'd left his watch back in camp when he'd run for his life.

Not that he could have focused on his watch; his vision was growing progressively more blurry as the afternoon wore on. Possibly the glancing blow he'd taken to the side of the head during his escape hadn't been that glancing, after all. He was too experienced an explorer to ignore the possibility of concussion. The infection in his arm would greatly reduce his chances of survival. Adding a concussion on top of that and he might as well pronounce himself dead on the spot, regardless of whether or not he was still breathing.

The expedition had started out well enough. The map had been a godsend; Farini had laid out the steps they were to follow with a surveyor's precision, and Humphrey had taken his team from one waypoint to the next with minimal difficulty. Each time they'd located another of Farini's landmarks, Humphrey had grown more convinced they would find the Lost City of the Kalahari. Just as Farini and his son had done nearly a century earlier.

Everything had been progressing just as planned. That was, until Barnes shot the San tribesman.

The mean-hearted bastard claimed it was an accident. But Humphrey had overheard talk of "bagging a trophy," as if the natives of the Kalahari, a society that had existed for thousands of years practically untouched by modern influences, were no better than the wildlife around them.

Clearly Barnes hadn't anticipated just how fiercely the tribe would react.

They had awoken the morning after the San's death to find the tires on all their vehicles slashed and all their gas tanks punctured and empty. A look under the vehicles' hoods had revealed even more damage. While the destruction was bad enough, what frightened Humphrey was the fact that all this had been done while the men slept only a few feet away. Not one of them had heard the San.

Humphrey knew he had entirely lost control of the

expedition at that point. His pleas to try to communicate with the tribesmen had been shouted down by the more militant members of his entourage and soon there had been a minicoup as he was supplanted in his role of expedition leader by none other than that idiot, Barnes.

Fool. He deserved everything he'd gotten as a result.

They'd tied Humphrey's hands and lashed him to a nearby baobab tree to keep him from interfering as they'd settled into defensive positions around the camp, ready for the tribesmen should they return.

Stumbling along, Humphrey shook his head at the memory. The San had come with a vengeance and within moments of their arrival the entire camp had been engulfed in chaos. He knew he would never forget the sight of the San leader on a massive bull elephant as it reared over Barnes, ready to crush him with its forelegs.

Humphrey had somehow managed to free himself from his bindings and fight his way out of the camp. The knife wound had come from one of his own men. The possible concussion was a gift from a San tribesman with a club made of elephant bone.

Humphrey had been on the run since.

The Kalahari Desert was not a forgiving place and even in his fevered state he knew that if he didn't find help and shelter soon he wouldn't live to see next week. Initially, he thought he could make his way back along the path to where they had encountered a group of Dutch naturalists, but that plan fell by the wayside once he lost track of where he was and what direction he was traveling in.

It took everything he had just to keep moving forward.

A full moon—when had it become night?—gave him just enough light to avoid the major obstacles in his path. Not that there were all that many; aside from the occasional baobab tree, the Kalahari was pretty much flat pans and scrubland. He used the moon as a guide, stumbling toward it to prevent himself from traveling in circles. It wasn't the most effective compass bearing, but it was big and bright and easy to find in his fevered state, which was about as much as he could hope for.

At the incongruous sound of laughter to his right, Humphrey spun in that direction, nearly toppling to the ground. All he saw was the mottled brown back of an animal keeping pace with him.

Before he could begin to panic, he heard the laughter again, this time to his left. A similar animal was tracking him on that side, as well.

Fear pooled in his belly.

Hyenas.

In that moment Humphrey knew he was going to die here.

He'd been in Africa long enough to recognize the laughter for what it was, a hyena call to alert the clan of a food source.

In minutes he would be surrounded. Contrary to popular belief, hyenas were not cowardly or timid animals. In fact, they could be both bold and dangerous. They were no doubt sizing him up, smelling his blood, sensing his sickness, and it wouldn't be long before one of them grew daring enough to try to take a bite.

He couldn't outrun them. His only hope was to find a

place where he could hole up away from them and wait for the clan to grow bored and wander away.

In other words, he needed a miracle.

Humphrey staggered on, lost in delirium, and when he came to his senses next his two hyena companions had grown to a pack of six or more. They moved through the scrub on all sides of him, their yipping and howling letting everything within a half mile know that he was their prey and to keep back.

Tears began to course down his cheeks, matching the blood now running down his arm as his exertion reopened his shoulder wound. *One foot in front of the other. One foot in front of the other.*

The lead hyena, a big female that had to weigh a good one hundred and twenty pounds, dashed toward him from the side. He turned to face her, waving his arms and screaming, and she broke off her charge, disappearing into the darkness.

The attacks would become more frequent now, more aggressive.

He glanced around, searching desperately for something, anything, that could help him, when his gaze fell upon a large baobab tree about a hundred yards off to his left. He angled his path in that direction.

The hyenas swooped in twice along the way, the last time coming within just a few feet of him before turning aside. The next time Humphrey wouldn't be so lucky. He wanted to shout for joy when he reached the massive trunk of the baobab tree. He couldn't climb it—the nearest branches were thirty feet above his head—but with his back against it he would at least be safe from an attack from behind.

Humphrey had reached the end of his rope. His legs wouldn't even hold him upright anymore; he slid to the ground, his feet splayed out before him. His hands fell on some of the hard baseball-size fruit scattered at the base of the tree and he snatched them up. They were a poor excuse for a weapon but they would have to do.

He got to test them out a few seconds later as the first of the hyenas made a cautious approach, sticking its head out of some nearby brush and baring its teeth at him. Summoning as much strength as he could, Humphrey threw one of the fruits at the hyena's head.

Fate was with him. He struck the hyena's nose, startling it enough that it retreated into the scrub. Unfortunately, the effort to throw with that kind of accuracy also drained him. He'd be able to manage the stunt once, maybe twice, more.

The hyenas, it seemed, weren't going to give him the chance, though. Three of them advanced out of the brush, snarling and growling as they cautiously made their way forward. He tried shouting and yelling, but it did no good.

Without looking away from the advancing beasts, he felt around on the ground beside him until he found a good-size rock. He clutched it, determined to defend himself to the last.

The hyenas crept forward, their muzzles low to the ground, their lips pulled back.

Suddenly the lead hyena's ears pointed forward. A moment passed and then the trio turned as one, dashing into the darkness.

Even in the depths of his fever, Humphrey knew their sudden departure wasn't a good sign. Only a lion or some other large predator could make a pack of hyenas abandon an all-but-certain kill. The way they'd run off without even the slightest resistance told him that, whatever it was, it was much bigger and nastier than the hyenas.

He gripped his makeshift weapon tighter and prepared for the worst.

A minute passed.

Two.

Humphrey's vision swam and his head began to sag toward his chest as darkness sought to drag him down. He shook it off for what felt like the hundredth time since escaping the camp, determined to meet his death when it came.

As his vision cleared he jerked back with a start.

A San tribesman was squatting a few feet in front of him, watching him with eyes as emotionless as slate. He wore nothing but a loincloth, the rest of his skin covered with some kind of muddy paste that would make it easy for him to blend into the background. In his left hand he held a spear, the butt of which rested on the ground, the tip pointing skyward.

Without a change of expression the San warrior raised his other hand to his mouth and blew through it.

Humphrey watched a cloud of dust burst from the man's closed fist and before he could stop himself he'd breathed the powder into his lungs.

His throat closed up immediately.

He fought to take in another breath, but it was no use. The darkness closed in quickly, his view of the

San warrior in front of him swiftly dwindling until all he could see was the man's dark eyes.

Then the darkness claimed him entirely.

1

"Did you hear that?"

Annja glanced across the platform to where her cameraman, Lenny Davis, was seated. In the dim light he was hard to see—his dark skin and hair blended nearly perfectly with the night around them—but she knew where he was because they'd both been sitting in the same place for two weeks. Right now, though, the vibe he was giving off was very different from his usual laid-back attitude. Something clearly had him spooked.

"I didn't hear anything," she told him, which was the truth, though that was most likely because she'd been daydreaming about getting out of this fetid swamp. After being here for this long, who could blame her?

The two were deep in the Jiundu swamp in northwestern Botswana, following up on a recent rash of bat men sightings and trying to catch some footage of the alleged creature. It was their latest assignment for *Chasing History's Monsters,* the cable television show Annja cohosted. The show focused on exactly what its name indicated—historical madmen, psychopaths, serial killers and even legendary monsters—hence the reason they were on a platform ten feet off the ground using low-light cameras to try to catch a glimpse of what their producer, Doug Morrell, was calling the "scoop of the century." Of course, he'd said the same thing about the past three assignments he'd sent them on. Including one where he'd had them trying to film the ghost of a man-eating great white shark off the coast of Indonesia, which was why Annja didn't place much stock in his assessment. Investigating murderous ghosts was one thing; investigating the ghosts of murderous sharks was something else entirely.

Annja was five feet ten with chestnut hair beneath her favorite Yankees baseball cap. Dressed in a pale blue tank top, khaki shorts and hiking boots, she stretched her legs out in front of her, trying to keep from cramping.

"There it is again!" Lenny climbed to his feet, silhouetted in the dim moonlight. "Listen."

This time, Annja did hear something. It was faint, hard to decipher over the typical night noises coming out of the swamp. Like the sound of…the flapping of large wings?

"I hear it," she told him.

But what the heck was it?

She didn't think for a moment that it was an actual bat man; she was expecting to find a perfectly natural explanation for the so-called sightings that had occurred over the past several months. An unusually large vulture, perhaps, or maybe some unknown species of bird, driven out of the deeper swamps by the recent rainy season. Either would make far more sense than the mysterious bat people Doug was convinced were hiding here.

She rose to her feet and tried to get a fix on the

sound. It was getting louder, and therefore closer, but she couldn't pin down which direction it was coming from. It seemed to bounce off the trees and water all around them. The quarter moon wasn't much help, either; what little light it cast added more shadows than it illuminated.

"Behind you!" Lenny cried, and Annja turned just in time to see a dark winged shape swoop down at her from the nearby tree line with stunning speed.

She didn't stop to think, dropping into a crouch and bringing her arms up over her head to protect herself as the thing flew past. She quickly got back to her feet, but it had already disappeared into the darkness.

"What the hell was that?" Lenny asked in shock.

Annja didn't have any answers. She'd barely gotten a glance at it. What she had seen left her with the impression of a winged creature about the size of a large child, but that could just as easily have been her imagination filling in the blanks for what she hadn't seen.

Of course, it could also be the very thing they'd come here to find.

The bat men of Botswana.

"Get those cameras rolling, Lenny," she said as she moved from side to side, trying to catch a glimpse of the creature.

Her suggestion was unnecessary. Lenny was already all over his equipment. "Cameras one, two and three are live," he reported. "Four is giving me some trouble but I should have it online in another moment or two."

"Good. We don't want to miss this thing a second—"

"Look out!" Lenny yelled, but his warning came too late. Annja was turning when she felt claws rake her left shoulder. Pain flared down her arm. And then the thing was gone again. Quickly taking stock, she could feel blood beginning to seep down her back but didn't want to lose her night vision by turning on a light to inspect the injury. She'd deal with it later.

First things first.

If it came back, which it most likely would, this time she would be prepared to meet it on its own terms. She'd been using a walking stick to help her navigate the uncertain terrain of the swamp for the past few days and she snatched it up now, holding it before her in two hands like a baseball bat.

"Do you see it?" she asked.

Lenny didn't respond. He was standing with his back to her, fumbling with something in front of him that she couldn't see and muttering darkly under his breath.

Something wasn't right.

The strange buzzing sound the creature made whenever it swiped at them. The lack of aerobatics from a creature supposedly born to fly. Her companion's current distraction.

The answer, when it came to her, seemed so obvious she was surprised it had taken her so long to figure it out.

Lenny straightened and, without turning, said, "It's coming back, I think!"

This time, Annja was ready for it.

She could hear the swoop of its wings as it approached. Underneath that, though, was the same dull whine she'd noticed before. She had some idea what was causing that sound now and she intended to put her theory to the test.

"Here it comes again!" Lenny yelled, and suddenly the creature was diving at them for the third time that night.

This time, Annja was ready for it. She brought her staff around in a vicious swing, getting the full force of her hips into it, like a baseball batter determined to knock the ball clear out of the park.

"No, Annja!" Lenny shouted, but it was too late.

Her strike was right on the money.

She heard a loud crunch, felt the shock of the blow reverberate all the way up her arms and saw the creature go careering off in an uncontrolled spin. A moment later there was a loud crash ten feet below them.

Not a thud, but a crash.

Annja headed for the ladder.

"What are you doing?" Lenny called.

"Putting an end to this right now," she replied. She descended from the platform and then pulled her flashlight out of her pocket. Flipping it on, she cast about for a few minutes before locating the object she'd struck with her staff. She hurried over and shone her light on the wreckage.

The so-called bat man was in reality nothing more than a medium-size drone with a pair of motorized wings and some special effects added to give the suggestion of something more when glimpsed in the near-dark. Knowing that, it didn't take a genius to put two and two together. After spending days on end with nothing to show for it, Lenny must have been ordered to use the drone so the trip wouldn't be a complete waste. After all, footage of some barely seen flying creature was better than no footage at all, right? She knew just the producer who would think that way, too.

She looked up as Lenny finally joined her. Her expression must have reflected a fair bit of what she was feeling, because he winced.

"I think you have some explaining to do," she said through clenched teeth.

He held up his hands in a placating gesture. "Would you believe this was all Doug's idea?"

She would, she would indeed.

2

The sun woke Annja just after nine the next morning. She tried to go back to sleep, thinking she deserved a few more hours after the fiasco of the night before, but found she just couldn't. Bowing to the inevitable, she rose, dressed and ran through her usual routine of morning stretches to awaken her body in preparation for the harder exercise to follow.

After listening to Lenny's explanation about the drone the night before, Annja had decided she was done with the episode and stalked back to their rented Nissan SUV. Lenny had followed sheepishly in her wake. The ride back to their hotel had passed in silence, and Annja had retired to her room as soon as they arrived. There she finally got a chance to look at the shoulder wound. It turned out to be minor—a deep scrape most likely caused by the outer edge of the drone's wing as it swept past her. She cleaned it out, bandaged it and fell into bed exhausted.

This morning her arm was a little stiff but she quickly worked out the kinks as she ran through her warm-up exercises. When her muscles were good and limber, she reached into the otherwhere and drew forth her sword. It sprang into being in her hand with the speed of thought, fully formed, the hilt already warm to her touch as if she'd only been holding it seconds before. Who was to say she hadn't been? For all she knew time ran differently in the otherwhere—the mysterious place where the sword stayed until she pulled it out. Days here might be the merest microseconds there. Only one thing was certain. The sword was always there, waiting for her.

Her life hadn't been the same since that fateful day when she'd brought the broken, scattered pieces of the sword together for the first time since their original owner, Joan of Arc, had been burned at the stake five hundred years earlier. The sword had miraculously reformed in a flash of power right before her very eyes and, in some strange way she still didn't understand, had chosen her to be its next bearer.

The role came with its own unique set of responsibilities, protecting the innocent first and foremost among them. Her innate sense of justice seemed amplified when she carried the sword and as a result she'd found herself in any number of situations others would have walked away from. Numbers didn't matter, nor did the odds; what mattered was that she acted whenever possible to defend those who couldn't defend themselves.

It wasn't a life she would have chosen for herself, but now that she was in it, she couldn't imagine doing anything else.

Annja slipped into a series of movements designed to continue honing her already considerable skills with the weapon. Kata after kata flowed out of her as naturally as water from a spring and Annja quickly found herself lost in the synergy of thought and motion, becoming one with the sword in such a way that it ceased being a separate object but was instead an extension of herself. When she finally slowed to a stop over an hour later, she felt energized and ready to take on the day.

She released the sword back into the otherwhere, marveling at the way it vanished in the blink of an eye. She showered, changed and left the hotel behind, looking for a place to eat.

Upon arrival in Botswana, they had set up a base of operations in Maun, the district capital of northwestern Botswana that served as the jumping-off point for exploration of the Okavango Delta to the north and the Makgadikgadi Salt Pans to the east. What had once been a small village along the wide banks of the Thamalakane River had grown over the past couple of decades into a town of some forty thousand people. It was an interesting mixture of the old and the new, where hotels, lodges and even a rental car facility vied for room with square cinder-block homes with tin roofs and an infestation of donkeys and goats every morning when the local farmers brought their goods to market. Annja found a small café just down the street from the hotel and had a leisurely breakfast of fresh fruit and toast.

While she ate she eyed her cell phone, debating whether to call Doug now or wait until later. She was still pretty ticked off about the events of the night before but the sooner she dealt with this, the sooner she could move on to whatever was next on the agenda. She couldn't imagine going back to the swamp again.

When her breakfast was over, she snatched up her cell phone, dialed the familiar New York number and waited.

"Doug Morrell."

"What do you think you're doing?"

Doug recognized her voice, but not her tone. "Right now?" he asked. "I'm drafting a memo to Marketing about—"

"Don't give me that nonsense," Annja interrupted. "You know exactly what I'm talking about."

"Um, actually, I don't," Doug said. "I can hear that you're upset, Annja, but—"

"Of course I'm upset! Did you think I wouldn't find out?"

"Find out about what? I really don't understand—"

"You had the special-effects department create a simulated bat man and coerced my cameraman into using it when it looked like we wouldn't get any real footage. Something I told you would happen before we even left the States."

There was a moment of silence, and then Doug said, "I have no idea what you are talking about, Annja."

The smile that crossed her lips at his suddenly flat tone was almost predatory. "Good," she said. "Then you certainly won't mind that I practiced my Babe Ruth impression on it with my hiking staff and knocked it out of the sky in midflight."

"Wha-a-at?" Doug shrieked. "Are you insane? Do you have any idea what that thing cost? Effects is going to kill me, never mind what Accounting will do to my budget…."

"I thought you had no idea what I was talking about?"

Silence.

"Um, you see…" Doug finally stuttered.

This should be good.

"Ah, it was strictly a backup plan. You know, just in case the bat men were migrating or something...."

Annja let him babble for several minutes as she sipped her coffee. Doug had tried to enhance—his word, not hers—her shows with special effects in the past and each time she'd soundly shot him down. This time he'd conspired to do it behind her back, with her cameraman, no less.

A message needed to be sent.

"...and so I took it upon myself to support you—"

"Doug?"

"Yes, Annja?"

"I'm taking the day off, Doug. I'm going to do a little shopping, eat out at an expensive restaurant and generally enjoy myself in an effort to forget that you just tried to pull off a mechanical bat man. All of which will be coming out of your budget, of course. Come tomorrow, when I'm in a better mood, we'll talk about what we're going to do next. Understood? Good."

She could hear Doug spluttering for a reply in the background as she disconnected.

She finished her coffee, paid the check and then stepped out the door. There were several clothing stores around the café where she'd just had breakfast. If she didn't find anything there, she would wander back past the hotel to the large outdoor bazaar that filled the streets for several blocks in that direction.

The first couple of stores didn't have anything that interested her, but the third one was full of fabrics dyed in brilliant hues and she quickly fell in love with several items. The proprietor, a woman a few years younger than Annja, took particular pride in showing her around the shop. She quickly found her irritation at Doug and the events of the night before slipping away in the wake of the young woman's enthusiasm over helping her. In the end Annja bought several brightly colored tops and even a beautifully cut sundress just to show her appreciation.

She was headed out of the shop when a small white sign stuck in the corner of the window caught her eye. She leaned closer for a better look.

Public Notice of Auction
Personal Effects of Explorer
and Adventurer Extraordinaire
Robert C. Humphrey
Willoughby's Auction House
10:00 a.m., Today Only

Robert Humphrey. She knew that name.

A glance at her watch told her it was a few minutes before ten. If she hurried, she might just make it.

She stepped back inside the shop.

"Forget something, miss?" the proprietor asked.

"Willoughby's Auction House. Is it far?"

"No, miss, not far at all. Four blocks up on the right," she said, pointing for emphasis. "Above the post office."

"Thanks."

Annja hurried up the street. The post office wasn't hard to find and a quick question to one of the locals standing in line outside brought her around the side of the building where a staircase led up to the second floor. A door at the top opened up into a wide room that was clearly the site of the event, if the large Willoughby's banner across the back of the room was any indication.

The auction was already under way when Annja slipped inside and found a seat in the back. She was surprised by the turnout. About two dozen people, many of them clearly not locals, filled the rows of chairs in front of the auctioneer's podium. As each new item was introduced, a pair of assistants would hold it up in front of the group. At the same time a large image of the item was projected onto the wall behind the auctioneer.

The sale moved along briskly and Annja was amazed not only by the scope and variety of the items up for bid but also the amounts individual buyers were willing to pay for them.

Humphrey, she remembered, had once been a highly respected adventurer. He'd been the height of celebrity back in the mid-eighties, thanks to a series of well-publicized activities such as climbing—without oxygen—the highest mountain on each continent, dog-sledding solo across the South Pole and breaking the record for circumnavigating the earth by hot-air balloon. He'd even hit the top spot on *People* magazine's Most Eligible Bachelor list five years straight.

Then a tabloid paper had revealed that Humphrey had sunk several million dollars into an effort to prove the existence of the abominable snowman, or yeti. The public had laughed it off. Celebrities, even men like Humphrey, were allowed their pet projects, it seemed. But then other reporters began digging deeper and it quickly became apparent that Humphrey had more than just one pet project. UFOs. Pyramid power. Bigfoot.

Nessie. The hollow earth theory. Name just about any subject on the outer edge of science and myth and Humphrey was involved in it somehow. When the information came to light, he went public with his enthusiasm for all things esoteric and paranormal. That had pretty much sealed his doom. The reporters went on a feeding frenzy, like sharks in a pool of chum. Humphrey had withdrawn from the public eye for many years. From time to time you would hear that he was involved in some crazy expedition or another, like the time he'd tried to retrace the route taken through the Amazon jungle by Colonel Percy Fawcett in his quest to find the ancient city known only as "Z."

Listening in on the conversations around her, Annja learned that Humphrey had been living here in Maun for at least the past ten years, possibly longer. He'd disappear into the outback for weeks at a time, hunting for who knew what.

Maybe he'd been looking for the bat men of Jiundu, as well, she thought wryly. He'd certainly chased crazier ideas than that.

He and his entire expedition had disappeared two years ago while chasing down the legend of the Lost City of the Kalahari, an ancient city of enormous proportions supposedly built by the ancestors of the modern-day San tribesmen. Given that the San had been one of the most nomadic people on the planet, Annja found the idea that they'd built a massive city in the desert ludicrous. Then again, Humphrey and even *Chasing History's Monsters* had certainly searched for stranger things.

She was just about to get up and make her way out of the auction when a new item was introduced that caught her eye. It was a small drawing on what looked to be old parchment paper, mounted in a simple wooden frame.

"Our next piece shows an artist's representation of Lake Makgadikgadi in its heyday, somewhere around twenty thousand years ago. Mr. Humphrey's records indicate that this drawing was done by a man named Gilarmi Farini in 1895, though we have not been able to substantiate the claim. Is it possible? Certainly! Is it likely? I'm afraid I can't answer that. So, let's start the bidding on this fine piece at fifty dollars. Do I hear fifty?"

On impulse, Annja raised her hand.

"Fifty dollars from the lady in the eighth row. Do I hear seventy-five? Seventy-five dollars?"

A man a few rows in front of Annja raised his hand.

"Seventy-five, it is! Can I get one hundred? One hundred dollars?"

A sudden sense of need ran through Annja, so sharp it was almost painful, and while she didn't understand it she decided to listen to it. Her hand went up a second time.

"One hundred dollars! Do I hear one twenty-five?"

For a moment Annja thought the man a few rows ahead of her was going to bid again, but he must have thought better of it. He let the moment pass.

"One twenty-five, do I hear one twenty-five? No? Then it's one hundred dollars going once, one hundred dollars going twice, and sold to the woman in the eighth row!"

No sooner had the auctioneer's gavel rung out than

the doors in the back of the room were thrown open and a man rushed inside.

"Stop!" he shouted. "Stop right now!"

3

He was a big man, both in height and weight. Annja guessed he was a good six-two, maybe six-three, and an easy three hundred pounds. His blond hair fell just over the collar of his white Panama suit, and his blue eyes, a shade darker than his robin's-egg-colored shirt, were wide. Annja put his age somewhere around thirty.

He rushed down the center aisle toward the auctioneer, a mountain of a man moving with far more dexterity than Annja would have imagined possible. "That drawing belongs to me!"

The auctioneer cocked his head to one side and somehow still managed to look down his nose at the newcomer. "I'm sorry, sir, but you are too late."

"Too late?" he shouted. "Do you have any idea who I am? That drawing belongs to me, I tell you!"

"And I'm telling you, sir," the auctioneer replied, "that the image belongs to the young lady in the eighth row who just legally purchased it."

Annja watched as the big man spun around, his gaze first seeking and then finding her in her seat.

She watched as the big man stalked toward her. She could see he was younger than she'd first thought, definitely closer to twenty than thirty, but that still didn't give her any clue as to who he was or why he thought the drawing belonged to him.

She recognized the type, though.

Spoiled brat.

Annja had to hold back a smirk, realizing that any minute she was going to get a good look at that same behavior from a much closer vantage point and she didn't want to antagonize him any more than necessary.

He stopped and stood over her, glaring down. "That drawing belongs to me."

If it had been any other day, Annja might have let his rudeness go. She might have even tried to work something out with the auction house, as she didn't have an attachment to the drawing she'd purchased. The man in front of her clearly did. She might have tried to ease herself out of the situation before the confrontation blew up in her face.

But after the night she'd had, she wasn't all that interested in playing the peacemaker.

The idiot in front of her didn't know when to back off, either. "I said, that—"

"I know what you said," Annja replied, letting some steel seep into her voice, "but I'm afraid I have to disagree. The art belongs to me. If you wanted it, you should have been here on time to bid on it."

He scowled as he asked, "Do you know who I am? Do you have any idea how difficult I can make things for you?"

Annja laughed; she couldn't help it. If she had a dollar for every time a man like him had tried to intimidate her with his wealth or power, she'd be richer than her billionaire friend, Roux.

He leaned in close and shoved a finger in her face. "You have no idea what you've gotten yourself into."

Without a change of expression she reached up, grabbed his finger and twisted it. Then she stood. He'd have to be willing to let her break his finger if he didn't want to move in the direction she forced him to move and it was quickly obvious that he didn't have the stomach for that.

Annja applied pressure to his finger in such a way that he was forced to let her lead him.

"Didn't your mother teach you not to point?"

She was about to lead him down the aisle and out the doors when she heard the sound of running. She glanced up as four men in blue shirts and black slacks crossed the room toward her.

"Security, miss," one of them said. "We're here to escort Mr. Porter out."

"Be my guest," Annja told them as they grabbed his arms and pulled him away.

He didn't fight them, choosing instead to simply glare at Annja as they led him away.

She gave him a smile and a wave, just to show she wasn't intimidated in the slightest.

"Are you all right, miss?" a man at her elbow asked. She turned to find the auctioneer beside her, a solicitous look on his face.

"I'm fine. Really." She paused, then asked, "Did you know him?"

"Unfortunately. That's Malcolm Porter, the son of the late Mr. Humphrey. He's been calling our offices for weeks, ever since his father was officially declared dead, determined to get his hands on the man's property. But the will was quite clear that it was all to be auctioned off."

Family dynamics. Now, there was something Annja would never understand. She hadn't had one of her own. She'd been raised by nuns in an orphanage in New Orleans and had left as soon as she'd been legally able to. She swept the thought aside; it just wasn't a part of her life that she liked to think about and now was definitely not the time.

"Well, thank you for your concern," she told him. "I'd best be going."

"You can pick up your item in the next room," he told her, pointing to the connecting doorway not too far from where she had been sitting. "And might I suggest using the back stairwell rather than the front one. No telling what Porter will be up to and once you're off the property there is little we can do to stop him."

"Of course. Thanks again."

She bid him goodbye, double-checked she had her cell and then headed for the door he'd indicated. Her package was waiting for her as he'd said, wrapped in white paper and tied with a piece of twine to make it easy to carry. That was unusual, she thought, not able to verify she'd been given the correct item. Shrugging, she thanked the clerk and then took the back stairs as the auctioneer had suggested.

When she got into her hotel room, with some relief she unwrapped and set the framed picture on the table next to the bed, then dug her laptop out of her backpack. Firing it up, she began searching for information on Gilarmi Farini.

She immediately got a fair number of hits.

The man born William Leonard Hunt took the stage name Farini the Great for his tightrope-walking act over Niagara Falls. As his fame increased, he legally changed his name to Gilarmi A. Farini and moved his shows to Coney Island. When they did particularly well, he took them on the road, often to London.

He made several trips to Zimbabwe and South Africa, and it was after one of these trips that he returned to London with six bushmen, members of the Khoikhoi tribe from the Kalahari region. Farini convinced them to work for him as part of a show entitled Farini's African Pygmies, which was essentially an exposé of life in the Kalahari. It proved very successful in London.

Farini's relationship with the bushmen made him privy to many of their legends. He was particularly interested in their stories of a lost city deep in the Kalahari, especially after they told him the city was full of diamonds just waiting to be picked off the streets.

Annja smiled. If it wasn't gold, it was diamonds. When will these guys learn?

Farini, his son, Lulu, and a hired associate sailed for Cape Town in January 1895. They arrived by month's end and by mid-February they were headed for the Kalahari. They spent six months in the desert, returning in July claiming to have found a lost city of epic proportions. Annja was surprised to learn that they had accompanying photographs to support their claims.

She spent some time digging around on the net until she found the photographs. They showed massive stone blocks stacked on top of one another in what looked to be man-made fashion. In fact, it reminded her of the Great Wall of China.

Had Farini actually found something in the depths of the Kalahari?

It certainly was starting to look that way.

Farini had returned to London and given several lectures on his discovery, most notably to the Royal Geographic Society and later to the Berlin Geographic Society. A book, *Through the Kalahari,* which included those same photographs taken by Lulu, and a London-based Lost City Exhibition soon followed. After that Farini faded from public until he died on his ranch in Ontario in 1929. Without ever having returned to the Lost City.

He did, however, pen some poetry about the place in his later years. She read one of his poems aloud into the empty room.

A half-buried ruin, a huge wreck of stones,
On a lone and desolate spot.
A temple, or tomb for human bones,
Left by man to decay and rot.

Rude sculpted blocks from the red sand project,
And shapeless uncouth stones appear.
Some great man's ashes designed to protect,
Buried many a thousand year.

A relic, maybe, of a glorious past,
A city once grand and sublime.
Destroyed by earthquake, defaced by the blast,
Swept away by the hands of time.

Annja sighed. Good thing he hadn't given up his day job. Robert Frost he was not.

She picked up the framed map and compared it to some of the hand-drawn images Farini's son had included in *Through the Kalahari*. The style was the same—swift, sure pencil strokes with an occasional finer detail. If she had to guess, Annja would have said the drawing was most likely done by the son rather than the father. Still, the subject matter was unusual. Why draw what the lake might have looked like thousands of years earlier when sketching the flat pan of the lake bed would have made more sense in a map, given that they would have been staring at it during much of their expedition. They had probably crossed straight through the center of it, in fact.

No matter. It was a nice piece and would look good in her apartment back in Brooklyn.

Her curiosity satisfied on one account, she turned her attention to Malcolm Porter.

There wasn't as much information on Porter as there had been on Farini. Which was the opposite of what Annja had expected. Porter lived in the era of Google, Facebook and the paparazzi, after all. The son of a celebrity, even one known more for his general wackiness than anything else, should have generated more than just the occasional note in the society pages. There was no background data or information on what he might have been involved in at the time of his social notices. It piqued Annja's curiosity. How had he escaped notice with such a notorious father?

Then her eyes fell on the word used to describe him in each of the articles she'd managed to dig up.

Estranged.

"'Malcolm Porter, the estranged son of Robert Humphrey,'" she read, "'was seen tonight at the gala opening of Chef Hiroto's new restaurant. Hiroto, a three-time Michelin-star winner, was…'"

Because the two of them hadn't been speaking? Was that why Humphrey had left him out of his will? It seemed harsh, but she didn't know the story behind their estrangement. She had to believe it was something big that had set the two of them at odds. After all, Porter had apparently taken his mother's last name in protest against his father.

4

She couldn't stay angry at Lenny for doing what Doug had ordered him to do, so Annja agreed to have dinner with him that night. As it turned out she arrived at the restaurant—a quiet little place a few blocks away from their hotel—before he did. She took a table in the back away from most of the other patrons and ordered a glass of wine.

She was lost in thought, thinking about the sketch she'd purchased earlier that day, when she sensed someone approaching her table. Expecting to find the waiter with her glass of wine, she was surprised to see Malcolm Porter, dressed in the same tropical-weight suit she'd seen him in earlier.

Annja tensed. She didn't know what Porter wanted, but he'd already caused a scene in a public place once today. She was already thinking about ways to subdue him quietly if things got out of control when he held up his hands in a placating gesture.

"May I speak with you a moment, Ms. Creed?" he asked. He kept his tone conciliatory.

Annja hesitated. At last she indicated the chair opposite her.

"Thank you," Porter said as he settled into the seat.

He glanced around for a waiter and waved one over. Annja raised an eyebrow but didn't say anything. Porter asked for a seltzer and a lime. Then he turned to face her, with what he probably thought of as a disarming smile on his face.

"I want to apologize. My behavior today was unacceptable. I trust you will forgive me."

Annja was already regretting her decision to invite him to sit. While his words formed an apology, they were anything but.

"I'm willing to give you twice what you paid for the drawing," he continued, reaching into his suit coat for a checkbook. "Just tell me how you would like me to make it out."

Annja shook her head. "It's not for sale."

Porter gave her a fifty-megawatt smile. "Not enough, then? You drive a hard bargain, Ms. Creed. Three times what you paid, then!"

Annja hesitated again. She still didn't intend to sell it, especially not to Porter, but he had piqued her curiosity. What was it about the map that made him want it so badly?

"You seem to be going to an awful lot of trouble for such an innocuous item, Mr. Porter," she said. He wasn't the only one who had done his homework. "May I ask why?"

"It has a great deal of sentimental value to me."

"Oh?"

"Yes. My father gave it to me when I was a child and for many years I thought it was lost. That in my youth, I had mislaid it. I only recently found out that it was on the list of items to be auctioned, and hurried here to claim it before it went on the block." He grimaced. "Clearly my frustration got the better of me when I was too late."

"Seems an unusual gift for a young boy."

Porter spread his hands and shrugged. "I was enthralled with maps and images of faraway places as a child. My father knew that a drawing of a special location in the heart of 'deepest darkest Africa,' as they used to say, would interest me."

He paused before plunging ahead. "So, three times what you paid seems very fair. Do we have a deal?"

Annja shook her head again. "As I've already said, the image isn't for sale."

Porter's demeanor instantly changed. "I dislike being denied, Ms. Creed. Very few people get in my way and come out better off."

Annja's eyes narrowed. "Is that a threat?"

Porter shrugged. "Take it however you want. I'm just stating facts."

Annja leaned back in her seat. She let her right hand slip casually down into her lap where it was hidden from the sight of both Porter and the other restaurant patrons. With the barest of thoughts she reached into the otherwhere and called her sword to her, the hilt sliding smoothly into her waiting hand, the blade extending beneath the table toward Porter.

Annja pushed her arm forward just far enough that the point of her sword poked Porter in his ample gut. "If you so much as look at me the wrong way again, I'll make sure you come to regret it."

He glanced down, saw the tip of her sword and blanched. He looked up to find Annja staring at him.

"Get out of here before I have you thrown out of a second place," she said.

Porter scrambled from his seat and took several steps away. Annja thought that was going to be the end of it, but apparently Porter was too stubborn for his own good.

"No one threatens me. I'll have that drawing one way or another."

Annja's grip tightened on her sword, but she kept it beneath the table. "The next time I see you I won't be so forgiving."

The waiter appeared with Porter's water and Lenny in tow. Porter angrily pushed past them and headed for the exit.

Lenny watched him go. "Was that Malcolm Porter?"

"Unfortunately." She sent the sword back to the otherwhere before anyone could see it.

The waiter, an older gentleman with a thick shock of white hair, glanced after Porter uneasily. "Is everything all right?"

She nodded and waited for him to leave with Lenny's order before she filled her cameraman in on what had happened earlier in the day.

"Weird," Lenny said. "With all the stuff Humphrey collected before he disappeared, you'd think his estranged son would want something more valuable, you know?"

Annja nodded in agreement. "There were some really nice pieces up for auction, any one of which commanded a lot more than what I paid for that little drawing. If I was going to claim my old man left me something without telling anyone else, it certainly wouldn't have been that."

"I don't think anyone would have believed him if he'd tried," Lenny said. "There aren't too many fathers out there who wind up leaving the family fortune to a son who curses their name in public."

Interesting. "Do tell," she said.

"He and Daddy had a major falling-out several years ago, right about the time Humphrey went public with all that craziness of his. Seems Junior didn't like Daddy turning his legacy into a joke."

Lenny paused to sip his drink before continuing. "To make a long story short, the two of them ended up taking their argument to the media, sniping at each other every chance they could get. Daddy eventually had enough and wrote Junior out of his will. Junior, in a very public meltdown, cursed his father seven ways from Sunday, declared he was no longer his son and took his mother's maiden name."

"I'll bet that was effective."

Lenny laughed. "And you'd be right. Daddy barely noticed before he was off on another expedition, hunting a furry something-or-other halfway across the globe."

Annja thought about the kind of anger it took to drive a feud like that. "Do you think he had anything to do with his father's disappearance?"

"Nah," Lenny said, waving the suggestion aside.

"You've seen him in action. Not exactly the mastermind type, now, is he?"

But that didn't mean he wasn't capable of malice. His obsession with the painting was proof enough of that.

It seemed there was more to Mr. Malcolm Porter than she'd first expected.

5

Despite Porter's interruption, dinner proved to be a fun, relaxing affair. Lenny was new to the show, new to the network for that matter, and he hadn't been there long enough to learn which orders of Doug's were acceptable and which ones crossed any number of lines. Annja would report on what mystery they came across; she would even, on occasion, speculate about a particular topic of discussion, letting the audience make up their own minds as to what was real and what was not. That was where she drew the line. Special effects couldn't create something that wasn't there just to boost the ratings. On the few occasions where it had happened in post-production she had protested vigorously against it in the final cut. Doug should have known better.

At least it was behind them now. They spent the meal swapping stories, just as they'd been doing since first climbing into that hide in the swamp two weeks ago. Lenny had worked for a variety of cable stations as an on-location cameraman and he'd been on the road almost as much as she had over the past several years.

The owner came by to let them know that they would be closing soon and it was only then that Annja realized they were the last two customers in the entire restaurant. They paid the bill and then headed back down the street the few blocks to their hotel. They'd both had a few drinks; she was feeling reckless, and for a few minutes she considered inviting him to the bar for a nightcap. He had a certain sexy resemblance to a rocker she liked and there was no doubt that she found him attractive. In the end she went to her room on the second floor. She didn't need the added adventure of romance in this working relationship.

As she got off the elevator, she noticed the door to her room was slightly ajar. She stopped, staring at the narrow crack of light that spilled out between the door and the jamb.

She'd closed the door firmly behind her on the way out. She was sure of it.

Annja glanced up and down the hallway, but there was no one else around. She was alone.

Others might have been uncomfortable with that knowledge and gone for help, especially being in a foreign country, but Annja was not your average tourist. Far from it. In fact, she was grateful there wasn't anyone else around at the moment. It let her deal with the problem her way.

She reached into the otherwhere and pulled out her sword. The long, slim blade seemed to gleam in the dim light of the hallway and she felt infinitely better the moment the well-worn hilt fitted neatly into her hand.

Ready to take on whatever might be waiting for her, she quietly began to edge forward until she stood with her back to the wall, the open door just another step beyond. She leaned forward slightly and peeked inside.

Annja's hotel room was expansive by Botswanan

standards—a wide, open suite with a sitting/living room area, a sleeping area and a private bathroom. From her current position she could see a small slice of the sitting area—a corner table, the end of the couch—but that was all. Not enough to tell her what was happening inside. She was going to have to take more drastic action to figure that out.

Reaching out with the tip of her sword, she gently eased the door open farther. She waited for a response, but when one wasn't immediately forthcoming she took a deep breath and stepped into the room, the sword extended before her en garde.

There was no one there.

The room was empty.

It was immediately clear that someone *had* been inside. Her clothes and other belongings were strewn about as if that person had gone through them in a hurry. Her passport folder, and the assorted credit cards it contained, was still untouched on the bedside table.

Cross off robbery as a motive, then.

Truth was, she'd done that the second she'd seen the state of the room. Whoever had been in here had been looking for something specific and she had a good idea just what the something was. After all, Porter hadn't been shy about telling her he'd take the drawing by force if she wasn't willing to sell it to him. No doubt he'd hired some local to steal it and her decision to stay out late with Lenny had given them the opportunity they'd needed.

Hopefully her foresight in hiding it before going out for the evening had kept it safe.

As she walked toward the bathroom, she couldn't

help but wonder again just what was so special about the image.

What good would a sketch of a lake that hadn't existed for the past ten thousand years do anyone?

Annja was starting to suspect it was high time she figured that out.

She stepped into the bathroom, took the cover off the toilet and fished the zipped plastic bag out of the tank. She'd double-bagged the framed image, in fact. They either hadn't thought to look there or her arrival had scared them away before they'd had the chance. Either way, the drawing was safe.

Grabbing a towel off the rack on her way by, Annja took the package into the common room, drying it as she went. She put it down on the table and was about to sit when she heard a noise behind her.

She spun around, hands coming up to defend herself.

The room behind her was empty.

And yet…it wasn't.

She wasn't alone.

She could feel it in her bones—that sense that there was someone else in the room even though she couldn't see anyone there. She glanced about the room, searching out and then discarding various hiding places one by one, until her gaze fell on the tall wardrobe by the bed. The doors faced her directly and were open the barest fraction of an inch.

Annja wasn't the neatest of people. She couldn't be certain, but she thought she'd left the doors of the wardrobe open earlier.

"I know you're in there," she said. "We can do this the easy way or the hard way. Your choice."

She waited, watching and listening.

"Suit yourself."

Annja could handle herself in hand-to-hand combat, but there was no sense in approaching the wardrobe, and the potential enemy hiding inside it, unarmed if she didn't have to. She called her sword to hand, not caring if the intruder inside the closet saw.

Perhaps the sight of it would make whoever it was less inclined to give her a hard time.

She advanced toward the wardrobe, her gaze glued to the crack between the doors, watching for the slightest movement.

The room around her was silent, the swish of the ceiling fan the only sound.

As she drew closer, the hair on the back of her neck stood on end.

Someone was there all right.

Annja stopped about two feet in front of the wardrobe, her sword between her and the doors.

"Last chance," she said.

Nothing.

With a rueful shake of her head, Annja reached out with the tip of her sword and knocked one of the doors open wide.

She was staring at the empty wardrobe before her when there was a tremendous yell and the entire piece of furniture suddenly toppled toward her.

She threw herself to the side, rolling over frantically to get out of the way as the wardrobe crashed to the floor where she'd been standing. Out of the corner of her eye she saw a man dart out. He snatched the double-bagged image off the table where Annja had left it and turned toward the door, intent on making an escape.

But Annja, anticipating that move, scrambled to her feet and rushed after him. Her speed and agility seemed to have increased since she'd taken possession of the sword, and she proved to be slightly faster than he was, getting close enough to take him down with a diving tackle before he'd gone half a dozen steps. The two of them hit the ground, Annja's arms wrapped around the intruder's legs.

That did little to stop him, however. He began squirming like a fish out of water, twisting and turning, pounding her on the head and shoulders with his free hand in an effort to free himself. Annja's grip had been tenuous to begin with and so it only took him a few seconds to accomplish his goal. He pulled away from her, only to find that Annja was between him and the door.

She grinned.

Now that they were facing each other, she could see that he was just a teenager. He couldn't have been more than sixteen or seventeen. He wore clean clothes and a white pair of sneakers that practically shouted their newness.

To her surprise the cheeky kid smiled back, spun on his heels and raced across the hotel room in the other direction. Annja watched him go, wondering just what he thought he was doing. There wasn't anything in that direction except...

"Oh, no, you don't!" she shouted.

He never stopped; he just charged forward as fast as his feet would carry him. He brought up his arms to cover his face at the last minute and threw himself into the wooden shutters that covered the threshold to the narrow balcony just beyond.

With a thunderous crash he burst through them and disappeared from view.

6

Annja couldn't believe it. Where did he think he was going to go?

She reached the shattered remains of the shutters just in time to see him leap over the low balcony railing and land on the brightly colored awning that extended from the hotel out into the street. He rolled once, twice and then, with impressive dexterity, grabbed the edge of the awning and swung down to the street below.

Annja didn't hesitate for the simple reason that she knew if she did, she'd lose him; the thief would disappear into the crowd and she'd never find him. So instead of pondering all the things that could potentially go wrong, Annja stepped past the wreckage of the door, put her hand on the railing and vaulted over it.

She fell about half a dozen feet before striking the awning, which slowed her fall and sent her into a rolling tumble down its length. She sensed more than saw the edge of the awning ahead of her and thrust out her hands, snatching the supporting pole as she rolled past, bringing her to an abrupt halt, hanging half off the fabric, her feet a foot or so above the ground. It wasn't as graceful as the exit the thief had managed, but it would do.

She dropped to the ground, determined which direction her target had taken and then took up the chase.

He'd put a good dozen yards between them and was just disappearing around the corner at an intersection up ahead.

By the time she reached it he was out of sight, but the commotion he left in his wake allowed her to follow him easily enough. She pushed herself harder and it wasn't long before she saw him moving in and out of the crowd ahead of her.

She could see immediately that he had slowed down, no doubt thinking that he'd left her behind following his unorthodox exit from the hotel, and so she was able to close the distance between them without too much effort. Once she had, he seemed oblivious to that fact that she was there. She decided to take the risk of following him instead of taking back what was hers.

Annja was already convinced that Malcolm Porter had hired the kid to steal the drawing. Getting the local police to take Porter into custody might be difficult because of his standing in the community, but if they refused to do anything about the situation, their inaction would at least allow Annja to handle this theft her way.

She was now less than ten yards behind the thief. She could see the package he'd taken tucked under one arm as he made his way through the streets. He was intent on his destination, and Annja suspected she could have walked up and tapped him on the shoulder before he would notice her.

From her explorations earlier in the day, Annja knew that the route he was taking would bring him to a large open-air plaza frequented by many locals. It was an ideal place for meeting someone without fear of being hemmed in.

She also knew that there were other, faster routes to the same location. If she could get there ahead of him, she might be able to see who he was going to meet. Of course, he might not be headed that way at all, and if she took a chance and broke away from him, she might end up losing him entirely.

So be it, she thought before darting down a side street and pushing herself faster. She must be quite a sight as she raced down the alley, dodging pedestrians, donkeys and vendors' carts alike. She didn't care; all that mattered was getting there before her target.

Which, thankfully, she did.

The plaza was roughly one hundred feet square, with entrances of arched stone at each of the cardinal points of the compass. Annja slowed down as she approached an entryway, not wanting to call attention to herself, and then stopped in the shadow of the arch to look out across the plaza.

She saw Porter almost immediately. He was hard to overlook in that white suit he favored. He was standing on the far side of the square, in the shade of an umbrella that was held by an extremely fit-looking man next to him who all but screamed former military. For a moment she thought they had seen her, as well, and she tensed, ready to dive back into the crowd. When they didn't react after several seconds she relaxed and settled in to wait for the thief.

Several minutes passed with no sign of him.

Had she been wrong? Had he been headed somewhere else? Porter's presence here might just be an unfortunate coincidence.

Another anxious moment passed and then the thief appeared in the mouth of the arch to her right, just as she'd expected he would. He glanced out across the crowd, obviously looking for someone. When his gaze fell on Porter, Annja saw his expression of distaste before he smoothed it into one of congeniality.

You know you've got a personality problem when even the hired thieves don't like you.

The youth lifted a hand in greeting and then crossed to Porter.

That was enough for Annja. She'd confirmed the connection between the two. Now it was time to take back what was hers.

She left the concealment of the arch behind and put herself on an intercept course with her target.

Unfortunately, the gunman standing beside Porter must have had formal training in executive protection at some point in his life. He picked her out of the crowd right away and switched his attention from the thief to her. One look was all it took for him to identify the oncoming threat. He drew his gun and pointed it at her.

He won't shoot, she thought, not with this many witnesses.

She couldn't have been more wrong.

7

Annja heard the sound of the shot right about the same moment she felt the bullet pass by her left ear. From behind her, a donkey screamed in pain.

The gunfire drew the thief's attention. Annja watched as he turned to see what Porter's bodyguard was shooting at and their gazes locked above the heads of the crowd. No sooner had he seen her than he jack-rabbited back the way he had come.

Annja flicked her gaze to the gunman, her body tensing for the next shot, and was just in time to see Porter knock the other man's arm upward, sending the bullet harmlessly into the wall of a nearby building.

She didn't wait around to see any more. Dodging panicked market-goers and anxious animals, she took off after her target.

He tried to lose her in the maze of outdoor shops and stalls, but Annja was unwavering in her pursuit. She matched him turn for turn, refusing to lose sight of him no matter what. This was personal now; the drawing belonged to her and she intended to have it back.

Her quarry was starting to get desperate; his head was snapping this way and that as he frantically looked for some way of throwing her off his trail. She stayed with him, relentlessly closing the gap. Her anger at Porter's backhanded attempt to steal what was rightfully hers fueled her efforts and she quickly closed the gap between them.

He glanced back, saw her closing in on him. They were passing a wide fountain to their left, an ornate stone affair with an elephant sitting in the pool of water, spouting water out of his trunk. As they came abreast of it the young thief flung the package away. Then he cut sharply in the opposite direction, no doubt betting that Annja would chase the package instead of him.

His bet was right on the money.

She watched the package sail through the air and splash into the fountain. She had no choice but to go in after it.

Bystanders watched as she jumped into the murky water and splashed her way over to where she'd seen the package disappear. She spent a few anxious minutes searching with both arms plunged beneath the surface before her fingertips brushed plastic. She gave a shout and snatched the package out of the water as she straightened.

The thief, of course, was long gone.

Porter and his man had apparently decided to make themselves scarce, as well, Annja was thankful to see.

As she climbed out of the fountain, her clothes sopping wet from the thighs down, she realized that the packaging had torn slightly at some point during the chase. Water had most likely reached the drawing inside. She clamped down on the impulse to scream and set about saving as much as she could. She stripped the packaging open, wiped one hand dry on the top half of her shirt and then used it to pull the painting out into the sunlight.

She saw immediately that one corner of the image had some water damage, but thankfully it wasn't extensive, only about the size of a half dollar piece, if that. With a little care she might even be able to restore it. To keep it from getting any worse, she quickly took off the wooden backing and then removed the drawing from the frame entirely. Seeing what she was doing, a vendor in a nearby stall offered her a hand towel and she used it to blot the image dry. To show her appreciation she bought the towel from him, both of them getting a good laugh from the soggy state of the money she drew out of the pocket of her pants.

After that, there was nothing left to do but return to her hotel. Once there the management apologized profusely for the break-in and moved her to another suite on a different floor to keep it from happening again. Annja wasn't happy to find that her belongings had already been sent to the new room. Having two sets of strangers pawing through her things in a single evening was not one of the night's high points. On the other hand, she was glad she wouldn't have to spend the next hour gathering up her things.

She needed a shower to wash off the grit and grime she'd picked up during her dunking in the fountain, but didn't want to let the drawing out of her sight, so she compromised by taking it into the bathroom with her and wrapping it in a spare towel to keep it from getting damp. After bathing she dressed in a pair of sweats and a tank top and took the bundle over to the sitting area for a closer look.

The damage jumped out at her the minute she removed the towel. The corner of the drawing that had gotten wet had separated, the top layer of paper lifting up and curling away from the one below it.

Except...

There was only supposed to be one layer, not two.

Annja stared at it in puzzlement for a moment, before picking it up to get a better look. On closer inspection she could see that they were actually two different pieces of paper, carefully fitted and glued together.

She took the drawing back into the bathroom and laid it on a towel at the edge of the sink. She turned the shower on full blast—hot. After making sure the drawing was far enough away from the shower to keep it from getting wet, she took a towel from the rack and left the room, closing the door behind her. She then laid the extra towel against the bottom of the door, effectively trapping as much steam inside the room as possible.

Now there was nothing more to do but wait.

She paced back and forth in front of the bathroom door for just over fifteen minutes. She was tempted, more than once, to open the door and take a peek, but doing so would release the steam and heat. She gritted her teeth and left it alone. She even gave it an extra ten minutes, just to be certain. By the time she finally opened the door and let all the heat and humidity out of the room, she was ready to scream.

As the steam cleared out, she got her first look at the drawing.

The top layer had curled up and separated from the layer below it, leaving her with two rolled tubes of parchmentlike canvas. A quick glance told her that the new layer also contained a hand-drawn image; she took them both out to the sitting area where there was more light so she could examine them in detail.

She set aside the top layer, the drawing of the prehistoric Lake Makgadikgadi. She already knew what it was and there wasn't anything to be learned there. Instead, she turned her attention to the newly revealed image on the second layer of parchment.

It was, she realized, a series of images, arranged one above the other in a vertical line. They were crudely drawn by hand but recognizable nonetheless.

The first was a building of some kind; two diagonal lines joined together to form a roof over two vertical lines that formed the walls. Written in the center was the notation *DM*.

The second image looked like the old pirate symbol of a skull and crossbones, but in this case the image of the skull had been replaced by the head of an elephant. As strange as it looked, Annja knew it couldn't be anything else; those oversize ears and long trunk were unmistakable even in a childlike drawing such as this.

The third symbol was of a baobab, a large fruit-bearing tree that could be found in Africa, India and parts of Australia. Often called a monkey bread tree because of the popularity of its fruit among the various species of monkey that liked to make their homes within its branches, the baobab stored hundreds of gallons of water in its trunk and was thought to live several thousand years.

But what really caught her attention was the fourth and final image. This was drawn much more carefully than the three before it and took up most of the lower third of the page. It was drawn as if the viewer were standing in the opening of a cave, looking out into a massive canyon filled with earthen buildings painted in brilliant colors.

She knew instinctively she was looking at the image of the Lost City that Humphrey had intended to find when he set off on his final expedition, but it was the words beneath the image that drew her attention.

The tulip stands amid the wild beasts,
Within its walls, the first of the answers you seek.
Find the gray crown that watches over the flock,
To receive a piece of the puzzle you hope to unlock.

Annja's breath caught in her throat as she finally understood what she was looking at.

It was a map!

The images, combined with the riddlelike verse, were clues to the route Humphrey had planned to take to find the Lost City. It couldn't be anything else. He'd hidden it behind a drawing supposedly done by Gilarmi Farini, the man who had originally discovered the city. It was like a neon signpost in the night to those who knew what they were looking for.

No wonder Porter had wanted it so badly.

If she could unravel the clues Humphrey had left behind, Annja was confident she could retrace his steps and discover, once and for all, what had happened to him during that final, fateful expedition.

As the night burned on toward morning, Annja got to work.

8

The first thing she did upon rising the next morning was put in a call to Doug Morrell. Given all the strange and unusual things Humphrey had searched for over the years, she knew Doug would not only know who he was but probably had a file cabinet full of information on him. Getting the chance to solve the final mystery of the man's disappearance would be a challenge Doug would leap at.

Unfortunately, the call went very differently than she expected.

Doug answered on the fourth ring, which should have told her something, but in her excitement she missed the lack of his usual enthusiasm.

"Forget the bat men," she said to him. "I've got something even better. What if I told you that not only did I know exactly what Robert Humphrey had been searching for when he disappeared into the jungle three years ago but that I also know where he went and exactly how to get there?"

Her producer didn't say anything.

"Doug? Did you hear me, Doug?"

"I heard you just fine," he said, more stiffly than usual. "But I refuse to fall for something that's so obviously a prank. When you're ready to be a grownup and put this behind us, let me know. Until then, I've got work to do."

He hung up.

Annja pulled the phone away from her ear and stared at it.

Doug hung up on her.

She couldn't believe it.

Hitting the redial button, she waited until he answered for the second time.

"I'm serious, Doug. I know exactly what Humphrey was looking for and I've got the evidence to prove it! All we have to do—"

"I've already apologized for the drone, Annja. I'm not going to do it again. If you can't accept my apology, fine, but stop trying to tease me with stories of Humphrey's Lost Expedition and the Vanished Tribe. It's just not going to work."

Then he did it again.

He hung up.

Annja gritted her teeth. She went to hit Redial again but stopped, her thumb poised over the button. Doug thought she was giving him hell for the stunt he'd tried to pull with the mechanical bat man and she knew from past experience that once he got an idea in his head it took a herd of stampeding elephants to get it back out. She was going to have to come at this from a different direction, it seemed.

She jumped out of bed, threw on some clothes and dashed down the hall to the stairwell, where she took the steps down two at a time. She emerged into the main first-floor hallway and hustled down its length until she reached Lenny's door and banged on it.

It took a minute, but he eventually opened the door a crack and blinked out at her.

"Annja? What are you—?"

She didn't give him a chance to finish, just pushed passed him and into his room. "I've got this terrific idea for the show but I can't get Doug to listen to me. He thinks I'm getting back at him for what he did the other day."

She turned to face him, only to come to a stuttering halt. "Oh!"

Lenny was standing just inside the door wearing only a tight pair of boxer briefs that left very little to the imagination. He had a hard, muscular body and Annja felt her gaze drifting down from his face....

She blushed and quickly looked up. "Sorry! Didn't realize you were, uh…"

Lenny, a mischievous grin on his face, made no move to cover up. "Come on in, Annja, by all means. No need to wait for an invitation."

Annja turned around, her voice steady as she said, "Shouldn't have barged in. You're right. Can you put some clothes on? I need your help with something important that I can't do alone."

"You're sure you want me to get dressed?" he asked. His voice had gotten lower, huskier.

Time to nip this in the bud right now.

"Remember what I did to that drone, Lenny?" she asked.

He got the hint.

After a moment, he said, "All right. Open your eyes and tell me what this is all about."

He'd pulled on a pair of cargo shorts and a loose cotton shirt.

She filled him in on what had happened, explaining about the robbery and how she'd ultimately discovered that there was a second set of images hidden behind the first.

Lenny raised his eyebrows in surprise. "So you think it's authentic?"

"Yes! I can't imagine anyone going through that much trouble for a fake, can you?"

Her companion had to admit that he couldn't.

"Porter knew the 'map' was there," Annja said. "It's the only explanation that makes sense. Why else would he want the drawing so badly?"

"So what's the problem?" Lenny asked.

"I called Doug to convince him to finance an expedition to follow in Humphrey's footsteps, using the clues as our guide, but he hung up on me before I even had a chance to explain what I had."

Lenny frowned. "Hung up on you? That doesn't sound like Doug."

"I'm afraid that's my fault. I was ticked when I spoke to him earlier this morning and now he thinks I'm just trying to get even with him."

Lenny laughed. "Ah, now I see. You want me to tell him you're not making this up."

"Exactly. He'll listen to you."

"I wouldn't be so sure about that. He's not very happy with me right now. I did let the drone get destroyed, after all."

"Trust me. The minute he realizes we're serious about showing the world exactly what happened on Humphrey's last expedition, he won't give the drone a second thought."

Lenny agreed to give it a try. He pulled out his cell phone and speed-dialed Doug. The two of them spent several minutes talking before Lenny handed her the phone.

"Yes, Doug?"

"If this is a joke I swear to you I'll—"

"It's no joke. Everything from the way the sketch was hidden to the notations on its face indicate it was created and intentionally left behind by Humphrey prior to his departure. He must have known that he might not make it back and he left behind some insurance. Just in case."

Doug grunted. "All right, fine. I'll take your word for it. Now what?"

"We go after him. With the show's backing, Lenny and I could buy the gear we need right here in Maun and be on the road before nightfall."

"Nightfall, huh? What does Lenny think of the idea?"

Annja glanced over at her cameraman, gave him the thumbs-up and said, "He's behind it one hundred percent. It's the opportunity of a lifetime and he knows it."

There was silence on the line as Doug thought that one over. Annja could see Lenny looking at her quizzically, no doubt wondering what she had just committed him to, but she waved him off, waiting on Doug's answer. Given how long it was taking, Annja was half convinced he was going to say no and she was preparing another round of arguments when Doug finally said, "You've got a week. Can you do it in that amount of time?"

Annja fist-pumped the air. "One week. With the map at our disposal, that should be plenty of time."

In truth, she wasn't exactly sure how long it would take, but she could always argue for more time if it turned out they needed it. Doug would be reluctant to pull the plug once filming was already under way.

They said their goodbyes and Annja got off the phone before Doug could come up with some crazy addition to what should be a straightforward expedition. They had Humphrey's map; all they had to do was decipher the clues and follow it.

Nothing to it.

The fact that they had already been buying supplies and equipment from the locals for the past couple of weeks during their ill-fated search for the bat men would make preparations for this new search easier. She would restock their gear and food supplies while Lenny saw about extending their Nissan SUV rental for another week. When he was finished, he would bring the vehicle around to the outfitters to be loaded. If all went well, they should be on their way before lunch.

9

The owner of the general supply was a jovial fellow named Michael Isooda—"Just Isooda to my friends." He welcomed Annja back to the store and then worked with her for the next forty-five minutes to gather the materials they were going to need. A week in the bush wasn't all that long, but it helped to be prepared for any eventualities. Her biggest concern, of course, was making sure they had enough water. The Kalahari was a desert, after all, and water would grow scarcer the deeper into it they went.

As she waited for Isooda's staff to package up everything she'd ordered, Annja reviewed one of his maps of the Kalahari, paying particular attention to the northern stretches of the Central Kalahari Game Reserve.

When she'd been up until almost dawn the night before, working on deciphering the clue Humphrey had left behind, she became confident she had figured out the first couple of lines.

The use of the word *walls* in the second line indicated that they were looking for a building of some kind and the reference to it being *amid the wild beasts* suggested that it was within the confines of the game reserve. Annja had been confused by the reference to the tulip until she figured out that it was code for something of Dutch descent, the tulip being the national flower of the Netherlands.

So the end result was that she was looking for a building associated with the Dutch in some way that stood within the boundaries of the game reserve.

Before she'd called it quits to grab some sleep, she'd also turned to the online community of myth hunters by way of the alt.archaeology.esoterica newsgroup for help.

She'd logged in under her usual pseudonym and had posted a request for any information connecting the Dutch to the legend of the Lost City of the Kalahari. Logging off, she'd then tried to get some sleep.

When she awoke a couple hours later, midmorning, she'd found several replies, one of which had caught her attention.

The post was by someone using the handle SirDrake. Farini and his son supposedly spent two days recuperating at a mission founded by an old Dutch priest on their return from the Lost City.

It was the connection Annja was looking for. She sent SirDrake a follow-up. Do you know the name of the mission or where it was supposed to be?

His reply had only taken a few minutes. No name given, but it was supposed to be located in what is now the northern part of the wildlife sanctuary in Botswana. Sorry I can't be more helpful.

Annja assured her new online friend that he had been more than helpful and signed off, happy to have a starting point. She was looking for a Dutch mission in central Botswana. There had to be records of that kind of thing, didn't there?

But try as she might, so far she hadn't been able to locate any. Having exhausted her usual sources, she was now left with staring at the storekeeper's map and trying to imagine the logic of where to build a mission.

She was so engrossed she didn't hear Isooda approach.

"Looking for something in particular, Annja?"

She glanced at him, smiling, and decided to take a chance. "As a matter of fact, I am," she said, and then went on to explain about the mission.

Isooda's smile deepened. "You need Dr. Crane."

Annja didn't know who that was.

"Dr. Crane is a good man. If you are sick, you can go to him and he will help you, even if you cannot pay."

Annja could certainly appreciate someone donating their time and skill to help those who were less fortunate, but she didn't see what that had to do with finding the Dutch mission.

"Dr. Crane's compound is here," Isooda said, pointing to a spot on the map that was about one hundred kilometers south of Maun within the northern reaches of the Central Kalahari Game Reserve. "His family built a medical clinic on the ruins of a much older facility. They have been helping the local people for generations. So much so that when the reserve was created, Dr. Crane was given permission to keep running his clinic inside the park. I would think that is the place you seek."

"Does he have a phone?" Annja asked, thinking to save a few hours of potentially unnecessary travel, but Isooda shook his head.

"I'm afraid not. If you want to speak with him, you'll

either have to wait until he comes to town or go out to his compound."

"How do you know when he's coming to town?"

Isooda shrugged. "I don't."

So the reserve it was, then.

Annja thanked him for his help when Lenny called to tell her that their truck had not one, but two, flats.

"Can't you just change them?"

"I could, if I had more than one spare. I've notified the rental company and they say it's going to take at least an hour to bring the extra tire on over."

So much for making an early start of it.

"So rent something else."

"Tried that, too. Apparently they're out of four-wheel-drive vehicles at the moment. I, for one, don't want to be driving around the African delta in a Ford Escort."

They had no choice but to wait.

This was not an auspicious start.

PORTER WAS ENJOYING a late breakfast when his cell phone rang. He glanced at the caller ID and saw it was Bryant, his personal bodyguard and right-hand man.

A former SAS commando turned mercenary, Bryant had few scruples and would do whatever was asked provided he was paid. Porter had hired him several years before and considered it one of his better business decisions. Where Porter was reluctant to get his hands dirty, Bryant positively relished the possibility. It was an arrangement they both appreciated.

Right now, Bryant was stationed in the lobby of Annja's hotel.

"Talk to me," Porter said, on answering the phone.

As usual, his subordinate's report was short and to the point. "She's in Isooda's buying enough gear for a couple of weeks in the bush."

Michael Isooda was the equivalent of the local quartermaster. If you were headed into the reserve on a safari or just exploring the more arid regions of the Kalahari, he was your man. He carried everything from firearms to dried goods, and if he didn't have it, he could usually get it for you quickly.

"Any indications where she is going?"

"No."

After a moment's thought, Porter said, "Wait until she leaves and then have a chat with our friend inside. Pay him the usual fee if the information is good. I want to know where she is going and when."

"Yes, sir."

Porter tried to return to his meal but he couldn't seem to enjoy it in the wake of Bryant's phone call. He wanted to move, to do something, to take back control of the situation, but he couldn't until he had the information he needed from Isooda. He wound up pacing back and forth across the room, imagining all the ways he was going to make Annja Creed suffer for daring to lay her hands upon his father's—no, *his*—map. She'd had the temerity to threaten him with a sword, for heaven's sake, and if she thought she was going to get away with that she had—

The phone rang.

Porter snatched up the receiver. "What have you got?"

"Isooda says Creed and her cameraman are headed

into the reserve. He didn't know anything more than that."

"You're positive?"

Bryant grunted. "He would have told me if he knew something else."

Satisfied his subordinate had applied the right amount of pressure, Porter considered what he'd learned. The Central Kalahari Game Reserve was a popular destination; there were half a dozen safari camps within its borders at any given time. Creed might simply be after a few pictures of the elephants, killing time between assignments for that television show of hers. That was what had brought her down here in the first place, wasn't it?

Still, something about the explanation didn't feel right to him. There was a deeper reason for her presence here. Her tenacity over the drawing indicated she knew more about it and the secret it contained than she'd let on and he was convinced that anything else was just a cover story for her real mission. She was after the Lost City and the treasure it contained, just as he was.

That was why he didn't find it surprising that she was setting out in the same direction his father had taken on his last, fateful expedition.

Clearly she had found the map; the one his father had left behind.

Porter intended to claim it as his own.

There wasn't much he could do against Creed here in the city. The aborted break-in and the subsequent fiasco in the square had raised her profile too high. But once she left the city behind, she was fair game.

"All right, listen to me," he told his subordinate. "We

don't have time to waste. We need to get out on the road ahead of them. Grab a couple of the men and get back here on the double."

"Okay. I don't think there's any need to hurry, though."

Gritting his teeth, Porter asked, "Why's that?"

"When you told me to keep an eye on them, I figured it would be easier to do if they couldn't go very far, so I flattened the back tires on their truck."

10

It was nearly 1:00 p.m. by the time Lenny finally showed up with the truck. It had taken almost two hours for the tires to be delivered and another forty-five minutes to swap them. Lenny had even tried to buy new tires but the rental car agency doubled not only as the local mechanic, but the only auto parts store within two hundred kilometers.

With nothing to do but make the most of it, the two set to loading the Nissan. Isooda sent a couple of teenage boys out to help and the four of them made short work of the stacked supplies. Since Lenny's camera equipment filled about half of the rear cargo area, some of the supplies had to be tied down on the roof inside the iron cargo rack welded to the frame for just that purpose. Finally finished, they said their goodbyes and started out on the road, with Annja behind the wheel.

They left Maun going south on the A3, toward Lake Ngami. The road was paved for the first twenty miles, but after that it abruptly turned to dirt. Their tires threw up a cloud of red dust that billowed behind them like the long tail of a comet. The road had them bouncing about in their seats with every dip and rut, but Annja didn't mind. She was back in the wild, chasing down another legendary locale and loving every minute of it.

Two hours after leaving Maun they turned south on a smaller dirt road that, if Lenny was reading the map correctly, should bring them to one of the few gates into the chain link protecting the park.

At thirty-three thousand square miles, the Central Kalahari Game Reserve was the second largest reserve in the world, covering an area roughly twice the size of Massachusetts. It had been established in 1961 and, thanks to the tireless efforts of the Botswanan government and wildlife preservation groups the world over, had become a popular destination spot for safari tourism over the past two decades.

Like the majority of the Kalahari region, the land was mostly flat, though they occasionally encountered long undulating hills. The desert dunes were covered with bush and grasses, dotted here and there with short stretches of trees.

When they reached the entrance, Lenny hopped out and opened the gate, then waited for Annja to drive through before closing it again behind them. They continued on.

It wasn't long before living proof that they'd entered the park walked right in front of them. A massive herd of wildebeest decided that they wanted to graze on the other side of the road, which forced Annja to pull over and wait while several hundred of them passed. She sat watching with delight at the sight of so many wild animals together in one place. Lenny took more than a few shots with his cameras. By the time the herd had thinned out enough to let their vehicle pass, Annja was almost sorry to go.

They'd been driving for another fifteen minutes when Lenny suddenly shouted, "Look! Over there!"

Annja followed the line of Lenny's finger to where it pointed to a large flock of carrion birds wheeling in the sky about a hundred yards to the left of the road. The black harbingers of death sent chills down Annja's spine.

Had to be something big to draw a crowd like that.

Without thinking, Annja turned the wheel in that direction. The truck bounced and clattered as they left the dirt road behind and made their way across the open plain.

"What are you doing?" Lenny asked.

"What does it look like I'm doing?" Annja replied. She kept her gaze locked on the knee-high grass she was driving through, not wanting to discover a boulder or fallen tree the hard way. "I'm going to take a look. Isn't that why you pointed it out?"

Lenny snorted in disgust but didn't say anything.

They got within twenty feet before the carrion birds took to the air en masse, squawking in indignation at having their meal interrupted. Their departure revealed the large, gray mound they had been feeding on and it didn't take long for either Annja or Lenny to recognize it for what it was.

A dead elephant.

Annja brought the truck to a stop and turned off the engine. She and Lenny got out and stopped a few feet away from the carcass. Lenny stayed standing while Annja squatted down to take a closer look.

The African bush elephant is the largest living terrestrial animal. The average male stands between ten and thirteen feet at the shoulder and can weigh between ten thousand and thirteen thousand pounds, while the female typically weighs half that. Unlike their Asian cousins, both the male and female of the species have tusks, from five to eight feet long. Annja knew elephants lost their teeth six times during their lives and that the most common cause of death for an older elephant is starvation due to the loss of those teeth.

It was immediately clear that this particular elephant hadn't died from natural causes, however. The missing tusks and bullet holes in its sides were testimony to that.

Poachers.

Anger swept through her at the thought. Elephants were highly intelligent creatures, possibly more intelligent than apes and even dolphins, and it hurt Annja to see one treated so brutally.

It also made her wonder where the other elephants were.

Elephants gathered in family units, led by a matriarch, and it was rare to see one of them alone. Even adult males tended to gather together and form alliances with other males.

This particular elephant hadn't been dead for long; aside from the coppery scent in the air from the tacky pool of blood that had formed around the body, there wasn't the stench one would associate with a carcass that had been lying in the sun for any length of time.

Which meant the poachers couldn't be far away.

Lenny must have come to the same realization as she did, turning in a slow circle, looking around them with the kind of intensity that suggested he thought they might not be alone.

Annja stood and did the same at the sensation of being watched. The plain stretched uninterrupted back to the road they'd left behind and she hadn't seen anything on their way in to indicate someone had been here before them. The grass to either side seemed undisturbed, though she'd be the first to admit that didn't mean much. If the poachers had been on foot, they could have moved through the area without leaving any obvious sign at all.

She took a few steps to the left, which gave her a better view of the area on the other side of the carcass.

The sun at her back brought the twin sets of tire tracks into sharp relief. They began about a dozen feet from the carcass and ran in a straight line toward a large copse of trees a few hundred yards away.

Annja was staring at the trees, wondering if the poachers were watching them even now, when she saw a flash of light.

It was only visible for a second, but that was all the time she needed to recognize it for what it was—sunlight reflecting off glass.

"Get down!" she yelled, and dove at Lenny.

The rifle shot echoed across the plain a split second later.

11

Annja felt the bullet whip past the spot where she'd just been standing as she flung herself forward. Poor Lenny had no idea what was going on. He was just turning toward her in response to her yell when she barreled into him. They slammed to the ground in the middle of the congealing pool of elephant's blood, splattering it everywhere.

"What the hell was that?" Lenny asked, unthinkingly starting to get up.

Annja yanked him back again. "Keep your head down," she said sharply. "Do you want to get it blown off?"

"Hell, no! But how are we supposed to see if they're coming when we've got our heads down in the dirt?"

He had a point. They couldn't stay here indefinitely. Whoever was out there had been willing to take a shot at them; they probably wouldn't have any moral dilemma about sending another gunman around to flank them and shoot them where they lay. If they were going to live through this, they had to take control of the situation, which meant getting out of here as quickly as possible.

Annja glanced behind them, gauging the distance

to the truck. Twelve to fifteen feet at most. She hadn't wanted to park too close to the corpse when they'd arrived, afraid of obscuring evidence for the park rangers to identify the killers. Now she was regretting that decision.

Even five feet felt like a mile when there was a gun pointed at your back.

Thankfully she hadn't parked straight on but at a forty-five-degree angle relative to the elephant. If she could reach the truck and get to the other side, she'd be shielded by several tons of Detroit steel and would have a better than average chance of survival.

If she could get to the truck.

She needed a diversion.

"Take off your shirt," she told Lenny.

He looked at her like she'd just lost her mind. "What?"

"You heard me. Take off your shirt," she repeated. When he still didn't move she gave up on him in exasperation and rolled over onto her back and began unbuttoning her own shirt.

She pulled first one arm and then the other out of her sleeves, leaving her wearing just her form-fitting tank top.

When she was finished she flipped back over on her stomach, the shirt bunched in her right hand. She kept her left hand flat against the ground. With her body as a shield to keep Lenny from seeing what she was doing, she called her sword to hand.

"We can't stay here forever," she said quietly, passing him her shirt, "so you're going to create a diversion while I make a run for the truck."

He stared at her and then down at her shirt in his hand. "I'm going to create a diversion…with this?"

"And this," she replied, passing him her sword.

Lenny's eyes nearly bulged from their sockets as she passed the English broadsword across the grass to him.

"Annja, that's a freakin' sword!"

"Yes, it is. Now here's what I want you to do."

She quickly explained what she intended. Lenny wasn't happy about it, but a sudden spurt of gunfire, designed no doubt to panic them into action, helped him understand they couldn't lie here all day. He wrapped the shirt around the tip of the sword and got ready to do his part.

"On the count of three," Annja told him. "One… Two… Three!"

As Lenny used the sword to lift her shirt over the far edge of the elephant carcass, two things happened almost simultaneously. Gunfire rang out from the copse of trees and Annja leaped to her feet and rushed for the truck.

She knew she had only a few seconds before the gunman's eye would be drawn by her movement, and so she didn't waste any time trying to zig and zag but just put her head down and ran full out. Her breath sounded overly loud in her ears; her heart was pounding in her chest and any minute she expected to take a bullet in the back.

She reached the truck and went sliding over the hood just as a fusillade of shots rang out, the bullets hammering into the side of the truck in her wake.

Damn, that was close.

She scrambled on hands and knees over to the

driver's door, yanked it open and pulled herself across the two front seats on her back, being sure to keep her head below the dashboard.

More shots rang out, but Annja focused on digging the keys out of her pocket and jamming them into the ignition. A quick flick of her wrist and the engine roared to life. They were only going to get one chance at this.

Annja took a couple of deep breaths and then she sat up, jammed her foot on the gas and dropped the truck into Drive all in one long, fluid motion. As the Nissan lunged forward she cut the wheel hard to the right, sending the vehicle slewing sideways until she brought it to a stop right next to the dead elephant.

"Now!" she screamed.

Lenny didn't waste any time, just yanked open the rear door, threw the sword into the truck and leaped in after it as Annja rammed her foot on the gas. She hoped he wouldn't notice that the sword had disappeared.

The window next to her shattered and suddenly she was aware of just how much gunfire was coming their way. Either the gunman was equipped with an automatic rifle or there was more than one gunman out there. Bullets were hammering the outside of the truck with staccato regularity.

She spun the wheel and raced across the uneven surface of the plain. The gunfire followed them for a moment, a final stray bullet smashing in the rear window, and then they were swerving back onto the dirt road and roaring south as fast as the truck would take them.

"You okay back there?" Annja shouted over her shoulder.

Lenny didn't say anything.

"Lenny?"

She chanced a glance behind her and gasped. Lenny was sitting in a pool of blood, his hands clamped tightly against the gunshot wound in his left thigh.

"Not as light on my feet as I used to be," Lenny grunted, and then promptly passed out.

12

A glance in the rearview mirror told her they weren't being followed—for now—so Annja pulled to the side of the road. Immediately she was out of her seat and climbing into the back to deal with Lenny.

She'd seen enough bullet wounds to know what she was looking at and it didn't take her more than a few seconds to determine that the bullet had entered the back of Lenny's leg and exited out the front about halfway up his thigh. There was a lot of blood, but it was seeping out of the wound rather than spurting in a stream. The artery hadn't been cut. That was good; it meant he might live long enough for her to get him help.

First thing she had to do was stop the bleeding.

She dug in the back of the truck until she located the medical kit. She pulled several thick pressure bandages out and put them over the entrance and exit wounds. She used an Ace bandage to hold them in place and then pulled the whole thing tight with the help of the leather belt Lenny was wearing. It wasn't the best field dressing, but it would do for the time being.

Annja hauled Lenny fully upright in the seat and then used the seat belt to secure him in place. After that she hauled herself back in front behind the wheel.

In the rearview mirror she could see they still had the road to themselves.

"Hang on," she told Lenny's unconscious form and then threw the truck in gear and slammed the accelerator. The SUV responded as if it understood the urgency of the moment, surging ahead.

Annja snatched the map off the dash and looked it over while trying to keep one eye on the road. Lenny's wound was a bad one; if she didn't get him help soon he might bleed out, tourniquet or no tourniquet. They were too far from Maun. She was going to have to find something closer if she wanted to do Lenny any good. The only place for miles around was the clinic they'd been headed toward.

Dr. Crane's, it was, then.

A little wooden sign staked into the dirt at the edge of the road was her only indication that she'd reached the turn. She almost missed it, necessitating a quick slam of the brakes that would have thrown Lenny to the floor if she hadn't taken the precaution of belting him into his seat. He didn't notice, though. Still unconsciousness. That, Annja knew, wasn't a good sign.

She threw the Nissan into Reverse, backed up a few feet to clear the turn and then took off down the track.

She only hoped she wasn't already too late.

Less than five minutes later she emerged from the trees and spotted a cluster of buildings behind a chainlink fence a few hundred yards ahead of her. She could see people on the other side of the gate and she started honking the horn as she raced forward. They had the gate open and standing wide by the time she reached it. She pulled up next to the main building and slewed to a stop.

"I've got an injured man here!" she yelled as she got out of the car and threw open Lenny's door.

With the help of several men, Annja was able to wrestle Lenny out of the Nissan and carry him inside the house. A tall, thin man with round glasses and a head of curly brown hair met them in the foyer, took one look and said, "This way, quickly now!" He led them into the room beyond, which turned out to be the kitchen.

"Get him up on the table," he ordered.

Annja and her helpers didn't waste any time, just swept the table clear and hefted Lenny's unconscious form onto it.

The newcomer, who turned out to be Henry Crane, the doctor in charge of the clinic, took one look at Lenny's injury and sent his people scurrying for supplies. Including, Annja was relieved to hear, a surgical bag.

"What happened?" Henry asked as he moved over to the sink and washed his hands.

"We ran into poachers and they started shooting."

Henry shook his head. "Those bastards are getting more dangerous every day." He dried his hands on a clean towel and returned to the table where he began to examine Lenny's wound in earnest. "You're both lucky to be alive," he said absently.

Given all she'd been through over the past few years since picking up Joan of Arc's sword and being drawn into the role of protector of the innocent, getting gunned down for being in the wrong place at the wrong time would have been the height of irony. She didn't say that, though. Instead, she nodded in Lenny's direction. "What's the verdict?"

Henry winced. "I won't know for sure until I get in there, but appearances suggest that the bullet struck the femur and started tumbling, which is why you have a much bigger exit than entry wound. No matter what, we have to get in there and stop the bleeding."

Annja didn't see any delicate way to ask her next question, so she just came right out with it. "Do you have any experience with this kind of surgery?"

He was already going to work on Lenny, cutting away his jeans and washing the wound with water so he could see what he was doing. "I'm a licensed internist, if that helps put your mind at ease, but I won't lie to you. Aside from a surgical rotation during my residency at Mount Sinai in New York a decade ago, I haven't had much experience with gunshot wounds."

Given that there wasn't much she could do one way or the other, Annja smiled weakly and said, "Guess I'd better stop pestering you and let you get to work, then, huh?"

Henry glanced over at her. "If by that you mean getting over here and helping me with this, then, by all means, step to."

13

Porter stood beside the Land Rover and used a pair of binoculars to scan the complex ahead of him. The Creed woman's Nissan was there all right, just as he'd expected it would be, parked close to the clinic's main building and currently being watched over by a pair of the doctor's hired hands. He didn't see either Creed or her male companion. They were no doubt inside somewhere, regaling their host with the tale of their narrow escape from a band of ruthless poachers.

Unfortunately, that left Porter with limited options to regaining control of the map. He wasn't particularly thrilled with any of them.

The simplest and most direct option would be for his men to storm the compound and take the map back by force. Only a handful of the doctor's people were armed and those just well enough to scare off wildlife. Ten minutes after Porter gave the order the entire compound would be in his control, he knew.

But taking such direct action brought troubles of its own. Once the shooting started he'd have to kill them all, from the doctor on down to his lowliest staff member. It wasn't the idea of shooting innocents that troubled Porter; he had plenty of blood on his hands and had no problem adding to it. No, it wasn't that at all. The problem was that the doctor was too well connected for an assault on his compound to be ignored or simply brushed off as a consequence of life in war-torn Africa. The authorities were sure to come after him with everything they had. He didn't know for certain how many individuals were currently inside the doctor's compound and would therefore be unable to say for certain that he'd managed to get them all.

A full-on assault on the compound was therefore out of the question.

He briefly considered waiting to waylay Annja on the road she left the compound behind, but he was afraid she would try to sneak out under the cover of darkness. And he would lose her as a result. He couldn't allow that to happen. She was his only link to the Lost City and the Vanished Tribe.

What he needed was a way to keep track of her without letting her know.

A smile crossed Porter's face as he realized he had just the thing.

TWO HOURS LATER Henry stepped out onto the back porch and sat on the step next to Annja. He handed her a glass of iced tea and then took a long swallow from his own glass.

When he was finished, he said, "The surgery went well. I was able to tie off the blood vessels to keep him from losing any more blood. Thank you for your help in there. He's resting quietly for now, but he's going to need constant care over the next few days and I don't have the facility here for that."

Annja nodded. "When can he travel?"

Henry grimaced. "Hard to say. These rough roads will bounce him all over the place in that vehicle of yours and that's not good for his leg. He could tear open that wound of his and undo all the work I just did. On the other hand, I'll run out of the antibiotics he needs to prevent infection in about forty-eight hours. It's six on the one hand, half a dozen on the other."

Annja was silent for a moment. "If I could arrange for a helicopter to pick him up, could you see to it that he gets aboard?"

Henry turned to face her with a frown. "And where will you be?"

"Our producer has only given us a week to get this story together and I'm already behind as it is. If I can't pull it together in time, we'll both lose our jobs."

It wasn't entirely the truth, but she didn't want to tell him the real reason she was afraid to stay in one place too long. Porter would come after her the minute he figured out she'd left Maun. He might already be on her tail. Staying here for two more days would give him all the time he needed to catch up with her and she had no idea what would happen when he did. She didn't want to risk putting Henry or any of his staff in danger.

If Henry was surprised by her willingness to leave her companion behind he didn't show it. He sipped his iced tea and then asked, "Television, huh?"

"That's right." She took a minute to give him a rough idea of what the show was about and then said, "We were actually on our way to see you when we ran into the poachers."

"Coming to see me?" He put his glass on the step. "Good heavens, why?"

"Three years ago explorer and adventurer Robert Humphrey set off to find what he called the Lost City of the Kalahari and was never seen again. We've recently come across information that might help us discover what happened to him and are doing what we can to retrace his final route."

Annja didn't miss that the doctor had stiffened when she mentioned Humphrey's name.

He knows something.

Henry glanced down at his drink, then smiled at her disarmingly. "I'd be happy to help, Ms. Creed, but I honestly don't know what I can do for you."

Annja knew better. His reaction had confirmed what she'd been able to figure out on her own. It was time to put her cards on the table and see how he responded. She unbuttoned the pocket of the fresh shirt she'd dug out of her pack and pulled out the copy she'd made of Humphrey's original drawing with its cryptic clue. Unfolding it, she laid it on the step between them.

Annja quoted from memory.

"The tulip stands amid the wild beasts,
Within its walls, the first of the answers you seek.
Find the gray crown that watches over the flock,
To receive a piece of the puzzle you hope to unlock."

Henry made no move to pick up the paper. He didn't even glance at it.

Gotcha.

"Once you realize you're looking for a building,"

Annja continued, "it doesn't take more than a few minutes on the internet to learn that this compound was originally built by a Dutch missionary back in 1865. Given that the building we're now in stands in the middle of the world's second-largest game reserve, I don't think I'm mistaken that this is the 'tulip' referred to in the verse."

The doctor steepled his fingers together pensively but still didn't say anything.

"That was all I'd managed to figure out when I left Maun this morning. When you introduced yourself the rest of the puzzle fell into place. Given the number of gray-crowned cranes we've seen since entering the reserve, I'm disappointed I didn't figure it out sooner."

Henry chuckled, finally looking her way. "Nothing to be disappointed about," he told her. "I certainly wouldn't have figured it out."

Annja felt her pulse quicken at the confirmation that she'd been correct. "Did Robert leave this puzzle piece with you?"

"I don't know about a puzzle piece, but he did leave me a letter. Asked me to give it to the one who came asking about that riddle. Come and I'll get it for you."

He led her back into the house and down the hall to the last room on the left. Bookshelves lined one wall, a collection of photographs another. A pair of armchairs with a lamp between them turned one corner of the room into a reading nook. A solid wooden desk, its top lost in papers and files, occupied much of the rest of the space. Henry went directly to it and began hunting for Humphrey's letter.

Annja stepped over to the photographs. There were

a few wildlife shots—elephants, zebras, that kind of thing—but most of the photographs showed Henry involved in one project or another. A photograph of him helping a pair of what looked like San tribesmen deliver a baby goat hung next to a shot of Henry talking with the mayor of Maun, according to a caption under the image. A picture of him digging a well was paired with an oversize shot of him playing in a group of giggling schoolchildren. It was a collision of the old and the new, ancient and modern, and to Annja it seemed to sum up life in southern Africa pretty well.

One photo of Henry and a heavyset man with curly hair and an infectious grin in particular caught her eye. The two men stood with their arms around each other's shoulders, smiling at the camera like high school chums, the plains of the Kalahari stretching away behind them.

The other man in the photo with Henry was Robert Humphrey.

"Ah! Here it is."

She turned to find Henry holding an envelope out to her. It was creased and faded, but other than that, not too worse for wear.

Annja stepped forward eagerly.

14

Annja's heart was racing as she took the envelope from Henry. If she was right, it contained another clue to where Humphrey had gone.

She turned it over in her hands, studying it. There was no writing on the outside. It wasn't thick. It probably held a single piece of paper, two at the most.

Annja looked up to find Henry watching her curiously.

"Aren't you going to open it?" he asked.

"In a moment. What did he say to you, when he gave you this?" she asked, holding the envelope up.

Henry shrugged. "Nothing much, really. 'Give this to the one who comes asking about the tulips and the crane,' or something like that."

"That's it? Nothing about what it was for or why he wanted you to hold on to it?"

"That's it. Robert wasn't one for long explanations."

"I'll say," Annja muttered under her breath as she turned the envelope over in her hands. It was just an ordinary envelope, like millions before it, the kind you could buy in any stationery store.

"Please, sit down," Henry said, indicating the nearby armchair, "and I'll try to explain."

Once they both found a seat, Henry went on. "Robert and I have known each other for years. High school chums and all that. He'd visited a time or two in the past, but was never enamored with Africa the way I was and as a result never stayed for long. Then all that business about bigfoot or whatever the hell it was he was chasing came out in the press and he wanted a place to get out of the limelight for a while, somewhere remote enough that the paparazzi couldn't be bothered to hunt him down. Can't get much more remote than this without the temperatures being below freezing."

Annja laughed. That was certainly true. "So you saw him a lot before that last expedition?"

"Oh, no," Henry replied. "If there's one fact I've learned about Robert in all the years I've known him it's that he can't sit still for more than ten minutes at a time. He wasn't in Botswana a week before he was off again on one of his quests."

She held up the still-unopened envelope. "And this? When did he give you this?"

Henry sighed. "He stopped here on his way out into the bush that last time. We shared a meal and he left the next morning. He was always asking me to watch over something or other, so I didn't give it any thought at the time. Now I wish I had."

Annja could hear the regret plainly in his voice.

"Over wine that night he gave me the envelope along with those crazy instructions of his. Tulips and crane? I had no idea what he was talking about until you read that verse to me earlier. To be honest, I'd forgotten I even had it until that moment."

"Time we find out what it's all about, then, don't you think?"

Henry nodded.

Annja carefully broke the seal on the envelope and looked inside. Just as she'd suspected, there was a single folded piece of paper.

She took it out, unfolded it and began to read aloud.

If you're reading *this,* it no doubt means that things haven't gone as well as I'd hoped they would on my search for the Vanished Tribe and their Lost City. That's too bad; it would have been nice to return home a victor one last time.

I have little doubt that I have, in fact, unearthed the location of that ancient city and, like Mallory before me, perished on my return trip before I could prove my success to the world. While unfortunate, I'm apparently not in a position to complain about it at this point. That's where you come in, my dear reader.

I've left clues to the location of the Lost City. If you're reading this, you've found the first of them. At the end of this letter you'll find the second. I hope you're like me—intrigued by the mysteries of the past and driven to solve them—and that you'll eagerly take up the search on my behalf.

Tell that old windbag Crane I'll miss him; he's a far better man than most.

Good luck and godspeed.

R. Humphrey.

In the place where Tantor goes to die,
Ahab's bane trumpets his call.

They say that music soothes the savage heart,
And makes allies of us all.

Annja looked over at Henry. "Windbag?"

The doctor lifted his hands and grinned. "He used to tell me I talked too much."

Annja laughed. She knew just the type; a particular producer back in New York came to mind.

"So what are you going to do now?" he asked.

This time it was her turn to shrug. "Try to solve the puzzle, I guess."

That was a given. The idea of turning back because Lenny had been injured frankly wasn't even something she'd considered. Forward, that was the direction Annja liked to take whenever possible.

"And the clue? Do you know what it means?"

The clue. Annja couldn't help but smile. Humphrey had been a clever man.

"Not all of it, no. But I've got a good start on it."

"Really?"

Henry's tone clearly showed he had no clue what it was referring to and Annja decided to take some pity on him. "In the first clue your friend Robert used plants and animals to represent the key components of the clue, namely the tulip and the gray-crowned crane. In the second clue, he's making literary references."

Henry looked at her in confusion. "I understand the Ahab reference, but Tantor? Is that an author's name?"

"Nope," Annja answered with a grin. "It's the name of an elephant, actually. From Edgar Rice Burroughs's Tarzan novels."

The doctor shook his head. "Robert must have been

into his cups when he wrote that one, Ms. Creed. What on earth do *Moby Dick* and an elephant named Tantor have to do with a lost city in the middle of the Kalahari Desert?"

Annja looked at him, her eyes sparkling with the challenge of it all.

"Believe it or not, your friend Robert is actually being very clear. To find the next clue, I have to track down a white elephant in the middle of an elephant graveyard and play it some music."

"Of course. How silly of me!" Henry said, but Annja just laughed.

"Sounds kind of fun, actually," she said with another grin.

15

"There's no such thing as an elephant graveyard, never mind a white elephant. Robert must be pulling your leg."

Annja shook her head. "I don't think so. It doesn't have the feel of a practical joke. He went to a lot of trouble to put these clues together and I can't see anyone doing that unless they were serious about the end result."

While she couldn't entirely rule out the possibility that it was an elaborate hoax, Annja believed Humphrey wanted someone to come after him. That much seemed clear.

"What if he wasn't being literal?" she asked. "According to legend, the elephant graveyard is a place where old elephants go to die, right? Can you think of anywhere that elephants gather in a group? Somewhere that might also be related to the word *white?*"

Henry waved at the landscape outside the window. "This is the Kalahari and in the Kalahari all creatures, great and small, including elephants, gather at the watering hole."

But that was too simple. Anyone with half a brain could figure that one out. Humphrey's previous clue had required more mental dexterity than that and she expected him to make things harder with each passing clue, not easier.

She frowned. "That's pretty obvious."

Henry shrugged. "You're the expert. Besides, you'd have a hell of a time figuring out which watering hole, anyway. Too bad we can't just ask the San."

Annja saw him stiffen as he said it and knew he'd just hit upon something.

"What is it?"

"The San!" he said, snapping his fingers. "That's got to be it."

Henry hustled over to his desk and dug in one of the drawers until he found a topographical map. He glanced at the piles on top of his desk and then opted for the floor in front of it instead, spreading out the map so Annja could see it, as well.

He pointed to an area south of their present position and just north of a low range of mountains.

"The government forced most of the San tribesmen to relocate out of the reserve, allegedly for their own protection. A small group of them refused to leave and retreated to a valley at the base of these mountains. It doesn't have an official name but the locals call it the 'white valley' due to the presence of a particular flower that grows there in abundance."

"A flower with white petals, no doubt," Annja said.

The doctor grinned. "Precisely. But it's even better than that."

Annja waited for him to deliver the punch line.

"This particular group of the San," he said smugly, "call themselves the People of the Elephant."

SATISFIED THAT SHE and Henry had deciphered the clue properly, Annja set about making arrangements to have Lenny transported to the hospital. Using the mission's satellite phone, Annja put in a call to Doug in New York, explained the situation and requested that he send a helicopter to pick up Lenny. Once he finally stopped ranting about the cost of aviation fuel, reluctantly Doug agreed. He suggested that Annja return, as well, but she reminded him that they needed the footage to replace the failed bat man piece and that they had very little time to get what they needed. The helicopter wouldn't arrive until midafternoon the next day, but Annja wasn't going to wait. She intended to be back on Humphrey's trail first thing in the morning, she told Doug. She gave him the number to Dr. Crane's satellite phone to pass on to the helicopter pilot in case they ran into any difficulty finding the place. With the details settled, she hung up and went in to see Lenny.

He was awake when she stepped into his room and even managed a smile.

"How are you doing?" she asked.

Lenny's skin had an odd gray pallor to it, no doubt a result of the blood he'd lost, but he was sitting propped up by a couple of pillows behind his back.

"All right. Guess I jigged when I should have jagged," he said.

"You're just not used to having people shoot at you, but I'll give you points for trying," Annja replied with a laugh.

"Thanks. You're a doll."

"Anytime, man, anytime."

Lenny changed position slightly and winced. Apparently the pain meds were wearing off. "So now what?" he asked once he was comfortable again.

"Now you get to take a little helicopter ride back to Maun and spend about a week in the hospital waiting for that leg to heal."

Lenny didn't miss what she'd left unsaid. "And you?"

Annja shrugged. "The show must go on."

"You can't be serious?" Lenny exclaimed. "Somebody was shooting at us! What if they're out there lying in wait even now? The minute you leave the compound they'll be all over you again, except this time you'll be alone."

Annja held up her hands. "Whoa! Easy there, big guy, we don't want you pulling out any of those stitches."

"Be serious, Annja!"

"I am being serious. Tear out those stitches and Dr. Crane will have my head on a spike. Now, why on earth would poachers who we never got anywhere near, wait around to finish off the nonwitnesses?"

Lenny looked annoyed as he said, "I mean it about the gunmen."

"You mean the poachers. And don't worry. Dr. Crane called the authorities to let them know about the elephant."

"How do we know they were poachers? Did you get a look at any of them? What if they weren't poachers at all? What if it was that idiot Porter again?"

Annja bit off the hot retort that was already forming on her lips. Lenny was right. How *did* she know it had been poachers? There was circumstantial evidence to suggest that was the case, but if she really looked at it closely that's all it was—circumstantial. And Porter had tried twice before to take his father's drawing and notes from her. While chances were good that it had been poachers who'd attacked them and were now long gone, she couldn't afford to ignore the possibility that her new enemy had set a trap for her and she'd been lucky to survive.

Fine. I'll be careful. And I'll make sure that Porter can't follow me, if indeed he is out there watching us.

Lenny must have seen the change in her expression. "What are you going to do?" he asked, more gently this time.

"Just what we planned to do," Annja replied. "Find out what happened to Humphrey."

"Annja…"

She waved away his concerns with one hand. "Don't worry. I've got a plan."

ANNJA ROSE ABOUT AN HOUR before dawn, grabbed her backpack and slipped out of her room. She found Henry waiting in the kitchen, a thermos in his hand.

"Thought you might need this."

"Coffee?"

Henry shook his head. "Lenny said you preferred something stronger."

Annja twisted the cap off. The sweet aroma of hot cocoa wafted out of the open thermos.

"Leave it to the doctor to have just the right medicine," she said with relish.

"You sure about this hunt, Annja?" he asked. "Might be better to just catch the flight back with your cameraman."

She shook her head. "I'll be fine, Henry," she said

in a tone that made it clear she would brook no further argument. Truth was she'd been in far worse situations than this since taking up Joan of Arc's sword, but the doctor didn't need to know all that.

"All right, all right," he said, holding his hands up in surrender. "Anything special I need to do once the medevac flight arrives?"

"No. The network's people should handle everything. You might want to keep Lenny sedated, though."

"Why's that?" Henry asked. "Does he hate to fly?"

"Oh, it's not flying he hates," she said with a smile. "It's helicopters. Probably be best if he's already aboard— no, better yet, in the air—before he wakes up."

They laughed together and then said their goodbyes. As Annja climbed into her truck she felt strongly that Lenny was in good hands.

Now the rest of the expedition was up to her.

16

One of Porter's men shook him awake shortly before dawn. "She's leaving, sir," he said, and that was all it took to get Porter up and moving. He had no intention of letting Annja Creed get away from him.

He stepped out of the truck and over to where Bryant was leaning against a large rock, watching the compound through a pair of binoculars. Even without them Porter could see the headlights in the distance, the fencing surrounding the property momentarily visible, caught in the vehicle's illumination.

"What have we got, Bryant?"

The other man spoke without taking his gaze off the moving target. "It's the Nissan they arrived in, sir. The tracker confirms it."

Porter glanced at the satellite map on the laptop computer set up on the tailgate of the truck. A red blip could be seen moving slowly away from the dot on the map symbolizing the compound before them. He couldn't hold back a grin. Bryant had the foresight to plant that transmitter on the undercarriage of Creed's vehicle when he'd flattened the tires. It had been a stroke of genius. Now all he had to do was wait until she got a fair distance away from the compound and then move in to take back what was his by right.

He'd have that map soon enough.

"Tell the men to load up. I want to be ready to move out after her in ten minutes."

Bryant nodded. "You got it, boss."

In the end it took them closer to fifteen, but that was good enough for Porter. He sat in the back of the lead SUV, with the computer in his lap. Bryant was driving and another of Porter's armed guards rode in the passenger seat. The plan was simple. Once they caught up with their target they would box her in and bring her to a stop. Then they would take the map from her, by force if necessary. If Creed ended up injured in the process, so be it.

Perhaps the next time she'll think twice about interfering in family business.

Bryant had activated their GPS system, so now Porter had two dots to follow on the laptop screen—a red one, signifying Creed's vehicle, and a blue one, indicating their own. He took particular glee from watching the distance between the two shrink, until they were practically on top of each other. He was about to say something to Bryant when the other man beat him to it.

"There!" Bryant said, pointing at the red taillights that had just come into view ahead of them.

Creed tried to run—Porter would have been disappointed if she hadn't—but with three vehicles against her one it didn't take long for them to force her to a halt.

Bryant brought their vehicle to a stop about ten feet behind Creed's. The vehicles driven by Porter's other men were stopped roughly the same distance ahead of

Creed's, but on opposite sides of her vehicle and angled toward each other to keep her from driving forward.

For a moment, no one moved. Creed's Nissan was pinned in the glare of the headlights from Porter's Land Rover. Porter could see someone sitting in the driver's seat, but the angle kept him from seeing her, never mind making out the expression on her face. He'd been hoping to see Creed cower in fear, given the trouble she'd caused him over the past few days.

Now he had her, though. Like a rat caught in a trap.

He got out of the car and sauntered toward the other vehicle, savoring the moment. He would make Creed grovel in the dirt before deciding whether he was going to let her live or not.

His vision of what that would be like was interrupted when the driver of the Nissan threw open the door and stepped out into the glare of the headlights.

"What's the meaning of this?" Henry Crane asked, none too politely.

Porter couldn't believe it. She'd tricked him again. It was all he could to do keep from rushing forward and beating the man senseless with his bare hands. He took a couple of deep breaths to calm himself before stepping forward into the light.

"You're out rather early this morning, aren't you, Dr. Crane?"

Crane glared at him. "What business is that of yours? Tell your men to move their trucks before I report you to the authorities in Maun."

Porter let a hard smile cross his features. "We're a long way from Maun, Dr. Crane."

"I don't care how far away we are. I'll have your

ass thrown in jail the minute you set foot inside the city limits if you don't get those trucks out of my way this instant!"

His grin turned into a chuckle. He couldn't help it. "I have to give you credit, Dr. Crane, you've got more spine than I suspected. But that's not going to get you through the night intact, I'm afraid. Where is Creed?"

"I don't know who you're talking about."

"Creed. Annja Creed. The woman whose truck you're driving. Surely you remember her?"

For the first time Crane looked uncomfortable. "The truck is a rental and I'm returning it to the dealer."

"I see."

Porter looked over at Bryant and inclined his head in the truck's direction. With a nod of understanding the other man stalked over, pushed Crane aside and climbed into the cab.

"What do you think you're doing? Get out of there!" Crane yelled at him, but that didn't stop Bryant from rooting around in the glove compartment. When he got back out of the car, he walked over to Porter and handed him some folded papers.

It was the contract from the rental car company. The truck had been rented in Maun, just as Crane claimed, but the paperwork was made out by someone named Lenny Davis. Porter didn't recognize the name but it didn't take a genius to put two and two together to understand that Davis was most likely the young man Creed was traveling with, the one Bryant had shot earlier that morning.

He looked up at Crane, who was now watching him warily.

"I'm not going to argue with you, Dr. Crane. You'll tell me what I want to know, one way or another. Where is Annja Creed?"

Crane stood taller. "Your threats don't mean anything to me, Malcolm Porter," he replied in a cold, hard voice, making it clear that he knew exactly who he was talking to. "Touch me and I'll have you up on charges faster than you can blink. We're done here."

Porter watched in amusement as Crane turned and took a few steps toward his truck. The arrogant idiot thought he was protected, did he? Perhaps it was time to teach him a lesson or two, then.

A wave of Porter's hand was all it took. Bryant stepped forward and drove a meaty fist into the older man's kidney, sending him to the ground in a squirming heap. Several of the other men moved in at that point and there were a flurry of kicks with hard-toed boots that left the doctor weeping in pain.

"Get him on his feet," Porter demanded.

Bryant and one other man hauled the wounded Crane upright. The man's lips were split and the right side of his face was already swollen enough to blind that eye. Porter stepped to the other side to make sure Crane could see him clearly and got in close.

"I told you I'd get my answers one way or another, Doctor. You should have listened to me when you had the chance."

He stepped past the others, leaned inside the truck and pulled the lever to release the hood. Moving to the front of the vehicle, he opened the hood and propped it up out of the way.

"Bring him over here," he said, and waited while

Bryant dragged the suddenly meek Dr. Crane around to the front of the vehicle.

Porter held his hand over the engine. The truck had been driven hard in the desert heat and waves of heat were still rolling off the engine block.

He pointed to the smooth surface of the top of the engine block and said to Bryant, "Make sure it's the left side, so he can see it coming."

Two of Bryant's men stepped up and held the doctor steady while Bryant began forcing the man's face downward toward the hot engine block.

Suddenly recognizing that the abuse he'd endured wasn't yet over, Crane began thrashing, trying to free himself from the men's grip. They were far too strong, however, and in seconds his face was inches away from the scorching metal.

"Wait!" he cried, the word garbled through his swollen lips. "I'll tell you where she's gone!"

Porter scowled at Bryant when the man glanced up at him. He hadn't given the order to stop.

Crane's face moved another inch closer to the heated metal.

"No! No! I can tell you where she's gone! Don't do this! Please!" Crane screamed.

Bryant exerted more pressure, the doctor's face moving inexorably toward the engine block.

"Please, I beg you! I'll tell you about the clue!"

Porter snapped his fingers and Bryant jerked Crane's face up.

"The clue? What clue?" Porter asked.

The doctor couldn't talk fast enough. He told Porter that the map he was looking for wasn't really a map, but an image of the destination his father had been searching for, the Lost City of the Kalahari. He told him how Humphrey had left a clue with the image that had led Annja to his doorstep and how he, Crane, had then handed off the envelope to her that Humphrey had asked him to hold on his behalf.

"What was in the envelope?" Porter asked.

"Another clue."

"Do you remember what the clue said?"

Crane nodded.

"Well?"

He told him.

Porter cocked his head to one side, studying the doctor. "Why wasn't I given this envelope after my father disappeared?"

Crane's one good eye trembled in its socket as he mumbled something.

"I'm sorry, what was that?" Porter asked.

The doctor sighed, as if accepting what was to come, and said, "Your father specifically told me not to."

Porter said, "I see."

He stood there a moment, considering. He wanted more than anything to put a bullet through Crane's simpering face for that remark about his father, but he knew doing so would take away the only advantage he had right now. Crane had clearly discussed the map, and the search for the Lost City, with Creed and more than likely knew where she was going. He could follow behind her, let her do all the work and then swoop in at the end and take the prize from her.

Then, when he had what he wanted, he could kill both of them and no one would be any wiser.

Porter nodded, satisfied that he'd come up with the right solution, and then turned to Bryant.

"Tie him up and toss him in the back of the truck. We're going to need him later."

17

Annja waited fifteen minutes after Henry left the compound, giving him time to draw off anyone who might be watching for her departure, before starting the aged Toyota minibus that he had swapped for her SUV. She left the headlights off, using the lights from the nearby buildings to help her navigate as she drove slowly through the compound, headed for the opposite gate facing south.

Switching vehicles had been Henry's idea. Annja wasn't convinced it was entirely necessary, but in the end she'd agreed to do it simply to get Henry and Lenny to stop nagging her. Annja was convinced that the bullet that struck Lenny earlier had been fired from a poacher's rifle; the two men, on the other hand, were not. If Porter was still on their tail, it wouldn't hurt to use sleight of hand to throw him off it, they had reasoned. Annja's counterargument that they'd be putting Henry in danger had been brushed aside.

"Porter won't harm me," Henry had argued. "I'm tied too tightly to the local community for him to risk it. Trust me."

In the end, Annja had decided to do just that. The Nissan had been driven inside the long, barnlike struc-

ture that served as the compound's garage and there it
had been stripped of all the gear Annja and Lenny had
brought with them. The truck was returned to its park-
ing spot outside while the gear itself had been trans-
ferred to the minibus.

The way the procedure was handled by Henry's men
suggested they'd done something similar more than
once before. Annja knew Henry had been active in trying to help the local people reclaim their ancestral land
when the Botswanan government had forced them out
of the Kalahari reserve a few years back and she found
herself wondering just what it was his people had been
smuggling into the interior. Food and water, perhaps?
Maybe medicine? She knew it couldn't have been weapons. The San tribesmen, not to mention Henry himself,
weren't prone to violence.

A man stood by the gate, waiting for her. When she
was close enough he pushed it open and waited for her
to drive through before pulling it shut and securing it
behind her. Now she was on her own.

The Toyota was an older model and had seen more
than its fair share of use. It didn't handle as well as the
Nissan she'd left behind, but it should be up to the task
before her.

She hoped.

Annja drove slowly away from the compound a good
distance before turning on the headlights and heading
out into the African night, away from safety and toward the mystery that lay before her. For the first time
in days, Annja felt she was right where she was supposed to be.

The road wasn't much more than a dirt track, but

the minibus took it without complaint. According to Crane, she was to follow this road due south for about eighty miles. From there, she would turn west and make her way deeper into the Kalahari, until she reached the White Valley. The villagers she was looking for never stayed in one place long, so at that point she would have to hunt them down by trial and error.

The directions weren't detailed, but they were good enough. She'd find the village; she had little doubt of that. The hard part, she suspected, would be convincing the tribe to help her in her quest to discover what happened to Humphrey during that final, fateful expedition. Especially if realizing her quest meant finding the Lost City and it turned out the San people couldn't, or wouldn't, help her.

Let's just hope they're in a sharing mood.

The first part of the trip passed without incident. Twice she was forced to wait while large groups of wildebeests crossed the road, and later she caught a glimpse of a lioness dragging a zebra carcass behind her and disappearing into the brush along the side of the trail.

The latter nearly proved to be Annja's downfall. While she was craning her head trying to get another look at the magnificent creature, she inadvertently swerved off the side of the road. She took the bus crashing through a series of camel thorn bushes, bumping over several newly formed termite mounds before regaining control and getting back on track.

After that, she did her best to keep her eyes on the road.

The sun came up, signaling the start of a new day

to the animals that made the Kalahari their own, and Annja began to see more and more wildlife the deeper into the reserve she went. Along with the zebras and wildebeests she'd noted earlier, she caught sight of herds of springbucks and oryx, a colony of meerkats, two packs of hyenas and even a pride of lions basking in the sun.

By midmorning the temperature had risen to somewhere in the low nineties and Annja was grateful for the minibus's noisy air-conditioning. She even left the vehicle running when she stopped to forage for something to eat in her backpack, not wanting to forfeit the steady stream of cool air coming out of the vents by turning the ignition off. Two cans of peaches and a bottle of water later, Annja was ready to continue.

Annja turned off the dirt track and headed west at the eighty-mile mark, just as she'd been instructed. If her rate of travel on the so-called road had been slow, it was positively glacial as she drove carefully through the knee-high scrub grass, on the lookout for hidden obstacles. An hour after turning off she glanced down at the odometer and saw that she'd only traveled another five miles!

Drumming the wheel impatiently, she continued onward. She hadn't gone much farther when a series of loud knocks began issuing from beneath the hood of the minibus. They came quickly, one after another, and grew louder with each passing moment. Annja wasn't a mechanical whiz, by any stretch of the imagination, but even she knew that wasn't a good sign. A glance at the dashboard showed the minibus's temperature gauge way up in the red. Concerned, she slowed the vehicle and came to a stop.

By then, however, the damage was done.

Steam billowed out along the edges of the bus's hood, evidence that it had overheated. Annja wouldn't be going anywhere until the vehicle cooled. But as she stepped out of the minibus and glanced back along the dirt track she'd been following for the past several hours, she noticed the real problem.

A thin black line stretched back the way she had come, glistening in the late-morning light.

Annja squatted down beside it. She reached out and dipped a finger in the substance, then brought it up to her face for a closer look.

Oil.

"Damn." She hurried over to take a look beneath the vehicle at a point just behind the front tire.

All it took was one glance to confirm her fears.

Oil was slowly dripping from a hole she'd somehow managed to tear through the bottom of the oil pan. That meant the knocking she'd heard must have been the pistons firing without any oil in the engine.

A simple engine overheat she could handle. But a hole in the oil pan? Not so much. Sure, she carried an extra pint or two of oil in the truck; you didn't travel in the outback without being prepared. But no way did she have enough to fill the engine, even if she was able to get the hole in the oil pan plugged up.

The minibus wasn't going anywhere anytime soon.

She swore again and then kicked the tire a few times in frustration.

Of all the luck.

If Crane's directions were right, the White Valley was at least another eight, maybe as much as ten, miles ahead of her. Not to mention whatever distance she'd need to cover to find the San village she was looking for once she reached the valley itself. Annja knew she could do three miles an hour on foot, which meant it was going to take her until midafternoon to reach the valley. What other choice did she have? It might be days, even weeks, before another vehicle came this way, if ever. It wasn't like she was on the main highway headed southwest out of Maun. This was the middle of the Kalahari.

Certainly no sense in staying here.

Once she made up her mind to continue on foot, Annja set to making preparations with her usual level of focus and attention. She filled her backpack with several days' worth of MREs—Meals Ready to Eat—that she'd bought back in Maun and as much water as she could carry. She added a flashlight, batteries, matches, water purification tablets and a few more odds and ends she thought she might need. She kept a careful watch on how heavy the pack got; she didn't want to overburden herself and wind up exhausted before she'd reached the valley. At the same time, she didn't want to end up in the middle of the Kalahari with nothing to drink.

The vultures wouldn't be far behind.

When she was ready, she slung the pack onto her back, tugged her Yankees baseball cap squarely down on her head and set off westward, into one of the last great wildernesses on the planet.

Annja could feel her heart pounding with excitement.

18

The terrain, mostly flat plains and knee-high grasses, was easy to navigate and Annja was able to keep a steady pace without much difficulty, which was a good thing because she didn't want to stay out here any longer than necessary. The sun beat down mercilessly from high overhead and she was soon thankful for both her baseball cap and her long-sleeve shirt despite the one-hundred-plus-degree temperature. Without them, she would have roasted alive. As it was she was able to keep her body temperature down to a reasonable level by periodically soaking her shirt with some of the precious water she was carrying.

She saw more wildlife now that she was on foot than she had driving. It was as if the animals had decided to put on a display for her and her alone. Giraffes, wildebeests, warthogs, gemsbok and jackals. The numbers and variety of the animals she cautiously passed were astounding. Above her head soared a cacophony of birdlife, from goshawks and kites, to kestrels and martial eagles. Twice she passed massive weaver nests suspended in the branches of low-hanging trees, the colonies stretching nearly fifteen feet in length and inhabited by more than a hundred of the yellow-breasted birds. Annja felt like a little girl on her first trip to the zoo, and every new sighting brought a wide smile to her face and an eagerness to see more. For a while she stopped worrying about finding the San village she was headed toward and just basked in the beauty that nature laid out for her to enjoy.

Eventually, though, her thoughts returned to the warning Lenny had given her that the poachers might not have *been* poachers. When she'd been safely behind the wheel of Crane's old minibus, putting distance between herself and the compound as rapidly as possible, she hadn't been concerned. By the time Porter figured out where she had gone—if it was Porter and if he even did figure out where she'd gone—her lead would have been so large she doubted he would have been able to catch up with her.

Now, however, stuck crossing the Kalahari on foot, she wasn't feeling so confident. If Lenny had been right, if it had been Porter and not some random poachers that had left that elephant carcass for them to find and had subsequently fired on them, it was clear he was far more dangerous than she'd given him credit for being. Theft was one thing. But his willingness to use violence, and deadly violence at that, took his confrontation to a new level.

Not that she couldn't handle that, too, if it proved necessary. Better men than Porter had tried to eliminate her in the past and had quickly discovered that she was not one to back down at the first sign of trouble. In fact, she was often the one who ended what others had started. She wasn't exactly comfortable with violence, but she didn't shy away from doing what needed to be done if and when the situation called for it. If Porter pushed things beyond the pale, she'd deal with him.

Annja banished Porter from her thoughts and turned her attention back to the task at hand. As far as she could tell, she'd been traveling at a steady pace of about three miles per hour, just as she'd anticipated back at the beginning of her hike. Given that she'd been walking for almost three hours now, she should be reaching the White Valley soon. At that point it was just a matter of locating the San village, which she didn't expect to be difficult.

As it turned out, she was right. It wasn't that difficult, because rather than having to try to locate the village, the village came to her.

Annja was taking advantage of the cooler air in the shadow of a large boulder to squat for a moment and take a few sips from her water bottle when she felt eyes upon her.

She gave no indication that she sensed a presence and just continued letting the cool liquid slide down her throat. She didn't see anything at first and was starting to wonder if it had just been a momentary interest from a passing animal when she finally spotted what she was looking for. A pair of brown eyes set in a dark face stared out at her from behind a nearby bush.

She let her gaze slide over him, not wanting to give away that she'd seen him yet in the hopes of observing him in turn for a moment or two. She had to give him credit. The boy was good; if she hadn't stopped to take a drink she probably never would have noticed that she was being followed. As it was she could barely make out his form, hidden by the vegetation he was crouched behind.

But she had a hunch she knew how to draw him out.

Annja dug into her backpack and removed a couple of the chocolate-flavored protein bars she carried. Unwrapping one of them, she made a big show of taking and enjoying a bite of it.

"Mmm, that's good," she said, before taking another.

She kept it up until she'd finished the entire bar. Then, unwrapping the second one, she held it out toward the bush where the boy was hiding.

"Here," she said, "you try some."

He didn't move.

"Come on. I won't bite." She smiled at him, doing her best to appear nonthreatening.

Given the number of safaris that operated in this part of the world, Annja was betting the boy had encountered strangers before and it turned out she was right. He slowly stuck his head out from behind the bush and watched her for a moment. Then, having apparently decided she wasn't a major threat to life, limb or liberty, he walked over and squatted in front of her.

"Go on," Annja said, holding the protein bar out to him. "Take a bite."

She didn't think he could understand her, at least not verbally, but that didn't stop him from taking the bar from her hand and sniffing at it. Tentatively he took a bite...and promptly spit it back out again.

"Yeah, can't say I disagree with you, kid," Annja said, laughing.

The boy appeared startled for a moment and then laughed along with her.

From the bushes came a chorus of laughter and before Annja knew it she was surrounded by children of different ages, all laughing and reaching for the protein bar to try it for themselves. She even dug out two more so that there would be enough to go around. The children chattered excitedly at her in their own language, melodious-sounding words mixed in with a collection of clicks, whistles and hoots that sounded more like bird calls than any speech she knew. When they were finished with the protein bars, they took her hands, drew her up from the ground and led her into the bush.

It wasn't long before the children introduced her to the village proper. A couple dozen grass-and-wood huts had been erected in a clearing, the doors all facing inward toward the communal cooking and eating area in the center. There were perhaps fifty or so people here. The men and women alike dressed in simple, loose clothing made of animal skins, many with their upper torsos bare. Their skin was dark, with a leathery appearance from all the time they spent in the sun, making it hard for her to guess their ages.

The women were all hard at work on one task or another. She spotted one group making jewelry from what looked to be ostrich eggs while another group a short distance away was butchering a pair of gemsbok antelope, no doubt for dinner that evening. The men squatted in a group on the other side of the camp, laughing and talking among themselves. They glanced at Annja as she and the children passed, but kept at their activities and made no move to interact with her.

Annja knew the San were a nomadic people, setting up camp in an area for an indeterminate period and then moving on again when food or water became scarce. At least, that's what her anthropology class had taught her. Something about this village spoke of a greater permanence, however. The huts seemed to be built of sturdy materials and didn't appear to be the type of structure that could be taken down with any ease or speed.

One other thing stuck out to her and that was the high percentage of implements, tools and other items made from bone. Annja knew that the San believed in using every available part of the game they killed, so she expected some items to have been crafted from bone, but there seemed to be a disproportionate volume of bones here, as if these people had access to a larger supply than usual.

A thrill ran through her. It was tenuous, yes, but it was the first evidence she had that she was on track.

The children led her toward a young man sitting beneath a monkey thorn tree talking to several children. He looked roughly her age and what little he wore showed off his powerful physique. As Annja and the children approached, he rose to his feet and smiled warmly.

"Welcome to our village," he said.

Annja hadn't been expecting anyone to speak such excellent English. "Thank you," she said. "I'm Annja."

"My name is Xabba." He stepped forward so that he could see back in the direction she'd come. "Where is the rest of your group? Are you here on a tour?"

Annja shook her head. "No, I'm on my own."

Xabba considered that for a moment. "It is not safe to be in the Kalahari alone," he said at last. "There are many predators."

You've got that right. And not just the four-legged kind, either.

She slipped her pack off her back and pulled a photograph of Humphrey out of one of its pockets. "I'm looking for this man," she said, holding it up to Xabba. "Can you tell me if you've seen him?"

For just a moment she thought she saw a flicker of recognition in his eyes, but it was gone so quickly that she wasn't sure it had been there at all.

He shook his head. "I do not know this man."

"Perhaps there is someone else who might have seen him…?"

"I will take you to Mmegi, our village elder."

As they walked, Annja asked, "Your English is excellent. Where did you learn it?"

Xabba's grin returned. "I went to school for a little while, when the government took our land. I learn quickly."

Annja knew about the land dispute from her research. When diamonds had been discovered inside the reserve, the Botswana government forcibly relocated most of the San tribesmen to refugee camps outside its boundaries. They were prevented from hunting and gathering and forced to live on government handouts. A number of human rights organizations came to the aid of the San and a few years ago the tribespeople had won the right to return to their ancestral home and way of life. Now, several years later, many still lingered in the camps, victims of alcoholism, boredom and depression.

Xabba led her through the village to where a group of older San were gathered together in the shade of several trees. They fell silent at their approach. One of them rose to his feet.

Must be the elder Xabba was talking about…

The old man said something in their native tongue and Xabba replied. They went back and forth for a moment, question and reply, until Xabba turned to Annja.

"This is Mmegi, our elder," he explained. "I've told him you are looking for help. Ask him what you wish and I will translate for you."

Annja nodded, then turned to face the old man. He was a wizened fellow, with bright eyes that seemed to stare into her. A mischievous grin played at the corners of his mouth.

"I'm looking for this man," she said, holding up the picture of Humphrey again. "Can you tell me if you've seen him?"

Xabba waited until she was finished and then translated what she'd said to the tribal elder. The elder, in turn, stared at the photo in Annja's hand for a moment and then shook his head before saying something in his native tongue.

"Mmegi says that he does not know that man."

Annja frowned. Something didn't feel right to her. The elder's answer had been straightforward enough, provided it was translated properly, which she suspected it had been, but something still felt…off. Even though she couldn't speak the language, she was left with the sense that the elder was lying.

Why would he do that?

She tried again. "It's been some time, so perhaps a closer look might help?" She handed the photograph to Xabba and indicated that he should give it to Mmegi.

"His name is Robert Humphrey. Big happy fellow with a keen interest in you and your culture. I'm all but positive he came this way. If he did, I find it hard to imagine that he wouldn't have stopped to enjoy your hospitality."

Xabba held out the photo but Mmegi didn't even look at it. All he said was one word and even Annja could hear the finality in it. He turned away, a sure sign that the audience was over, and that's when Annja saw it.

Tattooed on the old man's back was the image of an elephant skull, complete with long curving tusks. It started near the base of his spine and rose upward, with the tusks pointing over each shoulder, and filled nearly his entire back.

With nothing left to lose, Annja said, "I know Humphrey was here. He was searching for the elephant graveyard and thought you knew where it could be found. After all, you are the People of the Elephant, are you not?"

The moment Xabba translated her remark about the elephant graveyard there was silence.

Mmegi stared at her with hard eyes, his mouth stretched into a tight, angry line. Even Xabba was shaking his head in barely restrained anger.

Annja didn't know if it was because she'd all but called the elder a liar or her mention of the elephant graveyard that caused the shift, but it was clear she'd overstepped some boundary they held dear. She opened her mouth, intending to apologize, but the elder was a beat quicker. In the silence his voice rang loud and clear. Annja didn't need to understand what he was saying to know that he'd just passed sentence on her.

Xabba gave her the bad news seconds later.

"Mmegi says that you are no longer welcome among the People. He asks that you leave the village at once."

Six San warriors rose to their feet, spears and bows in hand.

Annja looked at each of them, one after the other, letting them see she wasn't intimidated by their actions. At the same time, however, she recognized that the situation had become untenable and it was time she left before things got ugly. She needed their help. Antagonizing them wasn't a smart way to go about getting it.

She faced Mmegi once again and bowed slightly, to show her acceptance of his request. "I'm sorry I have offended you," she said to him, trying to ignore his angry stare. Beside her, Xabba translated for her again. "I am just concerned about my friend. Please, if you have seen him, let me know. I am worried for him."

With that, she let them lead her out of the village.

19

As Annja moved off down the trail, she could've kicked herself for letting the events play out the way they had back in the San village. She'd pushed too hard and had no one but herself to blame for the results. If she'd been patient, if she hadn't tried to force the issue, she might still be there instead of wandering the outskirts of the village and trying to come up with some excuse for returning that wouldn't get her immediately thrown out again.

She stopped, brought up short by what she thought had been...a scream?

She glanced around, but didn't see anything besides the same thick grass and low trees that she'd been walking through for several minutes.

Had she imagined it?

She turned in a slow circle, straining to catch the sound again but to no avail. She was all but convinced that she had imagined it, when suddenly there it was again. This time, however, the scream was followed by a thundering roar and there was no mistaking that sound.

Lion!

Both cries had come from somewhere to her right,

on the other side of the thicket of monkey thorn trees. Time was clearly of the essence so Annja took off at a run, drawing her sword as she went.

The trees were low, no more than fifteen to twenty feet high at most. Their branches twisted and entwined, growing more outward than upward, creating a canopy overhead where two or more grew close together. As Annja made her way between the trees, she could hear the growls of the lion now intermixed with the crying of a child. She prayed she'd be in time.

Another few moments more and she emerged into a small clearing. Ahead of her, on the other side of the open space, a large jackal berry tree grew all by itself. A young boy presumably from the nearby village clung to branches as high up in the tree as he could go, his face wet with tears as he stared in horror at the lion below him. The beast stood on its hind legs, its body braced against the tree trunk as it swiped at him with its front paws. The tree shook, threatening to unseat the boy and send him spilling to the ground.

There was no doubt in anyone's mind—Annja's, the boy's or the lion's—what would happen if the boy fell.

Annja let out a yell to get the big cat's attention.

IT WAS NEARLY SUNDOWN by the time Porter and his men found Annja's abandoned minibus.

Unused to being subjected to violence, Crane had broken rather easily and revealed that Annja had headed south, deeper into the Kalahari in search of the White Valley and the San tribe known as the People of the Elephant.

Not the type to go roaming the desert for a needle in a haystack, Porter had ordered Bryant to turn their little caravan around and they had driven back to Dr. Crane's compound. There Porter had used the telephone to hire a helicopter pilot to search the area south of Crane's compound for trace of the missing minibus. He told the pilot he'd pay a handsome bonus if he could find the vehicle before the end of the day, more if he could do it in a few hours. With a bonus of what he could normally make in six months of flying, the pilot moved with alacrity and was airborne within moments of agreeing to take the job.

Unfortunately, the Kalahari was a big place and even with Dr. Crane's information Annja proved hard to find. The pilot spent the morning searching the road south of Crane's compound, returned just after noon to refuel and went back out again immediately. Porter spent the time in Crane's air-conditioned office, waiting for word. When it came, Porter, Bryant and his security team piled back into the SUVs and drove south for the second time in so many days.

According to the pilot, Creed had followed the road eighty miles south and then had turned west. She had apparently run into trouble at some point and the minibus was currently sitting out in the middle of nowhere with the hood up. The pilot had circled the vehicle three times, just in case the driver was taking shelter nearby, but no one emerged to flag him down. At that point, he'd called it in.

Now Porter watched from the coolness of the SUV as Bryant and a handful of his men checked out the abandoned vehicle and the surrounding area. It didn't take them long.

"She was leaking oil from a hole in her oil pan," Bryant said through the partially opened window next to Porter. "There's a long trail of it running back in the direction she came from. Looks like she blew the engine."

"So where is she?"

Bryant nodded in the direction they'd been traveling. "O'Neil found boot tracks that way, so I'm guessing she continued on foot."

Deeper into the reserve?

Porter turned to Dr. Crane, who he'd moved into the vehicle with him. "What's in that direction?" he asked.

Crane glared at him with distain. "The White Valley, of course. Why else would she go that way?"

Now that the immediate fear of losing his life had passed, the doctor had grown more insolent as the miles had passed. Porter considered shooting him then and there, but he might need the man for what lay ahead.

His father had made trip after trip to the remnants of that indigenous-people group in the months before his final expedition. Porter had long been estranged from Humphrey at that point, and his father had never been one to share his secrets, so Porter didn't know the result of his efforts. But given that Creed was now retracing his footsteps based on the clue Crane had given her, it seemed clear that the next missing piece of the puzzle could be found among the San.

Which made sense, of course, given that the Lost City was supposedly the ancestral home of the San themselves.

A glance at the setting sun told him they had less than a half hour of daylight left. He wondered if they should go on. The halogen lights mounted on the roof of each vehicle would allow them to travel after dark, but he was reluctant to take the chance of losing her trail a second time. If they lost it in the darkness they might travel miles out of their way without realizing it. Best to hunker down for the night and start fresh in the morning, he decided.

No doubt Creed would be doing the same.

20

The lion turned to look at Annja when she yelled. Mission accomplished. It stopped trying to knock the boy out of the tree…and instead focused its attention on Annja.

It was a healthy-looking specimen, she could see, with a great black mane. Annja guessed it to be in the neighborhood of four hundred pounds and roughly eight to nine feet in length.

"There's a good kitty," she said in a steady voice, doing what she could to keep its attention. If she could draw it away from the tree, the boy might have a chance to climb down and escape.

She began to back away, waving her hand in a come-and-get-it gesture. The lion watched her for a moment and then turned back toward the tree.

Oh, no, you don't.

"Hey! Fur face! Over here!" she yelled, waving her hands over her head to create a bigger target.

That got its attention.

The lion whirled back around and roared, no doubt letting her know just who was king of the beasts and who was the prey.

Annja wasn't having any of it.

She yelled back as loud as she could, brandishing her sword at the same time, keeping the attention firmly on her as she slowly began backing away again.

This time the lion advanced in her direction, then made a couple of warning-swipes with one giant paw, the way a house cat warned off another cat when it got too close.

"What's the matter?" she taunted. "Afraid of little ol' me?"

Her behavior was clearly confusing the animal—Annja's stubborn refusal to behave like proper prey caused it to hesitate instead of rushing forward and pulling her down beneath its massive form.

A glance over the lion's head showed the boy silently dropping to the ground.

Run! Annja urged him silently. Run and don't look back!

As if he'd heard her, he did just that. He was off like a shot, disappearing into the undergrowth as fast as his feet would carry him and barely making a sound in the process.

The lion didn't even notice, its attention now fully on Annja. It began to advance slowly in her direction again, one step at a time.

Every instinct screamed at her to turn and run, but she knew she wouldn't make it ten yards if she was foolish enough to try. Lions weren't built for long-distance running, and would tire easily if forced to, but they could put on an impressive burst of speed for a short period. A lion's preferred method of attack was to rush its prey and seize the throat in its massive jaws, crushing the life out of its prey by suffocation. Therefore turning her back was the last thing she should do. Despite what her primitive survival instincts were telling her, her best chance was to stay where she was and face the beast head-on.

If she could keep it in front of her and at arm's length, she might have a chance of surviving.

She could outwit the lion, scare it off or kill it. She didn't want to do the latter unless that was absolutely necessary. This lion was beautiful and with so few of them left in the world the senseless slaughter of such a magnificent creature didn't sit right with her. She wouldn't hesitate to kill it if it became a matter of life and death, but she'd put off doing so as long as possible.

Without warning the lion rushed forward, snarling as it came.

Annja refused to run, standing her ground with her sword pulled back over her shoulder as the lion charged her. She waited until it was almost on her and then stepped adroitly to one side, striking with the sword.

The lion twisted toward her, one paw lashing out in a terrible blow no doubt intended to knock her flat to the ground, but Annja's sword was there to meet it.

Sword struck flesh.

Blood flew.

Annja spun away from the lion as it recoiled in pain.

It didn't stay away for long, though. Annja might have scored first blood but she knew a minor injury like that wasn't going to slow the cat down in any significant way. The lion proved this seconds later by taking a few short steps and then leaping at her.

Time seemed to slow as Annja's mind went into combat mode, analyzing and rejecting possible courses of action in milliseconds as the lion crossed the distance between them. Teeth, claws and sword glinted in the afternoon light. If the lion got close enough to take her down…

As the king of the jungle reached the nadir of his leap, Annja took the only course of action that looked as if it might give her a chance of surviving the next ten seconds.

She took two steps *toward* the leaping beast, released her sword into the otherwhere and then dove forward directly beneath the lion.

One oversize paw lashed downward, the claws passing less than an inch above her diving form, and then her fingers touched the ground and she curled herself into a ball, letting her momentum carry her through the somersault and back up onto her feet.

There was a large monkey thorn tree directly in front of her with a trunk thick enough to protect her back, and Annja headed for it with due haste.

Behind her she heard the lion touch back down and knew it wouldn't waste any time in turning and coming after her. She had only seconds to be ready for its charge.

As she ran she called her sword to her again, feeling an almost physical relief as her fingers wrapped around the hilt.

Behind her, the lion roared again, the air shaking with the intensity of its frustration.

Annja knew by the sound that they had passed the point of no return. Only one of them was going to walk away from this battle if the lion had its way.

In her mind's eye she could see the lion rushing toward her unprotected back. As she reached the tree she reacted to the unseen attack, spinning around and lashing out with her sword.

The blade bit deep into the lion's shoulder, throwing off the animal's strike, and the claws that were meant to rip her down the middle lashed into the trunk of the tree next to her.

Roaring again, this time in pain rather than frustration, the lion backed off.

It didn't stay away for long, though, taking a moment to recover itself and then rushing in again, lashing with its other paw this time.

Again, Annja fended it off.

So began a series of repeat attacks, with the lion trying to break through her defenses and Annja doing all she could to keep the beast away from her.

When the lion hadn't backed off after the first few times she'd injured it, Annja had quietly told herself that she was going to need to kill it to survive, whether she liked it or not. Trouble was the wily beast refused to give her the opportunity. It had developed a healthy respect for the shining blade and danced in and out, feinting and striking, over and over again without getting close enough for Annja to deliver a fatal thrust.

It was almost as if it was playing with her.

Eventually, she knew, she would tire and the lion would get past her defenses. She would vanish just as Humphrey had with no one the wiser. She needed to find a way out of this before she reached that point. She was too tired to run; the cat would pull her down in seconds. She could keep fighting for five, maybe ten, more minutes, but she could already feel her responses getting sloppy, her recovery after each cut and thrust getting slower. She supposed she could try to climb the tree behind her, but that would mean turning her back and that wasn't something she wanted to do, not even for a second. Maybe as a last resort.

The lion stopped pacing and fixed its stare on her.

A chill ran through her.

This is it. It's going to charge.

Annja braced herself, the sword out before her. If it rushed she'd do her best to deliver a thrust deep into its heart, but its reach was longer than her own and those claws would get her for sure.

She readied herself.

But to her surprise, it didn't come.

Instead, she heard the sound of running feet and Annja was no longer alone. San tribesmen appeared out of nowhere to stand on either side of her, their wooden spears thrust out in front of them, creating a wall of deadly intent that would make it difficult for the beast to reach her without being injured in the process.

The lion checked its charge, rearing up on its hind legs. It slashed the air with its right front paw and roared at them, but didn't come any closer.

Rather than be intimidated, the San warriors roared right back, shaking their spears and jumping up and down, using the action to make themselves look bigger and therefore more of a threat. That was what Annja had tried to do earlier.

Seeing what they were doing, she joined in, as well, shouting and yelling with the rest of them while brandishing her sword in front of her.

It was too much for the lion. One lone woman, armed

or not, was prey. But this jumping, shouting mass was too much to wrap its feline brain around, and with a final roar it turned and disappeared into the brush.

Annja sagged in relief.

That had been much closer than she liked.

The San tribesmen were laughing and cheering, apparently as happy at the lion's departure as she was. In the resulting confusion, Annja released her sword back into the otherwhere when she thought no one was looking.

A small form darted between the cheering men and slammed into her legs with the force of a battering ram. Annja looked down to find the boy she'd saved from the tree hugging her tightly about the waist. She bent down and hugged him back, just as thankful as he was to still be alive.

Though she couldn't understand anything they said, the warriors made it clear through hand gestures that they wanted her to follow them back to the village.

Given that they were her link to the mysterious elephant graveyard, Annja was more than happy to oblige.

21

They threw a banquet that night in Annja's honor. A large bonfire had been built at the center of the village, and the San gathered in a group as the feast was being prepared.

The main course was to be the eland Annja had seen the women skinning earlier that afternoon, the antelope roasted over a crackling fire. The smell of the roasting meat had Annja salivating, but the food would have to wait until after the ritual dance.

Several of the women rose and gathered in a loose circle around the bonfire, led by the mother of the boy Annja had rescued, a woman a few years younger than herself, named Balanka. The women wore patterned headbands and wreaths of beaded necklaces, and bangles at their ankles and wrists. They moved in a circuitous line, stamping the earth, filling the air with the rattle of their jewelry and sending up clouds of fine dust with every step. First Balanka began singing, a short burst of song here and there, and then the rest of the group joined in, weaving distinct patterns of melodies acting in counterpoint to one another. They clapped their hands in complex rhythms as they danced, and Annja found herself swaying along with them. The dancers' dark skin gleamed in the firelight, their bodies slick with the sweat of their exertion.

As the song gained momentum, several men rose and joined the circle, their deep voices harmonizing with the women's. The singing grew louder, the dance moved faster, and Annja felt a swelling sense of delight and with it a need to move with the music. When Xabba stood in front of her and extended his hand, she didn't hesitate. She jumped to her feet and joined the dancing, clapping group, doing her best to follow along until the dance was finally over and she staggered back to her seat, a wide smile on her face.

Balanka brought her a plate heaped high with antelope meat and roasted vegetables, and Annja fell to it with a vengeance. The meat was tender, succulent and came apart in her fingers as easily as something that had been marinating in a Crock-Pot all day long.

It was absolutely delicious.

As Annja was finishing the last of her meal, Mmegi rose and began speaking. Xabba listened carefully, laughed and then turned to Annja.

"Mmegi wants to honor you with a story."

Annja knew that the San were a highly creative people who loved to express themselves artistically.

"Tell him I would be honored."

Mmegi's reply to her was swift and the group around them clapped in enthusiasm when he was finished.

Xabba said, "Because of your interest earlier, he will tell us of the story of how the elephant came to be."

Annja clapped with the others. "Excellent! I can't wait to hear it."

Mmegi launched into his tale without preamble and

had the audience captivated in seconds, even Annja, who didn't understand a word until Xabba translated it. Mmegi was a born storyteller, using facial expressions and body movements to enhance the telling.

"Long ago, when the world was young, the First People lived in harmony with the world and the rest of its inhabitants, enjoying the life that the Twin Gods had given them. They walked and talked and played in the valley without fear.

"One day several of them were out walking when they heard a cry for help. Following the sound, they at last came to a large mud hole near the banks of the great river. In the middle of the mud hole was an animal they had never seen before. It was about the size of a hippopotamus, with a large nose and ears that were too big for its body, but only a little.

"'Please help me,' the animal cried, upon seeing the First People standing on the bank above the mud hole. 'I'm stuck.'

"Xhosa, the leader of the group, hated to see an animal in pain and so he quickly convinced the others that they should free this strange-looking beast.

"Very carefully the four of them climbed down the banks to the edge of the mud hole. They made sure to stay on firm ground, not wanting to get stuck themselves, and got behind the animal. They pushed and pushed and pushed, to no avail.

"The sun was hot that day and it gradually began to leech the color out of the poor animal's hide as they worked. Before long its pebbly skin went from being dark gray to light gray to nearly white and still the First People were unable to free the great beast.

"Finally, Xhosa had an idea.

"He left one of his companions to push it from behind and placed the other two on either side of the animal, instructing them to pull on his ears. Xhosa himself went around to the front and grasped hold of the animal's nose.

"'I'm sorry, but this is the only way I can think of to free you from the mud,' he told the animal.

"'I don't mind,' came the reply, 'as long as you get me out of here.'

"So Xhosa counted to three and on the final count his friends pushed and pulled with all their might.

"'Harder!' Xhosa cried, and his friends obeyed.

"They were pulling so hard, that the animal's ears and nose began to stretch, growing larger and longer with every tug.

"Seeing this, Xhosa was about to tell his friends to stop when the animal cried, 'No, don't stop! I'm almost free!'

"And so the First People did as they were told. They pushed and pulled, harder and harder, until…pop! The mud released the animal and it stumbled forward onto dry land.

"But the damage had been done. The animal's nose was now longer than Xhosa's arm and its ears were as big as boulders.

"Xhosa knew that the animal would be sad when it saw itself in the watering hole later that day, so he acted quickly to save it some pain.

"'Look at you!' he cried in wonder. 'Out of the mud and muck comes a beautiful new creature. I name you

Elephant and declare you a friend of the First People as long as you live.'

"And so, from that day forth, the First People and the elephant were as close as family."

The San were whistling and shouting their approval of the story and Annja joined in. Mmegi caught her eye and winked, which she took as a good sign.

Perhaps she might get the information she needed from them, after all.

The celebration eventually came to an end and Xabba offered to show her to a hut where she could sleep for the evening. Annja tried to refuse, upset that she might be evicting someone else, but Xabba assured her that the small shelter had been empty. It would be good to have something between her and the local animal life, even it if was just a temporary structure.

Nemso, the boy she'd rescued, was waiting for her outside the hut she would be using. In his hands he had a cloth-covered bundle, which he handed to Annja.

"Mmegi would like to express his thanks and appreciation," Xabba explained, "and so would Nemso. They offer this gift as a token of their respect and a hope that you will remain a friend to the First People even longer than the elephant has."

Annja smiled, trying to put the boy at ease.

Taking off her baseball cap she held it out to Nemso, saying, "Where I come from it is the visitor that offers the gift, not the host. In this case, however, I will make an exception, provided you accept this gift from me in return."

Nemso's eyes grew wide as he listened to Xabba translate. He stared at the cap, then looked up at Annja.

"For…m-m-me?" he asked in halting English.

"Yes, for you," Annja said, catching the look of pride Xabba gave him. She showed Nemso how to adjust the strap for fit and then watched him race off, eager to show his friends what he'd received.

Xabba said, "He was very fortunate you were there today."

"I was happy to help."

Her companion glanced at her shrewdly. "Happy to get in Mmegi's good graces again, as well?"

"I didn't stop to think. I simply acted to save the boy's life," she replied.

"Of course. I did not mean to imply otherwise. But even you must admit that the Twin Gods have smiled on you today. It is not every day that you get to save the village elder's only grandson."

Xabba laughed when he saw her shock.

"We will talk more about Humphrey in the morning, eh, Annja? Good night."

And with that, he moved off in the darkness, leaving Annja with a host of new questions.

A few more days, and she'd be that much closer to unraveling what had happened to Humphrey's expedition.

22

The hut contained nothing more than a small bed of eland skins stretched over a pile of dried grasses. Annja sat on it gratefully. It had been a long, exhausting day in more ways than one and she was ready to get some much-needed rest, but first there was one more task to take care of.

Under the light of her flashlight, Annja carefully unwrapped the package Nemso had given her. Inside the bundle of animal skins was an intricately decorated horn made from what could only be the tusk of an elephant. The exterior was covered with carved symbols, reminding Annja of rock art she'd seen at digs in other parts of the world. The images were clearly telling a story but she wasn't familiar enough with San folklore to know exactly what was being represented. Both ends of the tusk were capped with what appeared to be a plug of silver, which made her pause.

Silver? The San weren't metal workers. Where had the silver come from?

Given the unique nature of the item, as well as its relative worth, Annja assumed that it was really from Mmegi, rather than Nemso. After Mmegi's public disapproval of her interest in the elephant graveyard earlier that day, she couldn't see him telling her what she wanted to know outright; that might cause strife with his people. But passing her some information on the sly through his grandson? That made perfect sense.

She tried to pull the caps off, but the seals were too solidly set in place and there was no way she was going to be able to get them loose without tools. She bent closer to get a better look at the larger of the two caps and noticed a thin seam running down the exterior of the tusk away from the cap. It looked too straight to be of natural origin. Cracks in the bone would be ir-regular and this particular line wasn't. The first seam bisected several others running in different directions across the surface of the piece.

There's something inside.

She knew it was true as soon as it occurred to her. She'd solved too many puzzle boxes, secret containers and carefully constructed hiding places not to recog-nize one when she saw it. All she had to do was figure out how to open it.

Of course, that turned out to be easier said than done.

She tried twisting, turning, pushing and pulling the various sections of the tusk, hoping to find a way to release the two sections, but nothing seemed to work. It was only after nearly a half hour of experimentation that she figured it out. She pushed down on opposite sections with the thumbs of each hand while simulta-neously twisting the ends in opposite directions and pulled them apart.

The two halves separated without a sound, revealing the hollow interior. Inside was a rolled piece of tanned animal skin. It reminded her of the cloth the villagers used for their clothing. This piece was small, however, only about two inches wide and six inches long when unrolled.

A series of symbols, five in all, had been drawn on one side of the cloth in what looked to Annja to be charcoal. In order, from top to bottom, Annja saw an antelope, a round disk with lines coming out of it that was probably the sun, three wavy lines that reminded Annja of water, an elephant, easily recognizable due to its long trunk, and what she thought was a snake. They were simple, even primitive in nature.

But she had absolutely no idea what the symbols were supposed to mean.

She tried to find a connection between them but aside from the fact that they were all natural instead of man-made objects, she didn't see one. She tried to view them as a pictorial, but couldn't come up with any kind of story that made sense, never mind telling her something she didn't already know about the location of the elephant graveyard and what had happened to Humphrey's expedition.

After puzzling over them for another twenty minutes, she finally gave up. She might have a better chance of unraveling the puzzle in the morning after a good night's sleep.

With her thoughts still churning, she lay down to try to get some rest.

A HAND TOUCHED Annja's shoulder, bringing her out of her sleep. She opened her eyes to find the young boy's mother, Balanka, leaning over her.

Annja opened her mouth to say something, but the

other woman quickly shook her head and put a finger vertically over her own lips in the universal signal for silence. Annja's eyes widened at the sight—who was the woman worried would hear?—but she kept her mouth shut and didn't say anything.

With a few quick gestures Balanka made it clear that Annja should put her things together and follow her.

Intrigued, Annja did as she was asked. She always slept clothed in the field, so all she needed to do was pull on her boots and toss the souvenirs and gifts she'd been given at the ceremony last night into her backpack.

As quietly as a ghost, Balanka slipped out of the hut. Annja followed.

In the gray dimness of the predawn light the village seemed deserted. Even the cooking fires were still banked from the night before, with just thin wisps of smoke rising from them to serve as harbingers of the flames to come.

Balanka looked around nervously. Annja got the sense Balanka was worried about being seen with her and could only come up with one reason why that might be the case: Balanka knew something about the elephant graveyard.

Satisfied that they were alone, Balanka slipped between several huts until she reached the edge of the village and then set out across the scrubland toward a large grove of monkey thorn trees. Intrigued, Annja hustled to catch up.

Once they were out of earshot of the village, Annja broke the silence. "Where are we going?" she asked.

Balanka glanced over at her and said something in the clicking language of her people, gesturing at the trees ahead of them. Or maybe it was the mountain in the distance. Annja wasn't sure. She wasn't even sure Balanka had understood her question.

Nothing to do but follow along, it seemed.

Fifteen minutes later they reached the grove of trees. They were a thick tangle of intertwining trunks, the space between and surrounding them filled with waist-high growths of thorny bushes with spines that looked as big as her pinkie finger. So thick was the growth that the copse looked completely impassable.

Thankfully Balanka didn't try to fight her way through it. Instead, she led Annja around the side, following the line of trees until they were no longer within sight of the village behind them in the distance. Balanka clearly knew where she was going; not once did she hesitate or look around as if trying to find a particular landmark. From the way she moved it was clear that she'd been here several times in the past and Annja began to hope that she might be back on the right track, thanks to the young tribeswoman's help.

When Balanka finally came to a stop facing a particularly nasty-looking section of dense and thorny undergrowth, Annja felt that hope slipping away.

The young tribeswoman smiled, pointed at Annja and then pointed at the undergrowth.

Annja looked at her in disbelief. "You want me to go in there?"

The tribeswoman pointed again, this time more forcefully.

Annja shook her head. "No way," she said, "not a chance. How do you think I could get through that, anyway?"

Balanka said something sharply and stomped over to where Annja was standing. She got directly behind Annja and peered over her shoulder. Balanka let out a short "ah" sound and reached up to turn Annja's head a few degrees to the left.

Just like that, a route through the trees came into view. It wasn't a narrow trail, either. This was a full-fledged thoroughfare by nature's standards, a pathway wide enough to let something the size of an elephant pass through it without difficulty.

At the thought, Annja let out a cry, spun around and hugged the other woman. The entrance to the elephant graveyard!

Balanka hugged her back, chattering excitedly in Annja's ear despite the fact that neither of them understood a word the other was saying. It didn't matter to Annja, though; she'd found the next piece of the puzzle.

The particular combination of sunlight and shadow had created an optical illusion that made the thicket ahead of her appear as dense and overgrown as everywhere else. Unless you were standing in a certain spot and looking at it from just the right angle, you would never know the pathway was there unless you stumbled into the opening by accident.

It was an amazing piece of natural camouflage.

Perhaps too good.

Struck by a sudden suspicion, Annja walked forward until she passed through the outer edge of the undergrowth and then turned to look back the way she had come.

From this viewpoint, the ruins of the arch forming the opening she'd just come through were clearly visible. So, too, were the remains of the low wall that ran out from either side of that arch and formed the outer edge of the thicket of trees that she and Balanka had just been following. Maybe the vegetation had simply grown out of control since the structure had fallen into ruin or perhaps it had been planted like that intentionally. Either way, the structure was all but hidden by dense undergrowth.

Annja retraced her steps and tried to get the San tribeswoman to join her.

Balanka, however, refused to set foot beneath the arch.

Annja did her best to reassure her that everything would be fine, a not-so-simple task when hand gestures and facial expressions are all you have to work with, but Balanka steadfastly refused. In the end, Annja was forced to go on alone.

She found the first piece of bone about twenty feet beyond the archway. A flash of white caught her eye, and when she walked over to it, she discovered an elephant skull partially hidden in the long grass. It wasn't very big, no larger than that of a wildebeest or water buffalo, and she might have mistaken it for a skull of one of those animals if it hadn't been for the protuberances where tusks had been. After examining it, Annja suspected it had belonged to a juvenile that had died far from its prime.

As she continued on, she spotted bones with increased regularity. It wasn't long before she was walking through a landscape dotted with rib cages, thigh bones and massive skulls the likes of which she'd never seen outside a museum exhibit for prehistoric mam-

mals. Many of the bones were yellow with age, some
so old that when she brushed against them they crumbled apart.

To know all of these majestic animals had found
their way here when their time had come was both
eerie and somehow beautiful at the same time. Annja
warred with her emotions as she tried to come to grips
with the place. It was overwhelming.

As she squatted down beside a particularly oversize
skull, hoping to get a better look, she was distracted by
something flapping at the base of a bush several yards
away. She couldn't tell just what it was from that distance, but the smooth surface and even design made
her think it wasn't natural but rather man-made. When
she walked over to investigate, she discovered a beat-up
old fedora trapped between the branches of the bush,
fluttering back and forth in the light breeze.

She felt her pulse racing as she turned the hat over
and looked inside. There, on the hatband lining the interior, were a pair of faded initials.

RH.

Robert Humphrey.

Just to be sure she pulled out the photograph of Humphrey. In the picture, the famed explorer gazed out at
the camera from under the rim of a dark fedora.

Annja stood there, overcome with a feeling of déjà
vu. She'd known, intellectually, that Humphrey had
come this way. After all, it was his trail she was following to discover what happened to him. But knowing something intellectually and standing there with a
piece of physical evidence in your hand, particularly an
item so personal in nature, was something else entirely.

She carefully folded the fedora and slipped the hat inside her pack for safekeeping.

Rising, Annja felt a presence at her back. Thinking her guide had decided to join her, after all, she turned around to thank her for bringing her to this place.

The comment on her lips died before she could give voice to it. It wasn't her guide at all.

Far from it, in fact.

23

The largest bull elephant Annja had ever seen stood roughly a dozen feet away, beneath the sheltering boughs of a eucalyptus tree. It was at least twice her height and probably weighed twelve or thirteen thousand pounds. Its tusks were enormous, a good three feet or more long and at least as thick as her thigh.

The tusks alone would make this an attractive target for any poacher in the vicinity, but where most elephants ranged from light to battleship gray, this particular specimen was white as a ghost, from the tip of its trunk to the end of its tail.

Annja stared in wonder even as her mind got busy cataloging and identifying what she was seeing. Clearly the elephant suffered from hypopigmentary achromia, or albinism, a congenital disorder that was caused by a partial or, in this case, complete lack of pigmentation in the skin. That it had survived to adulthood was astounding. Body parts from albino animals were highly prized in African society. Witch doctors in particular believed they lent added potency to potions or spells. She remembered a case from just a few years ago in nearby Tanzania where an albino child was kidnapped, his body dismembered and the parts sold. Who knew what kind of price an animal of this size would bring?

As if sensing her thoughts, the elephant grew agitated. It shifted from foot to foot, shaking the ground.

"Easy there, Tantor," Annja said in a calm voice, hoping to soothe the big animal.

But the sound of her voice seemed to do just the opposite. The elephant began to swing its trunk back and forth, smashing the vegetation on either side of it with what, from Annja's perspective, appeared to be purposeful intent.

Annja was growing more concerned by the moment and when the huge animal lifted its head and trumpeted its anger in a loud voice she was convinced that it was about to charge. She was seconds away from drawing her sword, just to have something in hand to try to protect herself should the animal lose control, when the words of Humphrey's last clue drifted through her mind.

In the place where Tantor goes to die,
Ahab's bane trumpets his call.
They say that music soothes the savage heart,
And makes allies of us all.

Music.

Without hesitation Annja began singing the first song that came to mind in a crisp, clear voice. She was surprised to find herself singing a simple children's song she'd learned from the nuns at the orphanage in New Orleans. A song that she hadn't sung in almost two decades.

"Sur le pont d'Avignon, On y danse, on y danse, Sur le pont d'Avignon, On y danse tout en rond. Les beaux messieurs font comme ça, Et puis encore comme ça."

No sooner had the first few words left her mouth than the elephant's anxiety began to subside. It gradually stopped stomping its feet and lashing its trunk.

Astounded at the change in the animal, Annja kept singing.

"Sur le pont d'Avignon, On y danse tout en rond. Les belles dames font comme ça, Et puis encore comme ça..."

The elephant's trunk began to swing gently back and forth in time with the music. It took a few steps forward, bringing it out from under the shade of the eucalyptus tree and for the first time Annja could look into its eyes.

Its all-*white* eyes.

Annja's song faltered for a half beat before she recognized the milky cataracts for what they were and understood that the elephant was blind.

The elephant hesitated in midstep, one massive foot held up in the air like at a circus performance. Annja was quick to pick up the tune again, however, and that seemed to reassure the great mammal. It continued forward until it stood directly in front of her as Annja finished her song.

For a moment the two of them stood nose to trunk and Annja got the sense that the massive animal was sizing her up. She had been around elephants in the past, so she had some expectation of what might be considered "normal" behavior. Nothing, however, could have prepared her for what happened next.

The elephant lifted its trunk and, with a gentle, featherlight touch, explored the features of her face.

Annja closed her eyes and held perfectly still. She could feel the animal's soft breath on her cheek and could smell the eucalyptus leaves it had been eating before her arrival. More important, she could sense the elephant's innate intelligence. Perhaps it hadn't simply been luck that had kept it safe from poachers for so long.

The elephant huffed in her face and then withdrew.

Annja opened her eyes to find it standing a few feet away, waiting.

"Aren't you amazing," she said softly.

She felt as though she'd passed some kind of a test, but a test of what, exactly, she didn't know. Still, she had the definite sense that the elephant—Tantor, she decided to call him—wouldn't hamper her search going forward.

All she had to do now was figure out where Humphrey had left his next clue.

She began moving in the same direction she'd been headed before Tantor had interrupted her, but she'd only taken a few steps when the elephant let out a short cry.

Annja turned to find it looking at her.

It's not really looking at you. It's blind, remember?

She made herself turn away.

But Tantor trumpeted again, louder this time, the minute she lifted her foot to take another step.

The elephant clearly wanted something.

It waved its trunk at her when she turned once more and then, quite deliberately, did it again when she was too busy staring at it to respond.

She tried to tell herself it was just coincidence, but she didn't believe it.

The elephant wanted her to go the other way.

The elephant trumpeted once, much more softly, and then turned and headed back the way it had come.

Annja stood there dumbfounded to find herself seriously considering following a blind albino elephant deeper into the ruins. She knew elephants were smart, but wasn't this taking it too far? Did she really trust that an elephant knew what she was doing there?

When she found herself following in the elephant's wake, she had her answer.

24

The sun was still making its way over the mountains in the distance when Porter and his men arrived at the San village. Excited to have more visitors, the children scurried out to greet them. But as the men got out of the vehicles with guns in their hands, the children raced back the way they had come with cries of fear and shouts of warning.

Today's visitors, it seemed, were very different from their guest of the night before.

Bryant and his men rounded up all of the people they could find—man, woman and child—and forced them to assemble as a group in the center of the village. Porter stepped forward and brandished a pistol to get them to quiet down. "I'm looking for a white woman, alone and on foot. She would have come through here last night or early this morning. Has anyone seen her?"

The villagers didn't say a word. From the expressions on some of their faces, Porter wasn't sure they understood him.

He turned and gestured to Dr. Crane, who reluctantly stepped forward. Several of the villagers called out when they saw him, but Porter didn't know if they were reacting to the man's presence or the fact that his hands were bound securely in front of him, indicating that he, too, was a prisoner. Frankly, Porter didn't care either way. All he wanted the doctor to do was translate what he said.

"I know you speak that damned language of theirs," Porter snapped. "Tell them I want to know where the American woman went."

Crane turned to the assembled villagers and spoke to them in their own language. There was a pause and then a man of about twenty-five stepped to the front of the crowd and addressed Crane. The two conversed for a moment.

"He says that they've only recently set up camp and haven't had any visitors from the tour companies yet," Crane translated. "They haven't seen this woman you are asking about."

Porter took in the well-built huts, the lived-in look to the village, even the amount of what looked to be recent ash in the fire pit. The man was lying. Just how stupid did they think he was?

Without a word Porter lifted his pistol and shot the young man in the chest. He went down like a sack of bricks.

For a second the only sound that could be heard was the echo of the gunshot and then the moment was shattered by cries of grief and horror. A few of the men surged forward but were quickly knocked back with hard, sharp blows from the ends of the assault rifles Porter's men carried.

Porter didn't want the villagers to have any time to think, so he stepped forward, grabbed a woman who was too slow to shrink back out of reach and pulled her upright in front of him with one arm locked around her neck. As the shouting and screaming continued, he raised his pistol in the air and fired again.

The sound of the shot brought silence in its wake.

Staring out at the crowd, Porter put the pistol to the head of the woman and addressed himself to Crane.

"Tell them I'm going to kill someone for every minute that I don't have the information I'm looking for, starting with this woman right here."

Crane's jaw dropped. "You can't do—"

"Shut up and tell them, Doctor, or I'll do it right here, right now!" To emphasize his point he ground the muzzle against the woman's skull hard enough to draw blood.

Crane bit back what he was going to say and turned to the crowd, speaking quickly but clearly.

All he received in turn were hard stares.

Porter wanted to laugh. Did they think he was kidding? No way in hell would a group of desert rats like these get the better of him. He'd waste them all if that was what it took to get the answer he wanted. He was all but certain that Annja had come this way and he intended to get the information he needed one way or the other.

So be it.

He let go of the woman's neck and then kicked her knees out from under her so she ended up on the ground at his feet. He pointed the gun at her and began counting. "Five…four…three…"

An old man in the middle of the group slowly stepped forward. Several of the others tried to stop him, but he shook them off, glared at Porter and said something to him.

Dr. Crane translated without being asked. "He says his name is Mmegi. He is the village elder."

"I don't care if he's the president of Botswana," Porter snarled. "I want to know what happened to Creed. Can he tell me?"

Crane ignored the remark, continuing to listen to Mmegi's slow but steady speech.

"He says there is no need for violence. The woman you seek is not here nor has she been here. They have not had visitors for many days."

Porter couldn't see any fear in the old man's eyes, just calm acceptance of whatever was to come, and for some reason that caused a shiver of unease to run through his frame.

"Perhaps he's forgotten that the man with the gun is the one in charge. Tell him that I'm only going to ask one more time and then I will show them the consequences of defying me, and trust me, they will not be pretty."

Crane dutifully relayed the message but Mmegi was shaking his head before he'd even finished. "No woman! No violence!" he said in accented but clear English.

So the desert rat can speak English, after all, Porter thought.

He raised the gun and pointed it at Mmegi's face.

"Last chance…"

Commotion to his left caught his attention and he glanced that way just as Bryant came around the side of one of the huts, shoving a boy of about ten or twelve ahead of him. The kid stumbled and fell but Bryant grabbed him by the arm and hauled him back to his feet.

Mmegi jerked as if he'd been slapped and an expression of dismay flashed across his face. The old man recovered quickly, but not quickly enough. Porter had seen the look.

"Caught him eavesdropping from behind the hut over there," Bryant said as he dragged the boy over to Porter and pushed him to the ground at his feet.

"I see," Porter said. The elder was too old to be the boy's father. Grandfather, perhaps?

"I was just about to put him in the group with the others," Bryant said, "but then I saw that he had this."

Bryant held up a baseball cap.

A New York Yankees baseball cap.

It didn't take Porter more than a moment to make the connection. He had seen the exact same cap on Annja Creed's head less than twenty-four hours before.

He turned and faced the old man, a gleam of triumph in his eyes. "No visitors, huh? You had better start talking or I'll start shooting," he said. "And if I do, I'll start with that boy right over there."

For a moment the old man stood straight and tall, trying to stare him down, but then his shoulders slumped in resignation and he began to talk.

25

The elephant led Annja back the way he had come, beneath the boughs of the eucalyptus tree and along a long, winding path with more dense undergrowth on either side, until they emerged into a sun-dappled clearing.

There, half-hidden in the undergrowth, was a temple.

Or, at least she thought it was a temple. It was hard to tell because of the amount of vegetation covering it, but she'd seen enough structures like this one to make an educated guess. It rose out of the bushes and trees around it, a squat structure made of large, oversize blocks of dark stone fitted together like a giant jigsaw puzzle of rock. It immediately reminded her of the photographs she'd seen from Farini's son, Lulu, which supposedly showed the remnants of the lost city that they had discovered in the midst of the Kalahari. This structure before her now had the same look and feel to it as the one in Lulu's photographs, a sense that it was so old it had stood here and been ancient when ancient was still young.

But what was it doing here, in the middle of nowhere? And who had built it?

While she stood there staring at it, she felt Tantor's trunk against her back and give a shove from behind.

The message was clear. What she was looking for was inside that building.

"Okay, okay, I'm going," she said.

He nodded that big, bony head and then turned his attention to the succulent green leaves hanging inches from his face and began eating.

"Right. You stay here and pig out while I go exploring," Annja said with a laugh.

She dug her flashlight out of her pack, turned it on and headed into the temple's interior.

The building was designed like a lollipop, with a narrow entrance hallway leading to a wide circular chamber that rose two stories off the ground and seemed to be some kind of gathering place. Narrow beams of sunlight shone down from where small sections of the roof had collapsed over time, allowing her to see that much of the floor was covered with what appeared to be stone benches arranged in a semicircle facing the far side of the room. She could see balconies lining the second story, as well, providing even more seating.

Annja pivoted, focusing her attention in the same direction those sitting in the chairs would have done so long ago, and that's when she saw it.

A large circular image had been carved into the face of the wall ahead of her. It showed three concentric circles made up of various images set inside one another and surrounding the carved image of an oversize elephant skull in the center. It reminded her of a Mayan calendar, though of course the symbols were different. Same layout and style.

She found herself wondering which one had come first.

Annja moved forward until she stood directly before the design. Switching on her flashlight to get a closer look at some of the carvings, she noted how they had been cut out of the stone so that they stood in bas-relief against the backdrop behind them. She could see an antelope, a wildebeest, what looked to be a giraffe, a set of wavy lines like water, a pair of humans hunting with what appeared to be spears, a sunlike object…

Wait a minute.

She took off her backpack and dug into the pocket where she had stored the cloth she'd taken from the elephant tusk the night before. Unrolling it, she compared the symbols on the cloth with those on the wall.

It took her only a few moments to find all five of them.

Excited, she realized that she was looking at the next clue. All she had to do was figure out what it meant.

She'd spent time the night before trying to decipher some coherent story from the symbols on the antelope hide without success and she knew now that that had been the wrong path to follow. The symbols weren't supposed to tell a story in and of themselves, she realized, but were markers for something else.

And she thought she knew just what that was.

She stepped forward until she stood before the first symbol on the cloth, the antelope.

Her hand trembling, Annja reached out and pushed against the symbol.

For a moment, nothing happened, and Annja began to suspect she'd guessed incorrectly, but then there was a sudden movement beneath her fingers and the antelope sank down into the surface of the rock behind it to disappear from view with a loud click.

Annja stepped back, waiting to see if something happened.

When nothing did, she turned her attention to the second symbol, that of the sun.

Locating that symbol, she reached out and pushed against it, this time harder. The sun immediately sank into the rock wall with another click.

It's a lock, Annja realized, and the symbols were the combination.

She quickly ran through the rest of the symbols—the river, the elephant and the snake—then stepped back.

For a moment nothing happened and Annja was afraid she had done something wrong, but then the room was filled with a strange series of clicks, one after another, as if different switches were being thrown, and then, with a clunk of finality, a symbol at the bottom of the carving popped out about an inch.

Shining her flashlight on it, she saw that it was a symbol of a building, much like the one she stood in now.

She reached down and pulled it, revealing the drawerlike compartment behind it.

Inside was a small, leather-bound journal tied shut with a piece of rawhide.

Carefully, Annja lifted it out of the drawer and carried it over to one of the sunlit benches where she could get a better look at it.

The rawhide was only loosely tied and came apart easily.

Annja turned to the first page, which was covered with a bold scrawl from top to bottom.

I first heard of the Lost City of the Kalahari while traveling in Kenya with my son, Malcolm. He was little more than a boy at the time—ten or eleven years old—and we had just returned from an expedition to…

Her eyes widened and Annja skipped ahead to a random page in the middle of the book. The same person had written there, as well.

The second expedition has ended in as spectacular a failure as the first. I don't know where my calculations went wrong. Based on the coordinates in Farini's notes I would think…

Annja leaned back. The book was Humphrey's private journal, it seemed, and given what she had read so far it contained an accounting of everything he had done in his pursuit of the Lost City of the Kalahari. It was an invaluable find and would be particularly useful in fleshing out the back story surrounding Humphrey's final expedition for the *Chasing History's Monsters* special she had promised Doug.

With more than a little trepidation, she gave her attention to the journal and turned to the final page with writing on it. There she found a note of a different kind.

We meet again. Congratulations on deciphering the clues I've left along the way. If you've managed to get to this point, I have little doubt that you'll be able to reach the final destination, as well.

I leave in the morning on the last leg of my own search for the Lost City of the Kalahari. I'm convinced I've located it and hope to stand within its walls in just a short time. Farini's notations have proved to be a godsend. I highly doubt I would have gotten this far without them.

I'm leery of becoming another Fawcett, so I've been leaving this record behind me as I go. I've been hiding each waypoint behind simple clues that will keep the rabble out but that any adventurer worth their salt could decipher. As before, if you're reading this, things did not go as well as I had hoped and I have been unable to clean up the trail after me. If, by following in my wake, you discover my fate, please inform the necessary parties. There is no harsher fate than to be lost and forgotten.

Good hunting!

Robert Davis Humphrey

Written beneath the signature was a set of map coordinates.

Before she had the chance to begin figuring out just where the coordinates would lead her, there was a loud report from somewhere outside the temple. Annja immediately recognized the sound as a gunshot.

A big one, too, from the sound of it.

She had no idea what anyone could be shooting at out here, except…

Tantor!

Annja stuffed Humphrey's note into her pocket, snatched up her backpack and ran back the way she had come.

26

Annja raced out of the temple and back into the sunlight. She was just in time to see Tantor crash to the ground with earthshaking force, blood leaking from a bullet hole just above his right eye and staining his hide red.

She rushed to the elephant's side, oblivious to the fact that she had dropped her backpack somewhere along the way. She fell to her knees and threw her arms around Tantor's massive head, hugging him to her breast, knowing instinctively there was nothing she could do. The elephant was already dead—had been since the bullet from a high-powered rifle had entered its brain seconds before—but its body just hadn't accepted the stark reality of the situation yet. Annja watched as Tantor's eyes rolled in their sockets, the big beast struggling in vain to understand what had happened to it. It let out one final lungful of air.

The elephant went still.

Annja slumped forward, her head against the animal's pebbly hide.

Behind her, a man said, "How touching."

Annja knew that voice. She stiffened, her mind

working to understand how they had found her, caught up with her, even as hatred and rage bubbled over.

She was going to make them pay for what they had done.

Blood smeared her shirt and stuck to her skin but she barely noticed as she spun around, searching for and then finding the owner of that voice.

Malcolm Porter.

He wasn't alone, however, not that she had expected him to be. His hired gorilla, Bryant, stood behind him, cradling a big-game rifle in his arms. Several of Porter's other goons stood behind them, standing watch over a bound and gagged Dr. Crane.

For a second she considered calling her sword to her and rushing Bryant. Obviously he had fired the killing shot and she was reasonably certain she could reach him and gut him down the center before he had a chance to bring that big gun to bear. Still, she suspected even an idiot like Porter couldn't miss her at that range.

It was tempting, though.

She looked Bryant in the eye and said, "I'm going to kill you."

No bluster, no boast, just a plain statement of fact.

Bryant seemed taken aback for a moment and then laughed it off. "You're welcome to try."

Porter scowled. "You've led us on quite the chase, Ms. Creed, but that's over now. Dr. Crane has told us about the clues my father left to the location of the Lost City. Be a good girl and turn them over to me now, why don't you?"

Annja stared at him without saying anything.

"Uncooperative to the end. I expected no less," Porter said with an unsettling smile. "So be it."

He extended a hand toward Bryant, who was already in the process of passing Porter something.

Realizing what it was, Annja charged.

She made it three steps before the dart took her high in the chest, near her neck. She yanked it free and managed another step before the world seemed to tip up on its side and she crashed to the ground as darkness closed in.

The last voice she heard before unconsciousness claimed her was Porter's.

"Search her."

27

Annja came to in the back of a moving vehicle with a pounding headache, probably a side effect of whatever they'd shot her with. Despite the pain, her thoughts were reasonably free of fuzziness, for which she was thankful. Getting out of this mess was going to be hard enough without having to fight through fifty feet of cotton between her ears.

She opened her eyes to find that she was slumped against the passenger door in the backseat of a moving sport utility vehicle. Her hands and feet were secured with plastic zip ties that provided very little room for movement, but were thankfully secured in front of her body rather than behind. In the front seat ahead of her were a driver and one passenger, both men in their mid-thirties. She didn't recognize either of them, but the assault rifle on the dash was proof that they were in Porter's employ.

In the seat next to her sat Dr. Crane. He was awake and staring out the window beside him with a dull and listless expression. His hands and feet were also secured with plastic zip ties, although his were stained with dried blood. The gashes in his flesh beneath the tight black loops of plastic told of his efforts to try to free himself.

He turned to face her when he realized she was awake.

"Are you all right?" he asked.

"Yeah. Where are we?"

"A few miles southwest of the White Valley, near as I can tell."

"Any idea where we're going?" She looked around outside the truck. They were bouncing along a barely beaten track in a westerly direction.

"Unfortunately, no. They took what looked like a journal from you and a few minutes later loaded us up and got under way."

Looking past the driver's shoulder, Annja counted four vehicles ahead of them. She twisted around to look behind them, saw one, possibly two, more. It was hard to tell with all the bouncing around they were doing.

"What do you think will—" Crane was cut off by an angry snarl from the man in the passenger seat. "Quiet, back there!"

Crane dutifully shut up, but Annja saw no need to cooperate in any way. Flustered guards meant distracted guards and distracted guards improved their chances of escape. If they wanted to get out of here, they were going to need to start taking control of the situation and not follow along like docile sheep.

"How did they find the temple?" she asked.

Crane glanced worriedly at the men in the front seat, but answered anyway. "They told the elder they'd start killing tribespeople if he didn't tell them where you were."

Annja was surprised. She hadn't expected coercion to work on a man like Mmegi. "He gave me up, just like that?"

Crane shook his head. "No, Porter killed Xabba and threatened Mmegi's grandson, Nemso, first."

"That son of a—"

"I said shut up back there!" the passenger snarled, snatching his gun off the dash and pointing it at Annja.

She laughed. "What are you going to do?" she taunted. "Shoot me? Somehow I don't think Porter would be all that happy about that, especially given the trouble he went through to bring me along on this little jaunt."

The driver gave the passenger a look, and Annja knew she'd won that round.

But the guard was more intelligent than she'd expected.

He laughed in her face and turned the gun on Crane.

"So I can't shoot you. Big deal," he said. "But no one said anything about keeping your friend here alive and well, so if you open your mouth again I'll shoot him instead. How's that sound?"

This time, Annja kept her mouth shut.

"See that?" he said. "A little cooperation and no one gets hurt. That's not so hard, now, is it?"

Annja refused to respond.

Laughing at what he clearly felt was a victory, the guard faced forward once more.

But Annja was far from done.

She caught Crane's attention with a soft snap of her fingers. When he looked her way, she inclined her head toward the guard sitting in front of him and then mimed slipping her arms over the back of the seat and pulling backward.

Crane understood what she wanted, but seemed dubious about his ability to pull it off. He grimaced and cocked his head slightly as if considering his chances.

Annja was insistent. All she needed was a few seconds of distraction and then it would be all over for the two guys in the front seat. What she was going to do to get them away from the rest of the convoy she didn't yet know, but she'd figure that out when the time came. For now, though, they had to gain control of the vehicle if they wanted to escape.

Crane looked a little shaky still, but she ignored his unspoken pleas for a different course of action. She nodded her head once, emphatically, in his direction and then pretended not to see the pleading expression he was giving her. He'd either pull through when the time came or not. There wasn't much she could do about it and so she just barreled ahead as if he'd accepted her plan.

Annja sat up a little straighter in her seat and put her hands in front of her stomach, palms up.

The guy in the passenger seat glanced back at her, but must have been satisfied with what he saw for he faced forward again without saying anything.

He was going to regret that oversight.

She looked at Crane and saw that he was starting to sweat. If they didn't act soon, the guard would notice something wasn't right.

She flashed her fingers in a countdown.

One…

Two…

Three…

Crane lunged forward, extended his arms over the head of the man in the passenger seat so that his Plasti-Cuffed hands were directly in front of the man's neck and then hauled backward with all his might.

That was all Annja had time to see before she reached into the otherwhere and drew forth her sword, the same sword that Joan of Arc had once wielded in a righteous battle of her own. The sword materialized in her cupped palms, the blade thrusting forward as it came into existence. The sharpened steel went through the seat in front of her, pushed through the body of the unsuspecting driver sitting in that seat and came out the other side just to the left of his sternum. The blade was so long that the driver was able to look down at several inches of solid steel where it emerged from his chest.

He coughed once, spewing blood down the front of his shirt, and died. Annja guessed he probably never even knew what hit him.

She didn't know if she had enough room to pull the sword back out of the driver's body without getting the hilt jammed up on the seat behind her, so she just left it where it was for the time being and brought her hands up instead, using the exposed edge of the blade to slash through the zip ties holding them together.

She turned her attention to Dr. Crane, intending to help him subdue his own guard, when the SUV bounced over a particular large bump in the road. Without the driver's grip on the wheel to keep it steady, the vehicle immediately yawed to the right, careering off the road into the scrublands around them. Even worse, the dead weight of the driver's foot pushed the accelerator down and the vehicle began to speed in an arc away from the rest of the convoy.

"No, you don't!" Annja yelped, and threw herself partially over the front seat to grab the steering wheel. At the same time she let go of the sword, returning it to the otherwhere. No longer pinned in place by the blade, the dead man's body slumped to the side.

A quick glance to her right showed her Crane was still fighting with the man in the passenger seat, both of them oblivious to the course the car was taking. Crane had slipped down into the well between the seats, still pulling. Porter's man, on the other hand, was turning blue in the face as he fought the pressure of Crane's hands against his throat, his hands alternately pulling against Crane's arms and flailing in search of the gun he'd dropped.

A sharp clang reverberated through the car as it careered off a boulder on its now runaway course, and Annja knew they couldn't stay lucky for long.

Time to settle the odds.

While fighting the steering wheel with her left hand, she brought her right arm up as high as it would go and then savagely drove it back down so that her elbow connected squarely with the guy's temple, knocking him unconscious with one powerful blow.

Which was good, because she didn't have time for another one. She had to gain control of the vehicle.

Beside her, she heard Crane ask, "What happened to the other—?"

That was as far as he got.

The sound of retching that filled the car told her

he'd finally gotten a look at her handiwork in subduing the other guard.

What had happened to her? Why didn't she feel anything?

Crane was having a harder time dealing with the fact that she'd just violently ended a life than she was. In all likelihood the man had had it coming, but that didn't change that she'd just become judge, jury and executioner. It wasn't the first time, either. Her life had certainly changed since she'd taken up the sword and she'd been deluding herself if she thought it was *all* for the good.

But she didn't have time to examine that too deeply right now, as the vehicle continued to accelerate and she had to keep them from driving into a tree.

A horn blared behind them and Annja knew pursuit wouldn't be far behind.

28

Porter was in the front seat, flipping through the pages of his father's journal, when he heard one of the men in the back mutter, "Where's he going?"

Porter turned to see who had said it, only to look beyond the man and out the rear window where one of the vehicles behind them had suddenly veered off the road. It hadn't slowed down, either. If anything, it had sped up and was now bouncing and jumping over the dips and cuts in front of them like a motocross racer determined to take a spill.

Porter's orders had been quite clear. The vehicles behind him were to follow him to their next destination. They were not to stop for any reason and were not to deviate from the route Porter set for them.

Clearly, someone had decided to change the rules. Given that his men were well acquainted with the price they would pay for disobedience, there could be only one explanation.

Annja Creed was at it again.

"Damn that woman!" he exploded, startling Bryant, who sat next to him behind the wheel. "Turn around! Turn around!"

Bryant did as he was told without question, tapping

the brakes and slewing the big SUV into a wide turn, nearly clobbering a startled pair of zebras in the process as they broke from cover behind nearby trees.

"There!" Porter shouted, pointing at the SUV headed away from them toward a large outcropping of rocks in the distance. "Stop them!"

Bryant altered course and stepped on the accelerator in an effort to close the distance between them. Dust and dirt filled the air as the other vehicles followed suit, making it hard to see. Porter cursed and pounded the dashboard in frustration as Bryant was forced to swerve sharply to avoid one of the other SUVs as it emerged suddenly from out of the mess, their front bumper passing scant inches from the rear of the other. Only Bryant's swift reflexes kept them from slamming into each other dead-on.

The getaway vehicle had a good lead on them but Bryant's efforts were helping them close the gap.

ANNJA WAS FINDING IT increasingly difficult to control the vehicle from the backseat. Her arms and lower back were starting to ache from the strain and she knew her chances of making a fatal error increased with every passing second. She had to get into the front seat and gain better control of the vehicle or this ride was going to be over sooner rather than later.

"Henry!" she called. "I need you to cut my feet loose."

Her companion didn't say anything, but after a moment she felt him sawing at the zip ties around her ankles with a knife. She didn't have time to wonder where he'd got it from because a few seconds later the ties parted with a snap.

As soon as her feet were free she braced herself and then grabbed the shirt of the dead man behind the wheel and tried to drag him to the right, without much success. Crane saw what she was doing and added his strength to the task. Between them they were able to drag the body out of the driver's seat and dump it onto the unconscious man in the passenger seat.

The SUV began to slow as soon as the dead man's foot was pulled off the accelerator, but Annja quickly changed that as she slipped between the seats and into the driver's position, ramming her foot on the gas.

The SUV leaped forward.

Their slowdown had given Porter and the rest of them time to turn themselves around and now Annja counted at least three vehicles, maybe more, in hot pursuit.

They needed a distraction.

She glanced at the men in the seat next to her, then said to Henry, "Get rid of them."

"What?"

She jerked her thumb. "One of them is nothing more than dead weight and the other might wake up at any moment. If he does, we're in trouble. We caught him by surprise the first time. The second time around he won't be so easy to subdue."

"Okay," Henry said. "As soon as you slow down—"

Annja didn't let him get any further. "Slow down?" she asked incredulously. "Are you nuts? We've got Porter and his hired guns hot on our tail and you want me to slow down?"

"Um, well…"

"Just open the door and push them out."

"I can't do that."

"Of course you can," Annja said calmly. "You already tried to strangle him to death. I'd say the points for that on the 'do no harm' scale are much higher than simply pushing him out of a moving vehicle, wouldn't you?"

Henry gaped at her.

"If it makes you feel any better we'll try to dump them out on a nice grassy spot, all right?"

He shook his head. "I can't believe you're asking me to do this!"

The unconscious guard chose that moment to stir and Annja knew he wasn't going to remain unconscious much longer.

"Henry!" she said sharply.

"Okay, okay. Try to keep us away from any big rocks," he said as he leaned across the front seat, reaching for the door handle. Annja hit the switch on her door that opened all the locks.

"On the count of three," Annja said, timing their release so the bodies would tumble out into a reasonably debris-free area and not end up splattered across a large boulder or slammed into the trunk of a tree.

"One… Two…"

On the final count Henry popped open the door and did what he could to manhandle the bodies out the opening. Annja helped by leaning to the right and pushing with that hand, while still doing her best to keep her eyes on the road.

The first body slid out easily enough, but as the second followed suit, their former captor regained consciousness. His eyes popped open, startling Henry, who let out a squawk and tumbled back into the rear seat, and then the man's hands shot out to grab the nearest support as he realized that he was falling backward out the door. One hand latched on to the doorjamb while the other caught Annja's right arm just above the wrist.

Annja tried to pull herself free, to no avail. He had a good grip and wasn't letting go. In addition, every tug she made pulled him another inch back into the vehicle.

"Look out!" Henry shouted, and Annja looked at the terrain in front of her in time to see the massive baobab tree looming ahead of them. She jerked the wheel to the right, barely clearing the tree's thick trunk and sheering off the driver's side mirror in the process with a shriek of tearing metal and smashing glass.

And still their unwanted passenger held on.

With every bump, the door swung shut, slamming against the desperate thug's back and then rebounding only to do it all over again. Still, he refused to let go, holding on to Annja's arm for dear life, trying to use the one leg he had inside the vehicle to leverage himself back inside. If it hadn't been for the bumpiness of the ride, Annja knew, he would have already used the leverage he had to push himself back across the front seat at her.

"Do something, Henry!" she shouted, swerving to avoid a group of boulders.

Henry grabbed the other man's hand and began to try to pull him off Annja, but the guy's grip was like a vise and Henry just didn't have the strength. So he opened his mouth and bit the man's thumb.

Their unwanted passenger let out a shriek of pain and involuntarily opened his hand.

That was all Annja needed. The minute the pressure on her wrist let up, she jerked the wheel first to the left and then immediately back again to the right, throwing their former captor off balance and sending him tumbling out the door.

Annja glanced in the rearview mirror, trying to get a glimpse of what happened to him, but her view was filled by the dark shape of one of the other SUVs. The driver had taken advantage of her inattention to close the distance between them and he announced his presence by slamming his SUV's front quarter panel into their rear one. The wheel jerked in her hands, the movement threatening to send the SUV into a skid that would put the front compartment directly in the path of the pursuing vehicle. Annja doubted she'd survive having a five-hundred-pound vehicle dropped in her lap, so she fought the turn with everything she had and got them running straight again.

Henry shouted, "They're going to shoot!" half a second before a bullet shattered the rear window and embedded itself in the back of the front passenger seat. Several more followed, the crack of each shot causing Annja to hunch over the wheel, but none of the other bullets found their mark and she continued charging hell-bent for leather toward the rocky ridgeline she'd picked out as their destination.

Just a few hundred yards left.

She heard the sound of a gunning engine and the other SUV moved in for a second strike, but Annja tapped the breaks and cut the wheel hard in that direction, slamming her own vehicle into theirs. The impact was enough to push theirs several feet to the side, where the termite mound Annja had spotted seconds before was suddenly lined up directly with the front of the SUV. As Annja raced safely past, the other driver was unable to avoid the obstacle and slammed into it. The mound acted as a kind of makeshift ramp, tipping one side of the vehicle higher than the other and launching it into the air, only to come crashing back down to earth several feet later with a thunderous crash and the long warbling cry of a horn that was stuck.

Annja hit the gas again, trying to regain some of the lead they had lost. In the rearview mirror she saw two other SUVs trying to close the distance, intent on boxing her in, but she was determined not to let them get the chance.

She cut the wheel to the right to avoid a massive boulder, burst through a dense clump of acacia thorn bushes, and found herself driving along the knife edge of a long-dried-out riverbank. The earth along the edge of the bank was little more than dry, loose soil and she immediately felt the SUV lurch in that direction as the tires began to slip and spin.

She knew in that moment it was too late.

Still, she gave it her best, throwing the wheel in the opposite direction and physically leaning into it, trying to add as much weight as possible to that side of the vehicle to keep them from going over, but the slide was already in motion.

"Brace yourself!" she yelled as the ground beneath the passenger's side of the SUV gave way entirely and the SUV tipped precariously in that direction.

Annja spared a glance toward Crane, saw him hunkered down in the well between the front and backseats, his head tucked between his knees, and hoped it would be enough to protect him from serious injury. In the next moment, the SUV careened sideways off the crumbling riverbank and rolled toward the bottom. Annja lost all sense of which way was up and which was down as she was thrown from side to side. The floor became the ceiling, became the wall, became the floor, became the wall again as the vehicle came to a crashing halt in a great, billowing cloud of dust.

Blood flowed down one side of Annja's face from a cut across the edge of her forehead, but the rest of her seemed intact. A few bruises and what was sure to be an egg-size lump on one side of her head, but no twisted limbs or broken bones, thankfully.

Satisfied that she wasn't going to injure herself just by moving, Annja took a second to make sense of her surroundings. The SUV had come to a stop on its roof, its wheels still spinning. Broken glass covered the "floor" around her, and the door closest to her was crumpled and bent into the driver's seat. It wouldn't budge when she tried to open it.

Annja crawled over to the other side on her hands and knees, doing her best to avoid jamming herself with any of the crumpled safety glass that littered her way, and then tried the other door. It, too, was stuck, though it didn't look quite as bent or damaged. She turned around so that she was facing the door with her legs out in front of her, braced herself on her elbows and lashed out with both feet, driving them into the door near where it met the frame. On the third kick the door opened enough that she'd be able to twist her way through it.

She heard movement behind her and turned to see Henry crawling through the space between the seats. He looked dazed and weary, but physically uninjured.

"Come on! We've got to get out of here!" she said. Porter and his cronies couldn't be far behind.

The two of them writhed and wriggled their way out of the narrow opening, then crawled a short distance from the truck just to be safe. Through the ringing in her ears from the crash, Annja thought she could hear the sound of racing engines.

She looked at Henry. "Can you run?"

He nodded. "I think so. Do you have a plan?"

Annja glanced back the way they had come, then turned in the other direction. "We've got to get out of here before Porter and his men catch up to us. Our best bet is to head up into those rocks," she said, pointing toward the ridgeline twenty yards away, "and see if we can lose them in the canyons."

"What are we waiting for, then?" he replied.

They had no water and no supplies, but that was secondary to getting as big a head start as they could get. Porter would come after them. If he caught them, it was unlikely he'd be as lenient as he'd been the first time around.

Their only hope was to put enough distance between themselves and Porter that he eventually gave up the search. They took off for the safety of the ridge as fast as their legs could carry them.

29

The terrain reminded Annja of the American Southwest, a boulder-strewn series of hills and free-standing rock spires clung to a stretch of interconnected canyons. Plus plenty of dead-end trails. What little vegetation there had been along the banks of the ancient riverbed quickly fell behind them as they climbed the nearest slope, the loose rock and earth slipping beneath their feet with every step. Annja could hear Henry cursing beneath his breath every time his foot slipped out from under him. She moved closer without making it obvious what she was doing. She wanted to be there in case of a fall; the last thing they needed was a twisted ankle or, heaven forbid, a broken leg.

The terrain evened out once they got to the top of the hill, which was a relief. They paused a moment to catch their breath. It had been a difficult climb and they had both been worn-out before they'd started. A glance back down the trail showed the three others SUVS slamming to a halt on the bank of the river. Seconds later, Porter and his men poured out and began scrambling down the riverbank. One figure remained behind and it was a moment before a bullet ricocheted off a rock on the slope below them, the sound of the shot echoing through the canyons.

They needed a better plan.

Henry was already breathing heavily from the excitement and exertion of the past few minutes. He wouldn't make it much farther. She was going to have to lead them away from him, give him time to regroup, perhaps even to double back to secure a vehicle to make an escape.

"How are you doing?" she asked as she pulled him behind a nearby rock just in case the rifleman grew more accurate.

"Didn't think I was going to be running around the Kalahari when I left the house this morning. I'm all right, though." He nodded. "Yep, I'll be just fine."

But he wasn't fine and they both knew it.

Annja looked back down the trail again. Porter and his men had crossed the riverbed and were now headed toward the very slope that she and Henry had just climbed. Ten, maybe fifteen minutes at most, and they would catch up.

They had to move and they had to do it now.

"Listen to me, Henry," Annja began. "There's no way you're going to outrun them. Not after what you've already been through."

He didn't give it a moment's thought. "You're right. I'll stay here and delay them while you go on."

There was such an earnest and determined look on his face that Annja felt a sudden surge of affection for the old man. He barely knew her and yet he'd not only saved her cameraman's life but had willingly put himself in danger for her. And here he was, ready to put her welfare over his own once more. The fact that he was even in this position was Annja's fault and she was determined to see to it that he got out of this alive and intact no matter what.

"That's not exactly what I had in mind."

She explained that, yes, she wanted them to split up, but not for the reasons he suggested. "I've spent most of my adult life hiking in and out of canyons like this on various archaeological digs. I'm confident I can keep ahead of them long enough to lead them away from you and then throw them off my trail. While I'm doing that, I want you to hunker down somewhere safe. When they come after me, you can double back and do what you can to get to the vehicles below us. I don't think they left anyone guarding them."

"How long should I wait for you?" he asked.

She'd anticipated the question and had her answer ready. "I don't want you to wait. Run for civilization as fast as you can. I've spent enough time in the bush. I can handle myself as long as it takes for you to come back with reinforcements."

Henry agreed reluctantly. Annja didn't care, reluctant or not, provided he did as she suggested. As he hurried off down a path they hoped would provide him shelter, Annja decided to give their pursuers a reason to come after her rather than him.

She bent and quickly picked up half a dozen rocks. Each was reasonably round and roughly the size of a racquetball. They were just large enough to cause some serious damage if they struck the right spot but not so big she couldn't throw them with accuracy.

Aware that the rifleman might still be out there waiting for her, Annja peeked around the boulder and then let out a breath. The former gunman was now climbing up the slope behind the rest of them.

Perfect.

She took a couple of deep breaths. She'd only get one chance at this and wanted every throw to count. When she was ready she stepped out from behind the rock, scanned for and then found her target and, with a throw to rival that of a major league pitcher, she let the first rock fly.

PORTER WAS LABORING up the steep slope, fighting to keep his balance in the loose footing, when something whipped past his head.

He heard rather than saw it and by the time he turned his head to look down the slope it was already out of sight, whatever it was.

He stopped for a moment and straightened, allowing himself a few seconds to catch his breath. The way seemed clear; Creed and the doctor must have continued onward.

No matter. He'd catch up to her in time, and when he did, he'd make her pay.

ANNJA SHOOK HER FIST in frustration and cursed her lack of thought. Her first throw had gone long and high; she'd been throwing from a height and had forgotten to factor in the slope of the trajectory.

Thankfully no one appeared to have seen her.

She gripped another rock loosely in her hand and got ready for another throw.

PORTER HAD TAKEN another half dozen steps when he heard that strange whistling again. He was just turning his head to look when something smashed into his right cheekbone, snapping his head violently back and knocking him to the ground, where he promptly began sliding back down the slope in an uncontrolled tumble. It was only the presence of Bryant behind and below him, and the man's iron grip, that finally arrested his descent.

By then, the pain from his shattered cheekbone was making itself known and he let out an involuntary scream that echoed across the canyon.

He rolled onto his hands and knees, then leveraged himself upright. Bryant reached out a hand to steady him and Porter noted the look on his face, the same look that was on the faces of the other men near them. Whatever had struck him must have done significant damage. His cheek pulsed like a heartbeat and it swelled so badly in just a matter of moments that he could no longer see out of one eye.

Being made a fool in this way was intolerable, and his anger bloomed like a supernova.

He opened his mouth to order them to get moving when a second projectile whipped down the slope and struck him in the upper chest, just beneath his collarbone. However, he had enough padding there that it didn't do anywhere near the damage the first blow had, but it hurt just the same.

Ignoring the pain, he looked up the slope and was just in time to see Annja send another stone whistling at them. This throw was the most accurate so far, the rock striking the head of the man standing a few yards to Porter's left. He went down hard and stayed down.

In that instant any thought of keeping Creed alive to help him with the final task of locating the Lost City vanished. He looked up at her with his one good eye, pointed a finger in her direction and shouted to the men around him, "Kill her!"

ANNJA WATCHED HER second throw fly true, the stone striking Porter in the face, and felt a surge of satisfaction.

That's for Xabba.

She'd thought someone had seen her for sure, but all eyes were on Porter and she was able to send two more blistering shots down the slope, taking at least one of her pursuers out of the game.

As Porter's shout reached her ears, she turned and dove back behind the boulder she'd been using as cover just in time. The crack of gunfire filled the air and bullets whined past her, ricocheting off the rocks. They wouldn't take long to cover the remaining distance between them once the shooting stopped, so she got to her feet and took off, using the massive boulder as cover for as long as she could.

The rock walls quickly rose around her as she ran deeper into the canyons. Her sense of direction was better than most, so she was confident that she could find her way back again provided she kept calm and didn't lose track of the twists and turns she made. She fell into the rhythm of taking the right-hand path every time the opportunity presented itself, heading eastward with every turn.

Shouldn't take long to lose them.

WHEN PORTER, BRYANT and the rest of his men made it to the top of the ridge, they found the area deserted. Porter could barely contain his anger as he whirled on Bryant.

"Which way?" he snarled.

Back in the days when Bryant was a legitimate member of the SAS, he spent most of his days tracking insurgents through the sands of the Middle East. He could have read the signs the two fugitives had left behind and followed in their wake, but that wasn't necessary in this instance. Instead, he simply reached into his pocket and took out the smartphone he carried. A touch of the screen brought up a gridlike structure laid over a satellite image of the local terrain. Within the grid were two icons, one blue and one red. The icons represented the GPS signals the phone was receiving from the tiny tracking devices Bryant had slipped into their captives' clothing while securing them in the SUV earlier. With the device in hand, Bryant could follow the fugitives while at the same time mapping their own route by tracking waypoints on the map with the phone's built-in GPS. A glance at the monitor told him their quarry had split up. The blue icon, the one representing Dr. Crane, was headed west, while the other, indicating Creed's current position, was moving northeast at a faster pace.

Bryant showed the display to Porter. "The doctor hasn't gotten far. We can grab him and get back on Creed's trail long before she loses us."

Porter began to shake his head, then stopped abruptly from the pain. "He can rot in the desert for all I care. It's Creed I want."

"Then it is Creed you shall have," Bryant answered. He indicated the northern trail. "This way."

FIFTEEN MINUTES LATER, Annja stopped for a quick breather. Behind her, the sounds of pursuit continued. Time and time again she thought she'd thrown them off her trail only to discover that wasn't the case. No matter what she did, she just couldn't seem to shake them. Even now they seemed to be closing the distance rather than falling behind because of her superior trail-craft.

She was thirsty, had been for a while, but she made herself ignore it. She didn't have any water, anyway. It would be a problem if she overexerted herself, but she didn't have any choice. She promised herself that if she got far enough ahead of the others she'd take a few minutes to figure out a solution. Right now, she just didn't have the time.

After only a few moments of rest, she set off again, doing her best to stay close to the walls of the canyon where the shade was thickest and the cool air seemed to collect.

She wondered how Henry was doing. She hoped he had made his way back to where Porter and his men had left their vehicles by now. Provided he could get one started, it wouldn't take him more than a few hours to reach any of the seasonal safari camps to the south. From there he should be able to get help, both in the way of resupply and in numbers to ensure his safety when he returned for her.

Annja continued forward, moving, running, one foot in front of the other over and over and over again, ignoring the pain in her muscles and the tightness in her throat from her deep thirst. After a time—twenty minutes? an hour?—she reached a wide fork in the trail and slowed momentarily, thinking about her next move. If she continued following the plan she'd set at the beginning, she was supposed to choose the right-hand path, but something didn't feel good. It was much narrower than the trail on the left, with far more debris along it.

The left path, on the other hand, was wide, well lit from the sun high above and relatively free of loose rock fall. It would be a much easier route, never mind that her strategy to lose her pursuers didn't seem to be working, anyway.

If they were on to her choices, then wouldn't it be better to shake things up and break the pattern?

It was that last thought that decided her. She turned to the left and raced down the wider path, even as the shouts of the men behind her became discernible. The high rock walls and narrow canyons wreaked havoc with acoustics but it still seemed to her that the others were getting even closer.

She forced herself to go faster, knowing she wouldn't be able to keep up the pace for much longer but equally aware that she would need to if she didn't lose them sooner rather than later.

If she could just get a big enough lead.

Annja charged around a corner…and skidded to a halt.

A few yards in front of her the canyon ended in a sheer rock face that rose a good twenty or thirty feet above where she stood. She looked frantically about, hoping she missed some opening somewhere that she could try to squeeze through, but there was nothing.

It was a dead end.

30

She turned, intending to race back the way she had come. If she could get to the fork quickly enough, she might have a chance of staying ahead of her pursuers....

But she was already too late. She could hear their cries echoing down the passage she'd traversed only moments before. There was no way for her to avoid them if she took that route. For a split second she thought about doing it, anyway, imagined herself charging into them, knocking them aside with enough speed and surprise to get through, but then common sense reasserted itself. She'd never make it past all of them.

Annja wasn't ready to give up. Abruptly changing course once more, she rushed over to the wall that formed the canyon's end and began searching for hand- and footholds that might carry her to the top. She was gambling that Porter still wanted her alive and that they wouldn't immediately shoot her down when they saw her. It was climb or stand here and surrender.

Annja wasn't the type to do the latter.

She grabbed another handhold and pulled herself fully onto the rock face, seeking and finding support for her feet and then reaching for the next hold with her other hand. Despite her need to escape, she had to force herself to go slowly. The rock was smooth and there were limited handholds to take advantage of.

She'd gotten about eight feet off the ground when the rocky little spire she was standing on crumbled beneath her feet unexpectedly just as she reached for a new handhold. As she felt herself falling, she scrambled against the rock, looking for something, anything, to stop her downward slide but there wasn't anything big enough.

Down she went.

She managed to twist as she fell, so instead of landing directly on her back she caught most of the impact on her hip and shoulder. The fall knocked the wind out of her and for a few seconds all she could do was lie there and fight to breathe. In the end it was her fear of being caught that way by Porter and his men that got her back to her feet.

She was just in time, too.

The sound of running feet echoed into the rocky cul-de-sac and a moment later Bryant appeared at the entrance. He had a 9 mm pistol in his hands that he quickly brought up and aimed at her. Behind him came several other men. All of were armed, some with pistols, some with automatic rifles.

Behind them, Malcolm Porter, brought up the rear.

"Well, well, well," Porter said as he pushed his way to the front of the group. "What have we here, boys?"

For the first time, Annja got a good look at the damage her stone had done to his face and it wasn't pretty. Porter's eye was all but obscured by the swelling, and from the way it was already bluish-black Annja knew she'd broken at least his cheekbone, possibly even fractured his skull. His grin was a horrible caricature. "Caught like a rat in a trap, are we, Creed?"

Annja glanced past Porter to the guns his men held and knew all it would take would be a few ounces of pressure on the trigger of one of those weapons to end this once and for all. She was a sitting duck; there was nowhere for her to go and at this range Porter's men couldn't possibly miss.

But she wasn't afraid. She didn't believe Porter would have her shot.

The man was a control freak. Simply killing her wouldn't do any good. He would know she'd gotten the better of him, that he'd been unable to bend her to his will and force her to hand over the information his father had left behind. That would be unacceptable to a man like him. Taking the journal from her wasn't enough, especially not after she'd hurt him. He had to control her, to cow her, to make her grovel for forgiveness for daring to harm him in the first place.

As long as she refused to bend to his will, she had a fighting chance at life.

That was all Annja ever needed, a fighting chance.

"I think it's time for you to understand who's in charge here," Porter said.

He turned to Bryant. "Give me your knife."

Annja watched as the former commando turned over a wicked-looking combat knife with a blade nearly half a foot long.

Porter's good eye widened with anticipation as he turned toward Annja, knife in hand. "Playtime!" he said, and began walking toward her.

He was expecting her to be afraid and shrink from

him. That was, after all, what most bullies got off on from dominating and controlling a weaker individual.

She, however, was anything but weak. If he thought he could make her cower with that little pigsticker of a blade, he'd obviously forgotten their earlier encounter in the restaurant back in Maun. She was going to show him what a real blade looked like.

"What's the matter?" Porter taunted as he twisted the knife back and forth so that the sunlight glinted off the blade. "Where's that smart mouth now?"

Take a couple steps more and I'll introduce you to her.

Annja fought to keep a grin off her face. She wasn't ready to accept that this was going to be her final showdown, but if it was, if Bryant and company gunned her down in the moment after she struck, at least she'd die with the satisfaction of having put Porter in his place.

"I'm going to enjoy teaching you how to behave properly," Porter told her, and took those final few steps to bring him into range.

Annja laughed. "Give it your best shot."

A sane, rational person would have stopped and wondered why Annja looked so unconcerned. She was, after all, unarmed and facing a man with a nasty-looking knife in hand, but Porter was caught up in the blood-lust of vengeance.

He held the knife up in front of him. "I have a friend I want you to meet."

"Sure, right after you meet mine," Annja said nonchalantly.

31

Annja's arm flashed out and by the time it was fully extended she held an English broadsword firmly in her grip. The hilt fit her hand as if it had been made for her and her alone, and even though she knew that wasn't exactly true she found the sense of familiarity comforting nonetheless. She gave a quick little twist with her hand and slashed the tip of the blade down the side of Porter's already injured face, from just beneath the eye, through the swelling and down to a spot below the ear.

The response was instantaneous.

Porter shrieked and clapped a hand to the side of his face. Blood welled up over his fingers. His good eye was as wide as a dinner plate as he stood there and stared at her sword, trying to make sense of what had just happened and where it had come from.

Annja took advantage of his bewilderment to cut him again, this time in a line right across the chest from shoulder to shoulder.

Porter bellowed in pain again but this time had enough foresight to dance backward out of reach.

Annja could have killed him with that first attack. She could have simply thrust the sword through his throat and it would have been all over except for the burial. She knew it but, more important, Porter knew it, as well; she could see it in his eyes.

For a moment they stared at each other.

Then Annja broke the silence.

"What the matter, Porter? Cat got your tongue?"

He screamed in rage and moved in. For such a big man he was quick and he seemed to think that his quickness would allow him to get inside the arc of her blade and inflict some damage.

Annja was more than happy to show him that wasn't the case.

She knew at that point she wasn't going to get out of there alive. Even if she killed Porter, she'd still have to fight her way through several men armed with guns, and the chances of her doing that without getting shot at least once were slim. But for every moment she kept them preoccupied with her, Henry could get farther away.

She kept her back to the wall, making it impossible for Porter to circle around and attack her from the rear. He did his best to trip her up, weaving back and forth in front of her, consumed, it seemed, by his need for payback. His eyes were bright and full of hatred. He'd gone beyond wanting to see her grovel; he'd kill her now, if he could.

He rushed forward, knife at the ready, but Annja was there with the sword, driving him back. He feinted and tried again, this time from the opposite direction, but only managed to get a slash across the outside of one arm for his trouble.

The new pain seemed to wake him from his frenzy.

Instead of rushing forward a third time, he suddenly stepped back and called out.

"Shoot her in the leg, please, Bryant."

As Porter's words sank in, Annja looked over at Bryant to see him unsling the rifle from his shoulder.

"With pleasure, sir," he said in response.

She already knew there was nowhere to run. She gauged the distance between her and Porter, deciding in that moment to rush him and use him as a physical shield to protect herself from Bryant's gunfire.

Who knew? Maybe she'd get lucky.

Annja kept her eyes on Porter, mindful that he might be using Bryant as a distraction to rush in and jab her with his own weapon while she was busy watching the other man. She could see Bryant out of the corner of one eye and that was all she needed. She'd move when she saw the gun come up toward his shoulder.

Any second now…

Twang!

Twang! Twang!

Two of Porter's men suddenly collapsed, arrows jutting from their throats. A third shot, aimed at Bryant, struck the barrel of his gun as he was in the process of bringing it up across his body and, as a result, the arrow was deflected away without hitting its target.

The half second it took Annja to realize that not only were they under fire but the shots were coming from above and behind her was enough time for the shooter to get off two more shots, taking down the third of Porter's men and narrowly missing Porter himself when he twisted to one side.

Annja dropped into a crouch, releasing the sword

into the otherwhere, and looked up at the top of the canyon wall behind her.

Several tribal warriors stood silhouetted against the sky, bows drawn. As with the San back in the village, they wore little clothing and their wrists and ankles were decorated with all manner of bracelets and charms. Unlike the People of the Elephant, however, this particular group's jewelry appeared to be fashioned from gold and jewels.

Bryant caught sight of the newcomers about the same time Annja did and they became his new target. He fired several quick shots and at least one of them must have hit its target for the body of a San warrior suddenly slammed into the ground a few feet from Annja. Bryant began backing up toward the entrance of the rocky cul-de-sac as fast as possible.

Annja was forgotten as the men turned their attention to this new threat. More gunfire rang out, the shots echoing in the narrow canyon with earsplitting intensity, and the sound of the natives' bows was soon lost in the roar of automatic weapons. Two more tribesmen were hit and fell back out of sight, which should have helped Porter's team recover their confidence, but the unerring accuracy of the enemy's efforts far outmatched their own. With the exception of Bryant, few of them had faced a foe who fought back. The death of several of their number in so short a time had them spooked. When another of their number went down with an arrow in the thigh, the rest of Porter's men broke and ran, despite the fact that their modern firearms were more than a match against traditional weapons.

Seeing his head of security abandoning the field,

along with the rest of his men, Porter did the same. He glared at Annja one final time, then turned and ran as fast as he could for the canyon mouth a few dozen yards away. Several arrows were fired in his direction, but by some miracle he wasn't hit. At the mouth of the canyon, Bryant waited for his employer to run past him, sent a few more covering shots toward the tribesmen on the ridge above and then followed in Porter's wake.

And then there was only silence.

Annja stayed where she was for a moment, looking out at the aftermath of the confrontation, troubled by something that seemed out of place. It took her a moment to realize that the injured were neither moving nor making any sounds. There were no cries of pain, no shouts for help, nothing. Just silence.

This wasn't right.

She glanced back up toward the ridge above her. Three of the tribal warriors remained, watching her like hawks, their bows at the ready. The rest had disappeared.

Headed this way, no doubt. What happened when they got here was anybody's guess. Yes, they had chased off Porter and his men, but that didn't mean they were friendly. More than one well-meaning archaeologist had lost his life dealing with lesser-known indigenous cultures. She kept her hands in view and did her best to look disarming.

The situation in front of her had her puzzled, however, and after a moment she couldn't resist her curiosity any longer. She cautiously made her way toward the nearest injured man, who had taken an arrow through the right calf. She could see the feathered end sticking up even now. The wound was by no means life-threatening but it probably hurt.

Yet he lay there, unmoving.

As Annja knelt beside him, she got her first look at his face. His eyes were open and unblinking in the sunlight, his features twisted in pain.

Somehow an arrow to the calf had killed him.

It could be only one thing.

Poison.

The San tribes used a kind of poison made from the larvae of a small beetle, but it was slow-acting and often required hunters to follow the injured animal for hours, sometimes days, before it succumbed to the drug. Whatever this stuff was, it worked much faster and with considerably more deadly results.

32

It didn't take long for the rest of the warriors to descend from the ridge and enter the canyon below. Annja heard them coming and rose from her crouch to face them, well aware of the three still above her with bows trained on her.

Two of these men also held their weapons trained on her while a third bound her hands behind her back with a piece of rough rope. They left her legs free, so she could walk.

"Who are you and where are you taking me?" she asked in case any of them spoke English.

The man beside her said something in response, but it was in a clicking language similar to the one she'd heard back in the village and she was unable to understand it. He might have answered her question, but could just as easily have been telling her to keep quiet, she didn't know.

Once her hands were tied, he took her firmly by the arm and led her to the mouth of the cul-de-sac, where they waited for the other men to finish searching the bodies of the dead. Guns were ignored but knives seemed to be highly prized; each time one was found it was held aloft and displayed to the others. The pigsticker Porter had threatened her with was collected by one of the men and handed to her captor, giving Annja the sense that he might be the leader of the group.

He was tall and well built, which was easy to see given that he was wearing little more than a loincloth around his waist. He had thick, dark hair and brown eyes. His nose, broken at some time, had healed slightly out of place. His skin was deeply tanned but Annja thought it was lighter than the People of the Elephant.

Perhaps an indication of a different tribe?

It would make sense. The nomadic groups in the region were generally respectful of territory and tried to keep to informally agreed-upon boundaries where available. They'd traveled some distance from the People of the Elephant so it was logical to assume she'd stumbled into some other groups' territory.

But who were they? And why had they attacked Porter and his men?

More importantly, what did they want with her?

Annja didn't have any answers, but it looked as if she might have some soon. The rest of the group had finished with the bodies of the dead and were now gathering around their leader. Bent Nose, as Annja decided to call him, said a few words and as a group they headed off, taking Annja along with them.

They left the dead-end canyon behind and followed a twisting trail that led deeper into the canyons and made it difficult for even Annja to keep track of. At first she'd been surprised they hadn't blindfolded her or made any attempt to keep their path a secret, but gradually she came to realize they didn't need to. The complexity of the trail was barrier enough for anyone who attempted to follow. They walked for well over an hour, taking only one break. When they stopped, one of the men offered her a drink from a water skin. It was warm and tasted of old leather, but she drank greedily, not knowing when she might next get the chance.

When she was finished they set out once more, traveling up and down hills and through various intersecting ravines until, after what seemed like hours, they entered what she took to be another dead-end canyon. She realized it was something far different when they came to its end.

A massive stone temple loomed out of the fading afternoon light. Like the ruins at Petra in Jordan, the front of the temple had been carved directly from the face of the rock, giving the impression that it was growing right out of the wall itself. Its age was immediately apparent, the wind and weather having dulled and rounded the carvings' once-sharp corners and fine lines. That didn't subtract from the sublime beauty of the structure itself.

Something about it looked familiar, but Annja dismissed it as her general familiarity with ancient ruins the world over. There were only so many different types of building materials and so many different ways of putting them together to create monuments and buildings of this size and scale. Really, it was unsurprising that ruins in the jungles of Guatemala resembled those of Papua New Guinea.

And yet...

There was something different about this place. It was only when she got closer and could see the faded remains of the paintings that covered the front of the temple—representations of elephants and lions and men around a campfire—that she understood where she'd seen it before. Nearly identical paintings covered the interior walls of the temple in the elephant graveyard.

Clearly the two were connected. But how? And why?

She wanted to stop and study the symbols covering the stone, to try to understand, but Bent Nose pushed her along in front of him, and bound as she was she had no choice but to go along. Her dismay soon turned to excitement, however, when she realized that they were headed inside the mysterious temple.

She might be chasing "monsters" all over the world on behalf of a cable television show, but she was, at heart, an archaeologist, and what she was seeing now was the kind of find that only came once in a lifetime.

Just beyond the doorway were four warriors. They were standing in the shadows and Annja didn't realize they were there until they stepped out to greet Bent Nose and his companions. The guards—what else could they be?—were curious about her, but Bent Nose seemed reluctant to talk and eventually moved her over to a table in the corner that held a stone bowl filled with pitch-soaked torches. Soon the room was filled with a warm, flickering glow.

Bent Nose stopped to confer with two of the men that had been guarding the entrance, giving Annja a chance to look at the paintings decorating the walls. Unlike those on the outside, these had been protected from the elements and still retained much of their original gloss and color. They were extraordinary samples of ancient art and Annja longed for a video camera to record their details.

The paintings ran along the wall at about chest height and it only took a moment for Annja to understand they were telling a story, each panel leading into the next. She quickly scanned what she could see, trying to piece them together.

The first few panels showed a peaceful people living in a small village on the banks of a great river. Wildlife was plentiful, it seemed, as there were many pictures of elephants and zebras mingling with the people and in some of the pictures it seemed the two were working together. The overwhelming sense Annja got from the montage was peace and prosperity.

The village grew into a stone city in the next few panels, the mud-and-thatch houses replaced by multistory buildings of stone. There were several depictions of the Elephant Temple, as she had taken to calling the building where she had found Humphrey's final clue, and the animal itself seemed to play a role in daily life for these people.

But then the tone and tenor of the images changed to dead elephants and dead people. In each were what appeared to be another group—perhaps another local tribe—that were depicted as the cause of suffering. To Annja it looked like a neighboring tribe had come in and begun to kill the elephants, and the people of the city fought to protect them.

Then the last three images caught her eye.

The first showed the city on the plain, deserted and abandoned. Sticks littered the ground, which seemed odd to Annja, until she realized that they weren't sticks at all, but bones.

Elephant bones.

Her thoughts flashed back to the other temple. Is that how the elephant graveyard started? In the aftermath of a war? Was that temple all that was left of the city in these images?

The second last image showed a long line of people, refugees from the ruined city, stepping into a dark hole in the trunk of a massive baobab tree.

In the final image, the tree stood alone. The hole in its trunk was gone, as were all the people. It was as if the tree had swallowed them whole.

The Vanished Tribe.

A chill ran up her spine.

The story told in the line of images before her reminded Annja of the creation myth of the Anasazi Indians. According to legend, the Anasazi, or Old Ones, entered the Fourth World—the earth—through a hole in the sky in the Third World. They settled in the American Southwest, building beautiful cliff cities and enjoying a thriving culture. Many years later the Anasazi moved on again, this time opening a hole in the bottom of the Fourth World in order to reach the Fifth. The fact that the Anasazi culture seems to have vanished practically overnight made this particular myth all the more believable for those who bought into such things.

Annja tried to remember what she could about San religious beliefs and mythology. She knew they had two gods, or godlike beings—one that lived in the east and one that lived in the west. Unfortunately, that was about the extent of her knowledge. The legend pictured on the wall in front of her might be an incredible find, something that hadn't been seen before. Then again, it might be common knowledge for any anthropologist who spent time in the field with the San.

Another thought occurred to her. Were these people even part of the San culture? They weren't, after all, known for building permanent structures, never mind a city like the one pictured. Could they be a precursor to the people who would later become the San?

Not for the first time Annja wished she could communicate directly with these people. She had so many questions she wanted to ask and not being able to was driving her crazy. Things would have been a lot easier if Henry was still with her.

She was thankful they split up when they did. There was no way he would have been able to keep pace with her and more likely than not would have resulted in Porter catching both of them. Hopefully Henry had gotten away.

Annja was so deeply lost in her thoughts that she didn't realize Bent Nose had finished his conversation. He stepped between her and the wall, startling her. He said something angrily to her in his language and then stepped toward her, shooing her back with his hands.

Bent Nose called out to the others, who held the torches high and moved deeper into the temple.

They passed through several chambers one after another, too quickly for Annja to get a good look around, though it was clear from the amount of dust that the building hadn't been used for its original purpose in a long time.

When they reached the last chamber Annja got her biggest shock of the afternoon.

A stylized painting of a giant baobab tree covered

the entire rear wall, its outstretched branches seeming to flicker and wave in the torchlight as if blown by wind. And in its center, just like in the earlier painting, loomed a gaping hole. As they drew closer, Annja realized that it was the opening to a cave. The same cave that had apparently swallowed an entire tribe of people.

Without hesitation Bent Nose led Annja and the rest of the group to it.

She felt her pulse kick up a notch as they stepped through the entrance. The torchlight splayed over the close walls and she saw that it wasn't a cave at all, but rather a tunnel running deeper into the mountain. To Annja's experienced eye it looked as if the passage had formed naturally but had then been expanded by years of painstaking work. There were sections where the surface of the walls had been smoothed out, and she could even see the impact of hand tools on the rock itself.

They followed the tunnel for what felt like another fifteen minutes. It twisted and turned with easy regularity, and twice even doubled back on itself for several dozen yards, but in the end it kept them moving down. The incline wasn't steep, just a few degrees, but it was steady and after a time Annja guessed that they had descended about seventy-five, maybe a hundred, feet, beneath the surface.

No one spoke. The only sound was the crackling of the flames from the torches and the occasional clatter when one of Annja's thick-soled boots sent a rock spinning away from them in the darkness. The one time she started to ask a question, Bent Nose nudged her and added a whispered "Shh."

At one point they came around a bend and were suddenly assaulted by the sound of water rushing past them in the darkness. Annja started and glanced around, expecting a wall of water to come rushing down the narrow tunnel at them, but nothing happened. Curious, she stepped closer to the wall. The sound of the river grew louder the nearer she got. A glance at the wall showed the stone literally sweating from the moisture that was running somewhere on the other side. Another decade or two was all it was going to take for the water to find a way through the barrier and into the tunnel they were now using.

Nature always finds a way.

Eventually the tunnel leveled out and even began climbing slightly back up the way they had come. Not too long after that daylight began to filter back down the tunnel toward them and Annja guessed that they were nearing its end. Her suspicions were confirmed when they rounded a corner to see the opening at the other end of the tunnel, guarded by four more warriors.

As they approached, the two groups greeted each other. Bent Nose and his party were obviously expected. Annja, however, was not, and the new tribesmen stared at her in undisguised surprise, much like the first group back at the temple entrance. She felt like a bug under a microscope. Hadn't they seen outsiders before?

There was more than enough light and those carrying torches dowsed them in a barrel of water set to one side and then left them there. With a light step Bent Nose led her toward the cave exit.

Reaching it, she hesitated for a moment, letting her eyes adjust to the sunlight after being in the dark for so long. She stepped out on the ledge in front of the cave mouth and stared down in wonder at the valley below and at the city nestled within it.

She had found the Lost City of the Kalahari.

33

While in the Azores several years ago, Annja had the chance to visit Furno do Enxofre, Sulfur Cave, a magnificent forest-covered subterranean grotto inside a dormant volcano on the island of Graciosa. She'd had the pleasure of descending to the bottom of the caldera by a set of spiral stairs cut into the wall of the volcano and had stood among the lush vegetation at the bottom looking up at the blue sky through the opening some three hundred feet above her head.

She was looking at something eerily similar now, except the forest had been replaced by a city of stone sprawling out along the shore of a subterranean lake complete with its own cascading waterfall. Red-orange sunlight poured in from the opening high above, striking the eastern side of the valley floor, leaving the west in shadow, and Annja knew that it would gradually stretch outward as the sun fell completely behind the rim above.

She could see people on the streets below, tending to their business in the late-afternoon sunlight, and here and there Annja thought she saw a dog at their heels.

As she gazed out at the incredible sight, she noticed two buildings set off by themselves near the summit of the waterfall. The first was a multistory structure that reminded her of a palace, with its curving lines and sophisticated design, vastly superior to the block-like construction of the rest of the city's buildings. The second building rose like a beacon behind the first, a tall, slender cylinder that towered over everything else in the valley. From this distance she couldn't tell if it was ornamental—like an obelisk or a stele—or if it was some kind of functional space such as a watchtower.

She made a mental note to investigate both buildings, when the opportunity arose.

If the opportunity arose, she amended, pulling at her bindings to see if they had loosened at all during the trek.

They had not.

Bent Nose stepped up beside her and swept his arm across the view in front of them, taking in the entire city with a single motion.

"!Ksanna," he said, making that odd clicking sound with his tongue in front of the first syllable.

When Annja looked at him questioningly, he pointed at the city and said it again. "!Ksanna."

Annja understood. The city's name was !Ksanna.

She tried it out a couple of times, working to integrate the click sound properly, and Bent Nose smiled at her efforts, though whether he did so out of appreciation or amusement was unclear.

Bent Nose led her over to a wooden platform built into the side of the rock ledge where a large basket constructed of tree branches woven together with ropelike vines sat. The makeshift gondola was big enough to carry fifteen men by Annja's estimate; their party fit into it without difficulty. Nestled into an alcove in the cliff face behind the basket was a sophisticated wheel-and-pulley system that ran this primitive version of an elevator.

When they were settled inside the gondola, Bent Nose grasped a lever standing upright just outside the basket and gave it a good yank. In response, the large wooden spool in the alcove began turning, letting out the rope coiled around it, and the basket began descending at a slow, measured speed.

Annja did a quick calculation and guessed that it would take at least ten minutes to reach the bottom at this rate, which only increased her impatience. She wanted to go faster; she couldn't wait to see the city she had been through so much to find. She also hoped she'd be able to discover exactly what had happened to Humphrey. The question of why he hadn't returned from his last expedition still hung over her. She hoped the answer to that was down below within the city proper.

She wasn't the only one impatient to get down apparently. Bent Nose abruptly turned to one of his men and barked out a string of orders. The warrior nodded, slung his bow over his shoulder and then hopped up on the edge of the basket.

A half moment later she nearly had a heart attack when he swung his legs over the outside edge and dropped over the side. She rushed to the edge and glanced down, only to find him shinnying down the rope stretched out taut beneath the basket, making his way toward the ground below as fast as his hands and feet could carry him. At the rate he was going, he was likely to reach the bottom several minutes before they did.

She wondered what was so important that their leader had to send word on ahead rather than wait for the group to reach the ground themselves. Could it be her, a stranger's arrival?

The trip to the valley floor took closer to twenty minutes than ten, but at last they touched down with a bump. They disembarked, with Annja in the middle of the group.

They had come down in a clearing inside a grove of green trees. The city itself was east of them, on top of a series of low rises, like a miniature Rome astride its seven hills. A well-marked and well-traveled footpath led through the woods toward the city. Annja rightly assumed that was the direction in which they were headed.

Before they got under way, however, Bent Nose paused. He stared at Annja for a long moment and then gestured for her to turn around so her back was to him.

There was a sharp tug on her wrists and then, to her surprise, her bonds fell away, leaving her hands free.

Bent Nose was just slipping a knife back into his belt when she turned to face him, rubbing the sore spots on her wrists where the rope had dug in. He shrugged before indicating with his hand that it was time to leave.

If she was going to run, now was the time to do it. Overpower those around her, scale the ropes back up to the ledge and head off down the tunnels she'd entered through. She was confident she could handle the warriors that had been left to guard the entrance; they'd be looking for danger in the other direction and wouldn't see her coming until it was too late.

But her need to learn what had happened to Humphrey kept her feet firmly on the ground.

She'd come this far.

As they stepped away from the basket, the lift's control mechanism came into view. It was a large wooden wheel set horizontally on a wooden post, wrapped with a thick series of ropes. Four large beams extended from the wheel at each of the cardinal points of the compass.

Turning the wheel clockwise by pushing against the beams would wind out the rope and lower the lift to the ground. Turning the wheel counterclockwise would do the opposite, winding up the rope and raising the lift to the ledge high above. It was simple, yet elegant. The leverage provided by the wheel-and-pulley system allowed the lift to be operated with only a few men, regardless of how many were in the basket.

There were four operators standing near the wheel, but all of them were facing away from Annja. Something about their stance told Annja they were reluctant, as if they had been ordered to turn away. Annja glanced at Bent Nose but he didn't seem to notice, neither her scrutiny nor the lift workers themselves.

Curious.

At a signal from Bent Nose, the group started up the path toward the city. The warriors were much more at ease now, walking with their bows strapped over their backs and a lightness of step that told Annja they were not afraid of anything in the forest around them. For her part, Annja was amazed at the vibrancy and lushness of the foliage. To her it felt as if the valley existed outside space and time and it was easy to forget that just on the other side of the tunnels they'd passed through was one of the driest parts of Africa. She was amazed that this place had existed so long without being discovered by the outside world.

Of course the warriors around her probably had something to do with that, she thought grimly.

Emerging from behind the trees, Annja could see the city just ahead of them. They continued forward, leaving the path behind and making their way down a wide street she took to be a major thoroughfare. Most of the structures they passed were one- or two-story buildings, though she could see taller ones poking above the skyline. All the structures were constructed of rough-hewn stone blocks held together with some kind of dried mortar. Straw and mud, most likely. Both materials were plentiful and easy to repair. The buildings reminded her of the walls in Farini's turn-of-the-century photographs, though smaller and more refined. It was difficult to tell the age of them by looking. They seemed old, but there was a lot less wear than she expected and it took her a moment to remember that the entire city was protected, in part, from the elements by its very location.

They could be hundreds, if not thousands, of years old and they still would have fared far better than any structure out on the open plain.

They entered the city proper and began moving down a winding series of roads. Wherever Annja looked she saw signs of an established, successful culture. The buildings were in good repair. The streets were clean.

Bright color could be seen everywhere, from decorations and paintings on the buildings themselves to clothing hanging out to dry in the sun on balconies and terraces. Even the air, crisper and cooler with more than a hint of humidity from the nearby lake, was clean and free of the smell of human presence that so often pervaded towns and villages throughout the third world.

One thing she didn't see, anywhere, was people.

The streets around them were deserted.

It was as if the throng she'd seen from the ledge high above had simultaneously decided they had something else to do, somewhere else to be and, at precisely the same moment, had acted on that impulse without hesitation or delay.

Ri-i-ight.

Now Annja understood what the warrior Bent Nose had sent on ahead of them had been instructed to do. That he'd managed to clear the streets on his own, in less than fifteen minutes, was astounding. It spoke of a highly regimented and highly organized society.

In her current situation, Annja wasn't sure that was a good thing.

They made several turns, traveling into the center of the city. Once, Annja saw someone peeking out at her from behind partially opened shutters, quickly disappearing at a glance from Bent Nose. Annja hadn't seen if it had been man, woman or child. Besides the group she was traveling with, that was the only other person she saw.

Eventually they found themselves at the foot of another hill that held a single building: The palace-looking structure she had seen from the ledge above. Bent Nose headed toward it without a word.

It seemed Annja was going to meet whoever was in charge sooner rather than later.

34

A phalanx of guards lined the steps leading to the building's entrance, spears and bows ready. As they drew closer Bent Nose placed a hand on Annja's arm, indicating that she should hang back with the others, while he stepped out ahead to meet with the leader of the guards.

Annja watched as the two men conferred for a few minutes. It was clear that the captain of the guard, a tall muscular fellow who looked more than capable of handling himself in a tight spot, was upset about something to do with her. He showed considerable deference to Bent Nose, however, which raised the other man's standing in Annja's eyes and caused her to wonder if he were more than just your average scout party leader. A minor noble, maybe? The son of an elder? It was hard to say without knowing more about the group's social structure.

Whatever the case, the two men apparently came to a compromise. Bent Nose returned to Annja's side, the captain in tow, and the two of them took up position on either side of her. Bent Nose gave a short speech to his men, waited for them to acknowledge what he had said and then turned to Annja, taking a firm grip on her arm, just above the elbow. He nodded to the captain, who quickly did the same. Satisfied that their prisoner was now in their control, the two men started up the stairs to the palace, bringing Annja along with them. Behind them, a pair of palace guards followed suit, while the rest of the existing guard, plus Bent Nose's men, remained where they were.

It seemed she was headed for a semiprivate audience with the rulers of the city.

Her captors led her inside, down several corridors, until at last they came to a stop before a set of double doors guarded by a pair of men. There was a brief exchange and then the guards were opening the doors and ushering them inside.

As they stepped into the room, Annja gasped at the sight before her.

It was some kind of audience chamber. That much was obvious from the dais with a throne sitting on it. The throne was extraordinary. It appeared to be fashioned from the largest elephant skull she had ever seen. The skull had been turned upside down, so the crown rested on the floor, and the skull cavity itself converted into a seat. In that position the tusks curved downward at an angle, creating a paired set of armrests. Long, curved bones—ribs, maybe?—had been attached to the back of the throne like the feathers on a peacock's tail, giving it a wingback appearance.

But what drew her attention was the oversize diamond set into the wall just above the throne. It had to be a foot across and must have weighed a hundred pounds. Even though it was rough and uncut, Annja recognized it for what it was immediately and knew that in its present state it would be worth tens of thousands of dollars on the open market. If it were to be cut and polished, that figure would grow exponentially.

Two concentric circles of symbols had been painted around it and Annja was reminded of the icons surrounding the Mayan calendar. Did these symbols have a similar purpose of keeping time?

Two men walked out of the shadows on the left side of the dais and crossed toward the throne. Beside her Annja felt both the captain and Bent Nose stiffen.

The first man was old, perhaps even the oldest human being Annja had ever seen. He was small and wizened, with a face so wrinkled it seemed to swallow his features, so that his eyes seemed to shine out of his face like a pair of searchlights in the dark. He was dressed in a colorful sarong that left his chest and arms bare, just like his feet. He crossed the dais, climbed into the skull throne and looked at her with interest.

The man accompanying him was much larger, a few inches over six feet, and wore a bright robe that covered him from head to foot. The hood on the robe was pulled up, hiding his face completely. After following the tribal elder to the throne, he took a few steps down the front of the dais and then stopped, standing between the two groups.

The elder said something Annja couldn't translate.

"I am Lato, elder and tribal chief of the People," the robed giant said, repeating the words of the man on the throne behind him in English. "Why are you here? What do you want?"

Annja stared at him in surprise.

He'd spoken in *English*.

It took her a moment to find her voice, but when she did she made certain to speak in a calm, clear voice.

"Myself and my companion were being held against our will by evil men. We managed to escape and sought refuge in the mountains, where your people found us."

"Where is this companion now?"

Annja shook her head. "I do not know. We were separated before your people arrived."

The elder turned to Bent Nose and had a brief conversation. The translator did not share what was said, so Annja didn't know exactly, but she had a hunch the elder was asking if what she was saying was true. After several minutes of back-and-forth with his subordinate, the elder turned to her once more.

"Nagamush says that you were surrounded by enemies when the People found you and yet, regardless of the odds, you were prepared to fight, like a lioness protecting her cubs. When the People captured you, you did not fight back. He is confused by this."

Annja glanced over at Bent Nose—Nagamush, she corrected herself—and then addressed her reply to the elder.

"The enemy of my enemy is my friend, Eldest. Until they took me prisoner against my will, the People had not given me reason to consider them anything but a friend."

The elder pursed his lips, clearly not happy with her translated answer. His response was quicker this time. Almost as if he hadn't needed to hear a translation.

"You invaded our territory with weapons in your hands. Did you think the People would simply let that pass? Did you think we were too weak to deal with our enemies?"

Even through the translation Annja could hear the anger in the elder's voice. Gently, she thought.

"I did not enter your territory with a weapon, nor did I have one in hand when the People took me prisoner. As I said earlier, I was not there of my own volition but rather as a result of my attempt to escape harm at the hands of my enemies."

This time, it was the translator and the elder who went back and forth for several minutes. Annja didn't know if they were arguing about the translation or if the translator was offering his advice to the elder. Either way the older man didn't seem happy with what he was hearing, scowling several times in Annja's direction.

Hey, I'm not too happy with you, either, bud. Wisely she chose to bite her tongue. Still, she glanced around, noting the position of the palace guards, as well as those of Nagamush and the captain of the guard, just in case she needed to fight her way out of here. What she would do after she got outside, she didn't know. One thing at a time.

The elder signaled an end to the discussion with a sharp slash of his hand, silencing the translator. He addressed himself to Annja.

"Knowledge of the People—" Annja's jaw dropped; the old guy knew English, too "—has been forbidden to outsiders since our passage through the Hole in the World. We have jealously guarded our city and will continue until the Twin Gods decide the end has come."

The elder paused, considering, and then went on. "Yet, according to Nagamush, you have not raised your hand in anger against the People, so I am loath to pass judgment. Death does not seem just."

Annja let out a breath she didn't realize she'd been holding. Nothing like escaping a death sentence to get your pulse going.

"You shall remain with us until I have had sufficient time to eat, drink and pray."

"So I'm to be a prisoner, then?" Annja asked.

"Think of yourself as an honored guest. Nagamush will see to your needs."

"Now wait a minute!" Annja began. "There's no way—"

She didn't get any further. "You want I carry out the first sentence instead?"

Annja knew how to quit when she was ahead.

"No," she told him, bowing her head.

With that the wizened old man rose and walked back across the dais, the translator at his heels. They retraced their steps to the door through which they'd entered and disappeared inside.

Annja turned to find Nagamush and the captain of the guards waiting for her. They led her back outside and turned her over to a squad of warriors, who, in turn, took her to a small house on the outskirts of the city. They ushered her into a bedroom at the back of the house.

The door closed behind her and, seconds later, Annja heard the distinctive sound of a bar being slid into place.

She was locked in.

35

Porter and his men had retreated nearly a quarter mile back through the canyons when he called a halt. They waited, listening for signs of pursuit.

They didn't hear any.

It appeared whoever it was that had attacked them in the canyon had refrained from following them.

Porter's irritation at being attacked was tempered by his growing excitement over who those natives had been. He had been studying the San tribesmen for months. While they were certainly skilled hunters, the men they had just encountered were far more than that. Not just hunters, but warriors.

For years the idea that there was a lost city somewhere in the Kalahari had been dismissed by the scientific establishment. The San were a nomadic people, migrating across their lands in the wake of the animals that formed their primary source of food. Critics claimed that these were simple hunters with no reason, and no skill, to build anything larger than a temporary camp. A city, especially one made from stone blocks the size of those in Farini's unsubstantiated photographs, was completely out of the question.

Countering this so-called evidence was the suggestion that perhaps the San hadn't built the Lost City at all, but that another tribe, possibly one not previously known to modern researchers, had.

Porter believed that he and his men had just run into that very tribe.

And if that was the case, then following the tribe might take them right to the Lost City.

Bryant was playing rear guard so Porter called him over.

"Is that locator working?" Porter asked.

Bryant nodded. "The signal's faint, but steady."

"Let me see it."

Bryant turned on the display, then handed the phone over to Porter. There was no sign of the blue signal, but the red signal that indicated Creed's position was moving slowly north, deeper into the canyons.

Porter thought back to the confrontation. The tribal warriors had directed their attack at Porter and his men. Not at Creed. At least, not that he had seen.

Could she be in league with them? Was that why she ran in that direction? Had she previously made contact with those who occupied the Lost City and counted on their protection?

That was it. It had to be!

He turned to Bryant. "Creed's working with the warriors who attacked us and there's only one place they could have come from. If we want to find the city, we follow them."

"Right."

Bryant took the map out and spent a few minutes studying it before sharing his thoughts with Porter.

"If they continue on their present path," he said, "we

should be able to follow the ridgeline here and catch up to them. Once we have, our position should keep us from being seen and all we'll have to do is wait for them to lead us to our destination."

Within minutes the group was back on the trail.

SOMETIME LATER, Porter and Bryant lay in the shadow of a large boulder perched on a cliff. Using binoculars, they looked down into the canyon before them at Creed and her companions.

Not companions, Porter corrected himself. Captors.

The ropes binding Creed's hands behind her back were obvious even without the binoculars. So maybe this tribe wasn't in Creed's back pocket, after all, not like he'd thought.

Serves her right.

Porter moved the binoculars from Creed to the massive stone edifice they were approaching. Possibly a temple, he guessed. Unlike his father, who would have been swooning over a find in such well-preserved condition, Malcolm really didn't see any value in the structure itself. It was just another old building in a lifetime of old buildings, as far as he was concerned. No, what interested him was the fact that Creed and her captors seemed to be headed directly for it.

What is in that temple?

He soon had his answer.

Four armed men stepped out to greet them. After a few minutes, they all disappeared inside the temple.

"What do you think?" Bryant asked.

Porter didn't take his eyes from the binoculars. "Not sure yet..."

He waited for the group to come back out, but when they hadn't after twenty minutes he reluctantly decided that they weren't going to.

The temple had to lead somewhere else.

He was about to turn away when motion caught his eye once more. A lone warrior emerged from the entrance, followed the wall of the canyon until he reached a small alcove and then stepped inside. He would be out of sight of anyone looking out from inside the temple, but because of their relative positions above him, Porter and Bryant were able to see him quite clearly. The warrior stepped over to a ditch dug in the ground, pulled up his loincloth and squatted to relieve himself.

Porter recognized an opportunity when he saw one.

"Go!" he said to Bryant, only to discover the big man was already on his way.

By the time Porter and the others caught up to him, Bryant was standing over the rapidly cooling body of the tribesman, a pool of blood spreading out at his feet.

"Well?" Porter asked.

Bryant shook his head. "Nothing but that damned click speech. Figured it was better if we didn't leave him in our wake."

Porter agreed. The last thing they needed was this guy sneaking up on them from behind.

"Now what?" Bryant wanted to know.

Porter grinned. "We keep on, of course."

The decision was made to sneak up on the entrance from the side. Bryant and two of his men would enter, while the others stayed with Porter until the coast was clear.

In the end, the strategy worked even better than expected. Bryant and the others slipped inside the building, discovered the other three tribesmen sitting around a small fire in one of the adjacent rooms, preparing to eat, and three quick shots eliminated them as a threat.

A few minutes of searching led them to the tunnel Annja and the other warriors must have taken less than an hour before. Without hesitation, they lit torches from the pile on the table and headed down the tunnel in pursuit.

Bryant took point, staying a good fifteen yards ahead of the main group, trusting his instincts and the night vision he'd honed over years in the service. Because of that, he was able to spot the final pair of guards before the others rounded the corner and betrayed themselves with their lights.

He took one final look, then hustled back to the others. After telling the group to dim their lights and remain where they were, the ex-soldier drew his knife and disappeared into the darkness ahead.

Porter waited, fully confident in Bryant's ability to handle the problem.

After several minutes there was a thud from somewhere up ahead, followed seconds later by another.

Then silence.

Success, Porter thought.

He was straining to make out the sound of Bryant's return, but the other man was able to get right up next to him before he even knew he was there.

"Sentries won't be a problem anymore," Bryant told them, wiping the blade of his knife on his pant leg before sliding it back into its sheath. "I can see daylight up ahead."

They traversed the remaining length of the tunnel without incident and stood within the mouth of the cave, staring out at the city before them in the late-afternoon sunlight.

"Want me to find a way down?" Bryant asked after a few minutes.

Porter pulled the binoculars away from his face and shook his head. "No, not yet."

He stepped away from the entrance and paced back and forth, his thoughts awhirl. The legends involving the Lost City always made note of its vast wealth. It stood to reason if the city was real, that the treasure was, as well. And if that was the case, which Porter believed it was, the city's rulers probably wouldn't be inclined just to give it to him when he came asking for it.

Fat chance of that.

He was going to have to take it. Just like everything else in his life. Take it by force.

He thought about that narrow entrance to the tunnel they'd just passed through. A small, decently armed force could hold off an army in that tunnel if they had enough preparation time. Even with modern weaponry, it would be tough to bring a group of the size he needed to take the city by force through that tunnel. There had to be a better way.

He turned back toward the cave mouth and his gaze automatically slipped to the opening high above the city where the last of the day's sunshine could be seen. It was like standing inside the base of a volcano, he thought, and looking out through the cone.

Out through the cone…

Just like that Porter knew how he was going to do it.

By this time tomorrow, the city, and its treasure, would be his.

36

The room was rectangular and about the size of a studio apartment back in Brooklyn. It had one entrance, the door she'd just come through, and a single window.

A quick check of the window revealed that bars covered it on the outside. Escape through that route was unlikely unless she was willing to make a fair bit of noise. The room was also lightly furnished, with just a bed and a table with two chairs of carved wood. A clay chamber pot stood in the far corner.

"Now what?" she asked herself, but no answers were forthcoming.

She sat on the edge of the bed, suddenly exhausted. It had been a long and difficult day and she'd had very little to eat. In fact, now that she thought about it, she hadn't had anything at all since getting up that morning.

Just then she heard the bar on the door lift. She came to her feet, hands loose and at the ready, in case the elder had changed his mind and had sent warriors to carry out his "preferred" sentence. They wouldn't be expecting her to be armed and that might buy her enough time to…

Thoughts of escape vanished as the door opened and her two guards entered the room, followed by Nagamush. In his hands was a tray full of food and a jug of what Annja suspected was water.

Her stomach rumbled at the sight.

Nagamush said something, then shook his head and tried again. This time it came out more clearly.

"Eeee-t."

Surprised by his effort to speak her language, Annja smiled at him and received a smile in return. Perhaps there was a potential ally in the making.

The three men stepped back outside the door, which was then closed and barred behind them. Annja barely noticed; all she had eyes for was the food.

The tray held several different fruits and a bowl of some kind of meaty stew. A wooden spoon had been included, as well. In the jug, she found water, just as she'd suspected.

Annja didn't waste any more time. She dug in with enthusiasm. After a few bites she decided the meat was some kind of antelope, chewy and with a distinct but not unpleasant gaminess that reminded her of venison or reindeer. She ate most of it, but set aside some of the fruit for later. She was going to need it for the energy required when she made her break for freedom later that night.

When she was finished, she used the chamber pot and then settled onto the bed.

She was asleep within seconds.

PORTER AND HIS TEAM retreated back down the tunnel as quickly as possible. They collected the bodies of the sentries they had killed on the way in and then stashed them in a small cave they found a short distance from the temple. With any luck, the bodies would soon be found by scavengers and any trace of them would disappear before the men were even missed.

The sun had long since set by the time they made their way back to the SUVs they'd had to leave behind at the dry riverbed, but even in the dark it didn't take the men long to set up camp. Fires were prohibited, but cold rations and spare water were passed around so that the men would be comfortable. Bryant established a two-man watch that would last them through the night and settled in to take the first shift.

Meanwhile, Porter was on the satellite phone, rounding up the men and materials he would need for what he had in mind. It took some time and more than once he had to call back on alternate numbers as some of his suppliers were with other clients, but in the end he got everything he needed. Some of it was going to take a few hours to arrive, but his suppliers assured him he would have everything by early afternoon.

What he did with it at that point, of course, was up to him.

Of course, Porter thought.

After hanging up, he filled Bryant in on the plan and the two of them spent the next few hours ironing out the details. With the firepower he had called in, Porter was confident they would be more than a match for anything the tribesmen threw at them.

By the time he called it a night, Porter was feeling very confident.

Very confident indeed.

37

Annja awoke several hours later. Moonlight streamed in through the window, telling her the sun had long since set.

She rose to her feet, stretched and then walked over to the window. The streets outside were deserted and the town itself was quiet.

She tiptoed to the door and put her ear against it, listening carefully. After a moment she was rewarded with the sound of someone snoring on the other side.

She leaned back and examined the door. While it was well built, it certainly didn't have the precision that modern tools would have given it, and there was a quarter-inch-wide crack separating the edge of the door from the doorjamb.

It was perfect.

No better time than the present.

Stepping back, she reached out and called her sword to her. It appeared in her hand the next instant, fully formed and ready for use. The blade seemed to glow with a life of its own in the silvery light.

Without hesitation Annja slid the blade into the crack, pushed it forward a few inches and then drew it slowly upward until she felt it hit the wooden bar placed across the door to secure it.

The snoring aside, it was clear the guards weren't paying attention; no one would see the tip of a sword emerge from the door of a room where the prisoner was supposed to be unarmed and not raise a fuss. Which meant Annja would have a few extra seconds from the element of surprise once she got the door open.

Hopefully those seconds would be enough.

She took two deep breaths to prepare herself and then yanked the sword up a good couple of feet.

She felt the bar slide up with the sword and then tip out of its metal brackets. It hit the floor with a clatter that sounded unnaturally loud in the stillness of the night. Annja barely noticed. She was already in motion and had no intention of stopping until she was free.

She came through the door with her sword up and startled the guard, who was staring wide-eyed at the crossbeam now lying at his feet. He had just enough time to register her presence before the flat of her sword caught him across the side of the head and he went down without a fight, unconscious before he hit the floor.

The sleeping guard had been startled awake by the noise and was just now sitting upright on the floor mat he'd been using as a bed. His eyes grew wide as he took in Annja coming toward him. He was so focused on the sword in her right hand that he never saw the haymaker left she threw. The solid punch connected with his jaw and that was all it took. One blow and he was out. As he slumped over, Annja caught him and lowered him to the floor.

She crouched next to him for a moment, listening, waiting for the sounds of alarm from elsewhere in the building that would indicate her escape had not gone unnoticed. When she didn't hear anything after a few seconds she breathed a sigh of relief.

Time to get out of here.

With her sword out before her in the ready position, she crept to the end of the hall and peered around the corner. The hallway was empty. So was the one after that. She made it all the way down the staircase to the first floor and over to the front entrance before she ran into someone.

Literally.

Annja glanced back up the stairs, searching for pursuit, as she stepped through the beaded curtain that covered the front entrance and never saw the young woman coming in from the other direction.

The two slammed into each other and fell out into the street, the buckets of water the woman was carrying splashing both of them.

The other woman recovered first, took one look at the sword in Annja's hand, opened her mouth and screamed as loudly as she could.

"No, no, shh!" Annja whispered urgently, but the damage had been done. There was only one way to stop this woman from screaming.

Annja glanced at the woman's fear-filled eyes and lowered her sword. She couldn't do it; the woman was an innocent and hadn't done anything wrong.

Annja turned and ran.

There were no streetlights, nothing to guide her way but the light of the moon high above. Shadows loomed everywhere and Annja did her best to keep to them as she raced down the street, headed, she hoped, toward the edge of the city and the exit back to the world above.

From behind her came the sound of a man shouting orders and Annja knew that pursuit would not be long in coming. After the woman's screams, it wouldn't have taken them long to find the guards unconscious and her missing.

She pushed herself to run faster.

The streets were narrow and the buildings loomed close, preventing her from getting a good sense of where she was. The uneven surface of the road beneath her feet didn't help matters much, either. She stumbled and nearly fell several times as she raced.

The road curved to the right and as she came out of the turn she spotted a search party coming, the lights of their torches bobbing in the darkness.

Annja skidded to a stop, glancing left and right, looking for another route.

From the direction of the search party came a loud, guttural howl that was immediately followed by several more, echoing in the narrow confines of the street.

What on earth...?

She'd passed the entrance to another street a few yards behind her on the left and she turned that way. She didn't want to wait around to see what made a noise like that.

Once off the main thoroughfare, the area became a tangle of interconnecting streets and alleyways that seemed to twist and turn at random.

Within minutes, she was completely lost.

At the next intersection, she came to a halt, trying

to figure out where she was and what direction she should take. Everything looked familiar and alien at the same time. Had she been down this road? What about that one?

She heard the eerie howling, this time closer.

Much closer.

Something sleek, slung low to the ground, raced out of the darkness to her right, snarling, and Annja spun in that direction, her sword coming around with blinding speed. She heard the scrape of claws on stone and felt rather than saw the thing as it leaped at her. Her sword flashed out, catching it in midleap and cutting it in two with a single, powerful blow. Blood splattered across the front of her face and shirt. She had a glimpse of fur and teeth—dog, maybe? lion cub?—and then she was rushing on again, trying to find some way out of what was rapidly becoming a maze of streets and alleys.

Shouts from up ahead forced her to change direction again. She turned left at the next corner, entering a narrow street with no doors on either side, but the road sloped downward here and she began to hope that she was headed the right way at last.

That's when she heard the laughter.

It was a giggling sound, high-pitched and full of excitement. It was answered immediately by other laughter, coming from the same direction.

Behind her.

The hair on the back of her neck stood on end.

She dashed down another street, turned left at the next intersection and raced down that road, as well. She ran around a wide curve…and skidded to a halt, staring in dismay at the dead end formed by the backs of the buildings in front of her.

There was nowhere for her to go!

Shouts could be heard in the distance, but closer yet was that eerie laughter that seemed to mock her. She ran over to the nearest building and put her back to it, striking a defensive stance with her sword up. Whatever it was it was going to have to come through the sword to reach her, and Annja intended to make them pay dearly for that.

Something moved in the shadows of the alley she'd just vacated, but she couldn't quite see what it was.

"Come on, show yourself," she said under her breath.

It crept into the light, snout first, its teeth bared and dripping saliva. It had a doglike snout with black eyes black and large, batlike ears that were twitching. A tuft of hair ran over the top of its head and down its spotted back.

It slunk forward, moving low to the ground, but one glance at its powerful rear legs was all Annja needed to know that it could move with sudden speed.

Annja recognized it immediately. You couldn't spend time in Africa and not encounter a hyena.

This had to be what she had faced in the alley a few minutes before.

She was in trouble.

"Come on, then!" she shouted, trying to get the leader to charge before others joined in. If she could whittle them down one at a time...

But the hyenas didn't move.

They stood their ground, alternatcly growing and

laughing that horrible laugh, but making no move to come any closer.

That's when she noticed the collar on the lead animal's neck.

Trained hyenas?

Several tribesmen, holding torches and weapons, appeared behind the animals. Annja gripped her sword tightly, determined to give a good accounting of herself in the fight to come, provided they didn't simply shoot her down with one of those arrows she'd seen them use with such precision against Porter.

The moment stretched out, with both parties staring at each other across the short distance between them.

A sudden sting in Annja's left arm was all the warning she had. She looked down to find the end of a small dart sticking out of her forearm.

Uh-oh.

She took two steps forward as the world began spinning and she fell.

38

Annja came awake with a jolt.

She sat up from the pile of blankets on the floor, glancing around at the unfamiliar room. Unlike the first room, this one was round. Aside from the pile of blankets, the only other thing in the room was a chamber pot.

A chamber pot that looked suspiciously like the one she'd been given earlier.

How nice of them.

This room had three windows, but the same wooden bars covered them.

She rose to her feet and walked, a little unsteadily, over to one of the windows and looked out. Two stories below she could see the roof of the palace and, beyond that, the rest of the city. It looked from this height like some miniature model.

It didn't take a genius to figure out that she was in the tall circular tower she'd seen upon first entering the city.

Annja took a few steps toward the room's only door, but before she could get to it, the door swung open and a man entered.

She recognized him immediately by the long hooded

robe and wooden mask he wore over his face. It was the elder's translator.

He stepped inside and closed the door behind him but not before Annja caught sight of the four armed guards standing in the hallway outside.

Someone had learned their lesson, apparently.

Annja stared at the translator.

The translator stared back.

"Are you all right?" he finally asked. "Any dizziness? Nausea?"

It wasn't at all what Annja had expected and she was surprised into answering truthfully.

"No. A foul taste in my mouth, but that's all."

The translator looked around the room. "They haven't given you any water? Or food?"

There seemed to be anger in his voice.

"No," she replied, again truthfully, but now curious what kind of response that would bring.

"My apologies." He turned and rapped once on the door, which was immediately opened from the other side. He said something sharply in their language and one of them moved with alacrity to do his bidding.

It seemed the translator had some authority of his own.

Satisfied, he closed the door and faced her again.

"I'm sorry for the..." He stopped, muttering, "Oh, the hell with this nonsense!" under his breath and then reached up to remove his mask and push back his hood. "There," he said with satisfaction. "Much better, yes?"

He was thinner than in his photographs and had shaved his head bald, but there was no mistaking him.

It was the missing man himself, Robert Humphrey.

"I thought you were dead" was all that Annja managed to get out.

Humphrey chuckled. "There's been a time or two when I thought the same, but thankfully that sad day has not yet come to pass." He looked her over for a moment, studying her features. "Have we met?"

"No, sorry," Annja replied, stepping toward him and extending her hand. "Annja Creed, archaeologist."

Humphrey took her hand in his own. "Robert Humphr—"

Annja gripped his hand and yanked him forward, pulling him off balance, while at the same time spinning around behind him and getting an arm locked securely around his neck.

"Enough of this nonsense is right!" Annja whispered fiercely in his ear. "What the hell is going on here and why am I being kept prisoner?" She yanked once, hard, on his neck to show him she meant business.

Despite the fact that she could snap his neck with a sudden, sharp twist, Humphrey made no move to try to escape. He kept his arms out to either side, hands open and visible, so there would be no misunderstandings.

"Please, Ms. Creed," he said in a strained voice. "I mean you no harm and am here to try to help you. If the guards come back with the food and find us like this—"

"You want to help? Get me out of here, then."

"I am trying to do just that," he said, gasping. "Please, hear me out. Quickly, before it is too late."

He sounded sincere. It was that sincerity, plus his refusal to try to break free on his own, that made her release him and step away.

Humphrey took a few steps away himself and put

his hands on his knees, taking a moment to catch his breath.

He opened his mouth to say something but before he could, the door opened and a guard entered, carrying a bowl of fruit and a pitcher of water. Humphrey pointed to the floor, waited for the guard to put his burden down and then waved him back out.

"Seems you are a rather resourceful woman, Ms. Creed. First you break out of a locked room and disable the armed guards standing watch and then you over-power a man twice your size and take him captive. Is that what they're teaching archaeologists these days?"

Annja shrugged. "A woman's got to protect herself."

Humphrey watched her carefully for a moment. Annja was doing the same in return. He didn't appear to be a prisoner, so why was he still here? Did he even know the world had declared him dead?

He broke the silence first.

"What are you really doing here, Ms. Creed?"

Annja didn't hesitate. "Looking for you."

She explained that she had acquired the Farini paint-ing at his estate auction, about her confrontation with his son, Malcolm Porter, and of how Malcolm's botched theft had led her to discovering the puzzle Humphrey had left behind. Of course, at that point, she explained, she had no choice but to see it through to the end. The legend of the Lost City of the Kalahari was just too amazing for the archaeologist in her to ignore, and the mystery of his disappearance made an excellent topic for a *Chasing History's Monsters* episode.

She shrugged. "It was tailor-made for me."

Humphrey walked over to the window and stared

out into the afternoon sunlight. He didn't say anything for a long moment. When he addressed her again, he didn't look at her.

"So you're going to share the story of the Sho with the world?"

Despite her nonchalant attitude, Annja had been watching and listening to Humphrey very carefully ever since he'd entered the room, and caught the sudden dearth of emotion in his voice. He was trying to hide the importance of the question but was overdoing it in the process.

Stalling, Annja asked, "The Sho?"

Humphrey faced her, surprised, it seemed, that she wasn't familiar with the word. He waved vaguely at the window. "The Sho. Ancestors of the San. Cousins to the Khoikhoi. The inhabitants of this beautiful city."

He said the latter with such tenderness and longing that Annja immediately understood he was attached to these people in a way that went beyond admiration.

She could use that to her advantage. Still buying time to learn as much as she could, she asked, "How did they end up here? In this remote place?"

Anger flashed across his face and was gone again just as quickly. "The same old story," he said. "Human greed. Once the Sho lived in peace out on the plains, in harmony with life around them, in a city far larger than this one."

Annja flashed back to the mural she'd seen earlier and to the ruins of the temple that had become the legendary elephant graveyard.

Evidence of that earlier city?

"The Sho claim that far in the distant past the Twin

Gods smiled on the People. To show their favor, they pulled a star out of the heavens and sent it down to their children here on earth. The People discovered where the star had fallen and took it from the impact crater. They built a city on that spot and for years they lived in peace. The Heartstone, as they came to call it, provided them with all they needed."

Humphrey frowned. "But like everything else, even the glory days of the Sho had to come to an end. Neighboring tribes envied them. They wanted the Heartstone for themselves, believing that if they had it, the favor of the Twin Gods would shine on them, as well."

He shook his head. "The Sho's fate was sealed the day they let word of the Heartstone leak beyond their walls."

"What happened?" Annja asked. She wanted to keep him talking. Who knew what might be important in helping her get out of here?

"War happened, of course! The Sho were invaded by another tribe to the east."

Again the image of the mural rose in Annja's mind, the pictures of the invading tribe, the dead filling the streets as the city fell around them.

"And was the Heartstone lost?"

"Lost? Oh, heavens, no. The shamans knew of the attack long before it occurred, warned, some say, by the Heartstone itself. They were able to evacuate the city before the invading horde arrived, leaving only a small force behind to delay pursuit as long as possible. The rest of the Sho fled into the mountains, to this valley, and rebuilt their shining city. They've been here ever since."

Not entirely sure he would answer her question, Annja asked, "And the Heartstone? Where is it now?"

Humphrey grinned. "The same place it has always been, my dear. You've seen it yourself."

"I have?" she asked.

Her visitor nodded. "They say the Heartstone whispers its wisdom right into the elder's ear and that's one reason his decisions are so respected. Whatever he says goes. The People believe the Twin Gods are speaking directly to him through the Heartstone."

It took Annja a moment to put the pieces together.

"The diamond!" she exclaimed at last. "In the audience chamber."

Humphrey beamed. "Quite right, my dear, quite right."

39

The pieces of the puzzle snapped into place. With Humphrey's tale of the Heartstone, Annja finally understood just what Porter really wanted from the Lost City.

For a prize like that, Malcolm wasn't likely to give up easily.

These people were in serious trouble.

"We don't have much time," she said. "We have to warn them."

"Warn who about what?"

"The Sho. About your son."

Humphrey looked confused. "Malcolm? What does that overstuffed weasel have to do with this?"

Annja already knew there was no love lost between the two men, so she filled him in on the rest of what Porter had done, from taking Henry Crane hostage to trying to kill them both in the canyons outside the city gates.

Humphrey stood there, mouth agape. "Malcolm threatened, no, *tried,* to kill you and Henry?"

Annja nodded. "He wants the treasure and he'll stop at nothing to get it."

The older man was incredulous. "Treasure? What treasure? The Sho aren't the Incas! They don't have gold or precious jewels lying around everywhere for the taking."

"No, but they do have the Heartstone," Annja replied.

"Oh, no. He can't have that. No way."

"I hardly think he's going to listen to you," Annja answered dryly.

Humphrey, however, was insistent. "You don't understand, Annja. The Heartstone is a sacred, religious object for these people. They will die to keep it safe."

"Well, your son is going to find this place sooner rather than later and he's going to come in here with guns and an attitude. Looking to recoup some of the fortune you denied him in your will."

He was pacing back and forth, and for a minute Annja thought he might work himself right into a heart attack.

A knock at the door brought Humphrey up short. He answered it to find a Sho warrior standing there. They had a brief conversation, Humphrey nodded and the warrior stepped back into the hall.

"The elder has made his decision about you. He requests our presence immediately."

THE NEWS ABOUT PORTER had unsettled Humphrey and he kept to himself as the guards escorted them out of the tower and along a short path toward the palace. Just before they reached it, they veered right and entered a beautiful garden full of flowers. Given the desolation of the rest of the Kalahari, the garden seemed lush and exotic to Annja and she found herself imagining that once, long ago, the entire Kalahari region had been like

this. It was like a tiny moment out of time and Annja
was captivated by its beauty and innocence.

The cry of an elephant reached her ears, followed immediately by several more. Annja tensed, remembering
the last time she'd heard such a cry, and she began scanning the foliage around them, looking for the source.

She glanced at Humphrey, hoping he might share
some information about what to expect up ahead, but
he was still absorbed in his own thoughts.

The elephants, as it turned out, were around the next
bend.

Annja and the others emerged from the dense foliage
to find themselves standing on the bank of the river,
just upstream from the waterfall. A series of large rocks
formed a shallow pool in front of them and bathing in
that pool was a herd of elephants. Annja smiled at the
sight; she couldn't help it. She counted half a dozen
adults in the water, tending to two baby elephants, while
off to the right, near the edge of the bank, stood an older
one, most likely the matriarch. Her tusks gleamed in
the sunlight, as if they had been polished.

Sitting on a stool with his back to them, halfway
between the water and where they now stood, was the
elder.

Almost as if he had eyes in the back of his head he
turned at their approach and then beckoned them. Humphrey stepped forward as Annja was flanked by two
guards and ushered along in his wake.

Humphrey bowed when they reached the elder, then
frowned when Annja didn't do the same.

The elder didn't seem to notice. Addressing himself solely to Annja, he said in near-perfect English,

"I dreamed of you last night. I saw you in a great fire, holding a sword aloft as you stared through the flames."

Goose bumps broke out over Annja's flesh. She felt the hair standing up on the back of her neck. The feeling of being watched was overwhelming.

Who was this guy?

"I saw you standing alone in the ruins of !Ksanna, a look of sorrow and dismay on your face as wind whistled through the empty buildings and the plants lay withered on the ground."

Humphrey didn't say anything to interrupt the elder. Annja was not so sanguine.

"What do you mean I was standing in the ruins of this city?" Annja asked sharply. "How did that happen?"

The elder ignored her, his gaze never leaving her face. "I do not know what these visions mean, other than that your destiny is somehow tied up with the destiny of our fair city. Because of this, I have no choice but to keep you here until the prophecy plays itself out or until fate changes the path before us all."

Just like that, Annja became a more-permanent prisoner of the Sho.

For an instant she considered drawing her sword, running the blade right through the man seated on the ground in front of her and then making a dash for it.

She didn't want to harm him, though, didn't want to harm any of them, for that matter. She allowed them to pull her back, away from the elder, who sat watching her, emotionless.

Humphrey and the elder had a brief conversation in the Sho's language and then he was dismissed. He led her out of the Elephant Garden and back toward the tower.

For several minutes Annja didn't say anything. Then, as they neared the tower, she said, "If you can get me out of the tower under some pretense or another, I can get us both out of here."

"No." Humphrey's tone was flat.

"No one will get hurt. I promise you that."

Humphrey shook his head.

"Once we're free, we can bring the authorities down on Malcolm for what he did to your friend Dr. Crane. Keep him from coming here, disrupting the lives of these people."

"I said no, Ms. Creed."

The entrance to the tower loomed ahead of them. Annja had one last chance to convince him. She played her trump card.

"Don't you want to go home, Robert?"

He stopped, then slowly turned and looked at her.

"Home?" he asked. "This *is* home. And I won't let you destroy it."

They led her inside, up the stairs to the room at the top and then locked her inside once more.

40

Porter heard them before he saw them, the rotors filling the air overhead as the four Blackhawk helicopters came in from the north. They circled once, looking for a place to land, and then settled in the ancient riverbed nearby.

He went out to greet them.

The team was one that Porter had used before, mercenaries out of the Congo staffed with former soldiers and guns for hire. They were no match for a frontline unit like the South African Reeces or the U.S. Marine Recon, but Porter was satisfied that they'd be more than a match for the tribesmen with darts he expected to encounter. The group was led by a grizzled Congolese sergeant named Hawser.

The men shook hands and Porter explained what they were going to do. Hawser listened carefully, asked a few questions, but in general had no problem with the plan.

He'd better not, Porter thought. He's being paid enough.

Once the men were briefed, they broke camp and boarded the choppers.

The lead Blackhawk held Hawser, Porter, Bryant

and nine of Hawser's men. Hawser had the pilot's chair, while Porter sat across from him.

The rest of Hawser's two-squad unit, plus Porter's men, divided themselves among the final three choppers. Twenty-nine men in four Blackhawks, with ample room to carry out the treasure.

Porter gave Hawser the GPS coordinates for the city center and they lifted off. They flew at a good pace, covering in moments what it had taken them more than an hour to do on foot, and soon they were approaching the target. Porter's plan called for a smash-and-grab assault, with the choppers landing in the middle of the city near the palace he'd seen during their earlier reconnaissance. There, the miniguns could be used for fire support if it became necessary.

Given the primitive weapons he'd seen the tribesmen carrying he didn't imagine much firepower would be necessary. Better to have it and not need it than be without it in a crucial moment.

They swung out and headed for the group of low peaks in the distance, with Porter updating Hawser on the route they should take from the information on Bryant's phone.

Five minutes later everyone began scanning the area through their windows, looking for the target.

Porter saw it first.

"There!" he said, pointing between two peaks where the mouth of the crater was just now becoming visible.

Hawser swung the chopper toward it.

Before they got far, however, something struck the chopper violently, rattling its frame. To Porter, it felt like a giant had seized them from below.

Alarms went off and Hawser was suddenly very busy at the controls, flicking switches and hauling back on the stick to right the aircraft.

"What the hell was that?" Porter demanded.

Hawser looked grim. "Turbulence."

Porter wanted to laugh. Turbulence? Here he'd thought they were under attack by heat-seeking missiles. "Well, can't you go around it?"

"Working on it, sir."

But after a few minutes of bouncing around the sky, Hawser had to admit defeat. "Seems it's localized to the area around these peaks, sir. If we want to get down into that crater, we don't have any choice but to go right through the turbulence."

"Fine," Porter snapped. The bouncing around was making his face hurt beneath the bandages. "Just get us down there without killing us."

Hawser didn't reply. He tipped the chopper on its side and headed for the green they could see poking up between several peaks.

It was a bumpy ride. Porter held on to the crash webbing and tried to keep his food down as they twisted and turned through the descent. Behind him, someone else wasn't so lucky and the stench of vomit filled the cockpit.

It was clear to Porter how the city had stayed lost for so long, even in this age of technological wonders. There was the remoteness of the area itself. Not even the safari companies came out this way; there just wasn't anything out here to see, that tour guides knew of, anyway. That same remoteness made the area of little interest to international satellites and national security teams. This part of Africa was not known for being a terrorist breeding ground. The eyes in the sky were aimed at more target-rich environments in the Middle East and Southeast Asia, not the back end of nowhere in the middle of the Kalahari. If they were looking this way, the angle of the nearby peaks combined with the cloud cover hanging about the region would make spotting that one stretch of green marking the open mouth of the crater difficult.

Even if they did find the valley, getting to it, both by land and, as they were finding out, by air was more difficult than the average individual was willing to pay for.

Not unless they had a really good reason.

Like a legendary treasure.

"Hang on!" Hawser shouted, and the helicopter whipped over on its nose into a steep dive.

Bile rose in Porter's throat as Hawser dropped the helicopter through the mouth of the ancient caldera, if that was indeed what it was, and into the airspace above the ancient city.

Once they were out of the slipstream the turbulence stopped. The beat of the rotors magnified tenfold by the cliff walls as they swooped low over the city, heading toward the open area in front of the palace Porter had picked out as their landing place.

Ahead of them they could see a group of warriors gathering in the street, pointing up at them. Porter could see that quite a few of them were armed, but as he'd expected there wasn't a single modern weapon among them. There were plenty of spears, knives and bows and arrows, but against the firepower his people carried that was like going into a knife fight with a wet noodle. They weren't going to last twenty seconds if they got in his way.

Porter fully expected them to scatter and run, but as the helicopter swooped, the tribal warriors did the unthinkable.

They fired!

Everything from rocks to arrows to spears were launched at the chopper. Another place and time Porter might have found it interesting, admirable even. But he'd had his fill of people trying to prevent him from securing his goal.

Anger flared in him, hot and feverish, and the wall he had built to contain all the rage and frustration he'd felt since this expedition began finally gave way.

It was time to teach these people a lesson.

"Kill them," Porter said. "Kill them all!"

Hawser didn't need to be told twice. He turned and pointed at the door gunners. Without hesitation they pointed the barrels of their miniguns at the buildings whipping past on either side and opened fire.

A thunderous growl filled the air as the weapons fired four thousands rounds per minute. Wood splintered, walls collapsed and bodies bled as the bullets tore through anything in their way. People ran in every direction, screaming as destruction and terror rained down on them from the sky.

It was an utterly horrific attack against a people unable to defend themselves and Porter laughed to see it. He'd had enough of chasing after what he wanted. Now he intended to reach out and take it.

He had the choppers make several passes, and by the time he ordered them to turn and head for the palace, entire sections of the city were little more than smoking ruins.

No one was firing on them now, Porter noted with satisfaction.

The men were cheering and shouting in the back, their bloodlust high, so when Porter spotted the group of warriors standing in front of the palace steps like some kind of primitive guard, he ordered the mini-guns offline.

"I want those fools taken care of," he shouted, pointing out the window at the guards lined up like bowling pins, "but I'll personally shoot any man who tries to enter the palace ahead of me. Is that clear?"

There was a chorus of "Yes, sir."

Porter nodded. "Hawser, bring us down!"

The choppers settled in a diamond-shaped formation on the grassy area in front of the palace. As soon as the skids touched the earth the door sprang open and the troops poured out.

A barrage of arrows met them, but the wind from the still-circling rotors played havoc with the tribesmen's aim. Still, a few got through and at least one of Porter's men went down, a poisoned arrow in his chest.

Unfortunately for the Sho, the rotors had no such impact on the bullets from the soldiers' guns. Automatic rifles were brought to bear, riddling the group with a hail of burning lead. Limbs twitched and bodies shook under the impact of the firepower, making them seem to be doing some crazed sort of dance. Blood flew, splashing the steps and the doors behind them.

In seconds it was over.

41

Annja heard the helicopters first, the sound of their rotors quickly drowned by a thunderous roar that shook the tower she stood in.

She stumbled forward, trying to reach the nearest window while fighting to keep her feet. Something big and dark went whipping past the opening and Annja threw herself to the floor just as bullets chewed through the wall in front of her like a chain saw spitting teeth. Then she was rolling across the floor, feverishly trying to get out of the line of fire as the helicopter went flying past outside.

As the sound receded, Annja scrambled the rest of the way to the nearest wall and flattened herself against it, then rose and peered out the window.

Her heart leaped into her throat at the sight that met her eyes.

Blackhawk helicopters—at least three—were flying low over the town, gunners firing wildly as they strafed the buildings around them.

It was Porter. It had to be.

She had to stop him. Had to help these people.

Annja rushed over to the doorway and began pounding on it, desperate to get the guards to open the door.

She couldn't do anything from in here; she had to get out there, where the action was, if she had any hope of stopping Porter before things got worse.

When no one answered she stepped back and called her sword. The minute it was in her hand she tried the same trick she'd used the other night, sliding the blade between the door and the jamb, then using it to leverage the bar out of the way. Her captors had apparently learned their lesson, however. The bar was heavier than it had been before. So heavy, in fact, that she couldn't get it to move, never mind slide out of its groove.

The choppers came back around for another pass, and as the roar of the guns filled the small room, Annja began hacking at the door with the sword. Chips of wood flew with each blow, but at the rate she was going it would take hours for her to get through.

Hours she didn't have.

She spun around, looking for another solution, and her gaze fell to the remains of the window. The gunfire from the helicopter had shattered the wooden bars, leaving an opening wide enough for her to slip through.

Annja didn't hesitate. She ran to the window and stuck her head out.

The thunder of the choppers assaulted her ears and from where she stood she could see them headed toward the far side of the palace. It wouldn't be long now before they were inside and in possession of the Heartstone.

Not if I can help it.

She looked down. Tried to forget that she was three stories up as she examined the face of the tower. The stones had been carefully fitted and then sealed together with a thick coat of mortar. Their uneven nature created plenty of hand- and footholds. Climbing down shouldn't be much more dangerous than descending a ladder, really. All she had to do was get out the window without falling and she should be fine.

That first step was the hardest.

She used her sword to clear away what was left of the bars. Since the window was at chest height, she grabbed the chamber pot, unused thankfully, and turned it upside down as a stepping stool.

A barrage of gunfire rang out from the palace. Small-arms fire this time and not the choppers' guns. That wasn't much of a relief. It meant that Porter's men were engaged in the palace.

Faster, Annja, faster.

She stepped up onto the chamber pot, leaned out the window and drove her sword into the side of the tower as deeply as it would go. Then, using the sword as a kind of handle to balance herself with, she climbed through the window and let one leg dangle out.

Now the hard part. She kept one hand on the hilt of the sword and reached over her head with the other to grab the wall, while at the same time finding a foothold. When she was satisfied she'd found a spot that would support her weight, she pulled up with her hands, balanced on her foot and pulled the other leg out.

Once she had found two footholds, she moved the hand holding the hilt of the sword to the face of the tower itself.

She took a couple of deep breaths to steady herself and then began climbing hand over hand down the face of the tower. Above her, the sword vanished back into the otherwhere.

PORTER STRODE INTO the audience hall with Bryant and Hawser at his heels. Ahead of him was a raised dais. At the foot of the dais were three tribal warriors, bows aimed at them. On the dais sat a grizzled old warrior dressed in a colorful sarong on a throne made of bones.

Embedded in the wall behind the throne was the largest diamond Porter had ever seen.

As amazing as that was, his attention was compelled back to the dais and to the man standing next to the throne.

Porter would recognize him anywhere, even after so long apart.

His father smiled. "Hello, Malcolm."

Porter stared openmouthed for several long moments at the man he'd presumed dead for over two years now.

The gunshot was particularly loud in the silence.

Humphrey's eyes went wide as he slowly looked down to see the blood pumping out of him from the bullet wound in his gut, then he toppled over backward to lie jerking on the dais.

"Hello, Dad."

The gunshots that followed were almost perfectly timed with the twang of the bowstrings as both sides fired on the other. Unfortunately for the Sho, they had to reload after the first shot; Porter's men didn't.

It was over quickly, with the tribal warriors and their chief sprawled dead or dying across the dais and only two of the men with Porter sharing in their fate.

As far as Porter was concerned, that was a fair trade.

He stalked across the room and stepped up on the dais. His father, bleeding to death on the floor, grabbed his boot as he passed. Porter jerked his foot away without looking down. He ignored the body of the tribal chief, as well.

He stopped in front of the diamond.

It was enormous. Probably the biggest one ever found. Not only was he going to be rich, but he was going to go down in history, too.

Hawser whistled appreciatively and stepped forward, a thick-bladed combat knife in his hand. "I think I'll take my share of the booty now," he said, referring to the deal he'd cut with Porter for twenty percent of the spoils from the raid.

Porter's gun came up, barked once, and Hawser went down with a bullet through the skull.

Behind him, Porter heard Bryant's gun go off twice, followed in rapid succession by the sound of bodies hitting the floor. He turned to find his second-in-command standing on the first step of the dais, his gun trained on the men in front of him. Most of them were Porter's men, but a few had been part of Hawser's squad.

"Anyone else going to tell the boss how this job is supposed to go down?" Bryant asked, his gun steady.

A chorus of "No, sir" came back to him and he nodded.

He glanced at Porter and said under his breath, "Might want to secure that big shiny rock while we still can, sir."

Trusting Bryant and the rest of his men to cover his back, Porter stepped forward and began prying the stone from its resting place with the edge of his knife. It didn't take long; after just a few minutes the stone began to rattle in its setting. He called two soldiers up to help him hold it as he worked it over for a few more minutes before the stone popped out.

The three men lowered it carefully to the floor.

Bryant tossed Porter a thin nylon pack. He put the inside, zipped it closed and then hefted it up onto his shoulder.

It was heavy, but he'd make it.

As he turned toward the rest of the men, he heard the sound of an elephant trumpeting from somewhere outside. The elephant's cry was immediately followed by a thunderous crash.

The helicopters! Porter ran for the door. The rest of his men followed at his heels.

Outside it was chaos. Guns were going off, metal was shrieking and tearing like a living thing and over it all was the trumpet of an elephant gone mad. Porter stared in disbelief at the lurching, crumpled ruin that had been his helicopter. The rotors were snapped off, the cockpit glass shattered and the cargo bay containing the seats they'd ridden in nothing but a crushed hulk.

The helicopter behind that one wasn't much better. While the cockpit was still intact, the entire tail of the aircraft had been bent to one side at a perpendicular angle to the rest of the craft. Like the lead bird, this was another one that wouldn't be going anywhere soon.

Men were shouting, guns were firing, and Porter looked up in time to see a bull elephant come charging out of the nearby vegetation, lower its head and slam into the tail of the third helicopter just ahead of the rotor. Blood was pouring from half a dozen wounds on the elephant's hide but that didn't seem to slow it down any. It barreled its way forward and reared up next to the fourth and final helicopter. As it did, Porter could see that the elephant wasn't alone. There was a warrior riding on its back.

"Kill them!" he screamed, and began firing shot after shot. Behind him, the rest of the men followed suit, adding a punishing hail of gunfire to the efforts of the men who'd already been trying to kill the pair.

Bullets slammed into the hulls of the aircraft, ricocheting, the cacophony drowning out Porter's repeated demands that his men kill the elephant and its rider. Miraculously, however, the elephant managed to get through the fusillade without taking a mortal injury and, at its rider's urging, turned and rushed back into the dense foliage nearby, having accomplished its goal of destroying the craft that had rained down such pain and misery on the inhabitants of the Lost City.

Slowly the firing stopped, leaving Porter shouting furiously in the wake of his enemies and dry-firing a now-empty weapon. Eventually he realized what he was doing and stopped.

Behind him, Bryant began shouting orders for the team to grab what ammo they could from the wreckage of the helicopters and to form up around him.

Porter waited until Bryant had stopped shouting and the men were carrying out their orders before catching the other man's attention. "What are you doing?" he gritted, his fury still smoldering.

Bryant's reply was both calm and practical. "If the birds won't fly, our only chance to get out of here is that tunnel we came through yesterday. If we can get over there quickly enough, we can keep them from sealing off the route and trapping us here."

Porter frowned. "You think they would do that?"

"If a bunch of cowboys just shot up your hometown and were still within range, wouldn't you?"

Porter decided Bryant had a point.

42

Annja moved down the outside of the tower as fast as she dared, clinging to the wall like a spider and seeking out each new foothold with her toes, making sure it would hold her weight before releasing her hands. The biggest threat to her descent was her own haste. She had to keep reminding herself to slow down and move carefully. An inadvertent mistake would send her the short route to the bottom.

She was one third of the way down when an outburst of gunfire from the palace startled her. She missed the foothold she'd been reaching for in the same moment that her opposite hand slipped from the crack she'd jammed her fingertips into. Before she knew it she found herself hanging precariously by one hand as her feet scrambled for traction.

One of her flailing feet caught on the edge of a brick and she steadied herself, breathing a sigh of relief.

There has got to be a better way.

She glanced down, trying to gauge whether she was still too high to jump, and finally decided that she was. A two-story fall was likely to break an ankle or leg if she didn't land just right, and that was something she couldn't afford right now.

In the process, however, she spied another window, much like the one she'd climbed out of on the floor above, a few yards to her left. Thinking that it might prove a quicker route to the ground, Annja hustled over to it and peered inside.

It was a room like the one she'd been held in, except this one was empty.

Opposite the window, the door stood open.

Yes!

There were wooden bars over the window, but that didn't stop Annja. Getting a good grip on the wall nearby, she called her sword and used it to hack her way through the barrier. Once the bars were out of the way, and the sword returned to its resting place in the otherwhere, Annja shinnied through the window and dropped inside the room.

Creeping across the room, she peered out the open door.

No one was there.

Sword in hand, she stepped into the hall, descended the stairs and ran outside.

The gunfire had stopped. Annja didn't know if that was a good sign or not. It might mean there were no longer any targets worth shooting at. She hadn't seen the helicopters take off again from the other side of the palace, so that was where she decided to go.

She followed the path the guards had taken her on earlier, until she came to the rear of the palace. Spotting an open door, she slipped inside.

Her breathing was loud in her ears and her heart beat wildly as she crept down the hall. A short passage opened up on her right and she followed that until she came to a door.

She put her ear against it and listened, but didn't hear anything. Annja had no choice but to push it slowly open.

The door led into the audience hall and one glance was all it took to tell her that things had gone horribly wrong. Bodies littered the steps before the dais. Most were Sho warriors. It looked as though the Sho had been cut down where they stood, victims of firepower far superior to theirs.

Along with the bodies of the guards, Annja could see the forms of Robert Humphrey and Lato the Elder lying in pools of blood.

Behind the throne, the empty socket where the Heartstone had been kept glared at her accusingly.

She was too late.

It was a crushing blow, one that derailed her train of thought and left her wondering what to do next. Annja was standing there, staring at the destruction around her, when the elder twitched and groaned.

She rushed to his side. Kneeling beside him, she gave him a once-over.

It didn't look good. He'd taken at least three bullets to the chest and stomach. By the blood spreading out beneath him, Annja wondered just how much blood he still had in him. That he was still alive was a minor miracle.

Annja looked for something to stem the flow of blood from his wounds, before realizing there was no way she could put pressure on all of them simultaneously.

"Help!" she cried, not caring at this point if it was Porter's men who found her. "Somebody help me!"

No one came.

Annja did what she could, knowing it was futile, but she refused to give up. She tore several pieces of cloth from the elder's sarong and stuffed them into the wounds; infection was the least of her worries.

As she applied pressure to one of the makeshift bandages, his eyes opened. He stared at her, then grabbed her wrist in his aged hand.

"Return...the Heartstone...to the People," he gasped, blood dripping from his mouth. "Or we will all surely die."

He seemed to relax once he'd said it, and in the next moment his body went still.

Annja frantically tried to resuscitate him. It was only after she stopped giving him CPR that it dawned on her he'd spoken in English again.

A noise startled her and she whirled around, calling her sword into being.

Across the room, a bloody and battered Nagamush stood staring at the scene. His gaze drifted from the elder's corpse to the hole in the wall where the Heartstone had rested for generations and then back to Annja.

She didn't think she'd ever seen an expression so bleak.

Humphrey's words came back to her.

The Heartstone is a sacred, religious object for these people.

Maybe she could still stop them. She could still make this right. Wasn't that what she carried the sword for? To protect the innocent from the predators among them?

She hustled across the room, grabbed Nagamush's arm as she went past and headed out the front door.

Only to stop short at the destruction in front of her.

The bodies of more than a dozen Sho warriors lay scattered on the lawn, along with the mashed remains of the helicopters. Now she knew why they hadn't taken off. It looked as if a giant had used them as his playthings. Annja remembered the sound of the elephant she'd heard earlier and put two and two together.

So where was Porter?

The sound of gunfire drifted to her from somewhere in the distance.

The lift.

It had to be. He couldn't fly out, so he was trying to escape with the Heartstone through the only other entrance to the valley. The same tunnel Nagamush had brought her through the day before.

There might still be time to stop him.

43

Annja was about to rush off in the direction of the lift when Nagamush grabbed her arm. He shook his head and held out both hands. Then he put his fingers to his mouth and whistled.

At first there was no response. He tried again and this time a loud, trumpeting cry answered him. Annja spun around to see one of the elephants that had been bathing in the pool earlier stomp out of the vegetation on the other side of the wrecked helicopters. It moved toward them.

The majestic creature was in rough shape. Annja could see where it had been hit by several bullets, blood oozing slowly out of the holes in its hide, but the injuries seemed to have done little to slow it down. It walked up to Nagamush and trumpeted again, then bent down on one knee.

The Sho warrior scrambled up onto the elephant, seated himself behind its head, then leaned down, extending a hand to Annja.

This is a first, she thought to herself as she climbed up behind him. Going into battle on an elephant.

She let her sword vanish back into the otherwhere, then wrapped her arms around Nagamush's stomach.

He said something, then tapped the elephant twice on the head.

The great mammal responded without hesitation, lumbering down the street in the direction Porter must have taken his men.

They reached the base of the lift and the two of them dismounted. They raced over to the elevator mechanism, only to find their worst fears confirmed. The great wheel that powered the lift had been smashed and the ropes that normally controlled the movement had been pulled up to the ledge high above. The basket stood up there, as well, effectively marooning Annja and everyone else at the bottom of the cliff.

Or so they thought.

Annja took one look at the shattered mechanism and then turned her attention to the cliff instead. She estimated it to be maybe three pitches to the top, which would put it somewhere in the neighborhood of three hundred feet. It was a long way to go without adequate protection, but there looked to be a fair number of hand- and footholds. If she was careful, she wouldn't have trouble.

Except she didn't have time to be careful.

If she wanted to get the diamond back, she needed to catch up with Porter. Once back in Maun, he could hide behind the walls of his estate outside of town and she would have a much harder time gaining access to him and the gemstone.

She caught Nagamush's attention and then pointed to the cliff. Annja did what she could to make him understand her plan by pantomiming climbing the wall and then throwing down a rope so he could follow.

He nodded.

"Here goes nothing," she said beneath her breath, and started climbing.

To her surprise, the climb went quickly. She'd been correct; there were plenty of holds and with the exception of one ten-foot stretch of glassy smooth rock where she was scrambling for the next move, she didn't feel she was pushing the margins of safety far.

Then again, her margins of safety would make the average person quake with fear, so maybe that wasn't saying much.

She was about halfway up when she glanced down. Nagamush had sent the elephant away and was now climbing steadily behind her. He was doing all he could to help save his people from a catastrophe. In his position, would she have done any less?

Buoyed by his fearless determination, Annja climbed on.

Her arms were shaking from the lactic acid buildup in her muscles when her fingers finally slipped over the top. She'd made it. With a final pull, she heaved herself up over the edge and rolled onto her back, closing her eyes in silent thanks.

The sound of footsteps was so unexpected that it took a moment for her to recognize what they were. By the time she did, she opened her eyes and found herself staring into the barrel of a pistol.

"Well, well, well. Look what the cat dragged in."

Annja had never seen the man before, but the paramilitary fatigues and combat boots made it clear that he had to be one of Porter's men. His finger was on the trigger of his weapon.

Not good.

Annja heard the clatter of small rocks falling down the cliff face and then Nagamush's hand came up and gripped the edge.

The movement shifted the soldier's attention away from Annja. "What the…?" He swung the gun toward the ledge.

Annja lunged forward, grabbed his ankle and pulled with all her might.

The gun went off with a deafening bang, the bullet missing Nagamush by inches as the man's leg was yanked out from beneath him and he found himself headed for the cliff's edge with considerable speed.

Recognizing the danger, he dropped the gun and flailed his arms, trying unsuccessfully to grab Annja to stop his fall. With a final bloodcurdling scream, he slid over the edge and out of sight.

If he hadn't fallen to his death, she would have run him through with her sword.

The two of them took a moment to catch their breath and then set out once more. Nagamush led the way this time, unselfconsciously taking her by the hand and leading her through the tunnels without the benefit of a light, not wanting to give them away if Porter was up ahead.

As they neared the end of the tunnel Annja made him slow down and advance more cautiously. Porter had already left one guard to watch the trail behind him and she expected he'd do the same at this end. Annja didn't want to go blundering into anyone in the dark. But as they moved through the rooms of the temple, it became increasingly clear that they were the only ones there.

When she stepped out into the canyon, Annja knew they were too late. Porter and his men had already disappeared.

She turned to her companion. The look on his face told her he already knew.

They had lost Porter and, in doing so, had lost the Heartstone, dooming the Sho people to what they believed was certain death. The ones who were still alive, that is.

Nagamush sank to the ground. He stared at nothing, his eyes full of tears.

It was heartbreaking, and for the first time in a long time Annja didn't know what to do or say. How do you comfort someone who thinks he's witnessing the death of his entire race?

The words of Lato the Elder echoed in her head.

Return the Heartstone to the People or we will all surely perish.

There was no way she was going to let it end like this.

She and Nagamush could catch Porter if he was on foot. If Porter had managed to find transportation, it was a different story, but for now he was traveling in exactly the same manner as she was. Her best bet was to figure out where he was going and then beat him there.

If anyone could take her through these canyons, it would be Nagamush.

The question was where was Porter headed?

When the answer came to her, she wanted to smack herself for missing the obvious. How could she have forgotten about that?

Kneeling in front of her companion, she gripped

his shoulders and shook him gently until he acknowledged her presence.

"This isn't over yet," she told him, shaking her head. "We're still going to catch this bastard and return the Heartstone to your people."

She pointed first to herself and then to Nagamush. She tipped her hand upside down and with two fingers pantomimed the two of them walking. She then pointed to where she had abandoned the crippled SUV and where she hoped the other vehicles still remained.

If they could only beat Porter there.

She pulled a reluctant Nagamush to his feet and the two of them set off to retrace the path Annja had taken before capture by the Sho.

The trek proved to be more difficult than she'd hoped. Nagamush was able to return them to the canyon where his people had first encountered her without difficulty, but knowing where to go after that proved hard to explain. After several frustrating attempts Annja sat on the ground and drew a picture of an SUV in the dirt. She then pantomimed her driving it, steering left and right and then pointing at the drawing.

Something she said or did finally clicked. Nagamush leaped to his feet, pointing out a particular path and dragging her along.

Annja acquiesced to his lead.

It was another hour's hike before they emerged from a canyon a short distance from the wreckage of her SUV. It was in sorry shape. Annja knew there was no way they were getting the thing to start, never mind travel all the way back to Maun in it.

The other vehicles were gone.

Just to be sure, they crossed the old riverbed and searched the bank above it. They found plenty of tracks where the vehicles had been previously parked and Annja knew that this time they really were too late.

Porter had beaten them to the punch.

Annja was staring at the ground, wondering what to do next, when Nagamush nudged her arm and pointed.

A few hundred yards away a beat-up pickup truck pulled out from behind a large pile of boulders and slowly drove toward them.

Annja tensed, ready to call her sword. *Please don't let them have guns.*

The driver's door opened as soon as the truck rolled to a stop and out stepped Dr. Henry Crane, a wide smile on his face.

Annja gave a shout and hustled forward, wrapping the older man in a hug. She was overwhelmed with relief. He had survived his ordeal in the desert when they'd been forced to split up and he was here now, with a means to get them back to civilization. She only wished he'd brought more help.

"You are a sight for sore eyes, Henry!"

He chuckled. "I can say the same for you. I've been waiting out here all night, worried sick. Then Porter and his mercenaries came blundering out of the canyon and I thought for sure you were in trouble."

"How long, Henry?" she asked urgently. "How long since you saw Porter?"

"Half an hour. Forty-five minutes, maybe." He glanced around nervously, as if expecting the other man to come charging out from behind a rock.

Forty-five minutes. It was a bigger lead than she'd hoped, but not insurmountable. If they hurried.

She grabbed Henry's arm and pushed him toward the truck. "We have to go. I'll explain while I drive."

Turning to Nagamush, she pointed at him and then at the truck. The implication was clear. *Get in.*

But Nagamush shook his head. He pointed back the way they had come and said something she couldn't understand.

Thankfully Henry could.

"He's saying he needs to return to…!Ksanna, is it? To help the injured."

Annja didn't even have to think about it. "Good. That's good. Tell him I'll find the Heartstone and return it to his people. Tell him I promise. I won't give up until it's returned to them."

Henry did but then frowned at the response he got.

"What?" Annja asked.

"He says thank-you, but it's already too late. The wheel has turned and the Sho must go with it. Annja, what is he talking about?"

Too late? Not on her watch.

"I'll explain as we drive. Get in!"

Turning to Nagamush, she said, "I *will* come back. I promise you. And I'll have the Heartstone with me when I do."

The Sho warrior smiled sadly.

Annja jumped in behind the wheel and fired up the truck's engine. She nodded once to Nagamush, then turned the vehicle around and went north in pursuit of Porter.

She glanced back in the rearview mirror to see Naga-mush standing where they had left him, watching them.

It was the last time she would lay eyes on the Sho warrior.

44

As they drove, Henry filled her in on what had happened to him. After separating from Annja in the wake of his escape from Porter, he found a small cave to hide in. He waited until dark and then tried to make his way back to where the trucks were waiting.

Unfortunately, or perhaps fortunately, he lost his way in the dark and wound up traveling in the complete opposite direction he should have been going in. After walking for several hours, he stumbled on a group of French zoologists who were studying the social behavior of the aardwolf. They were just getting ready to return to their home base in Maun, so Henry hitched a ride with them out of the wilderness. They dropped him at his compound on their way north.

After calling the local authorities on his satellite phone—they gave him such a bureaucratic runaround, he had no faith they'd ever come out to investigate— he'd borrowed his foreman's pickup truck since his own vehicle was still out in the desert where Porter had forced him to abandon it, and then he returned to try to find Annja. He hadn't wanted to put any of his staff in danger, so he'd chosen to come alone.

Afraid that Porter might return and find him, he

hid the truck in a small canyon. He'd been lying in the shade of some boulders, watching the SUVs, when he'd seen their enemy come stumbling up the riverbed. Henry stayed in place, waiting for them to leave, and then resumed his watch for Annja. He'd been about to give up and return to base when she'd walked out of the canyon with Nagamush in tow.

When Henry was finished, Annja returned the favor, relating all that had happened to her after she'd led Porter astray. Henry was amazed by her tale, especially the part where she told him that she had found his friend Robert living among the Sho. Except that he'd been gunned down by his own miserable excuse for a son.

"We have to get back to the authorities with this!" Henry exclaimed when Annja was finished. "With your testimony, they'll act. We could have Porter arrested for murder and—"

"Do you really think the authorities will move against Porter? Given the kind of individual he is, do you think he doesn't have them in his pocket already?"

Henry visibly deflated. "You're right," he said. "Their response when I called them about my own kidnapping proves it. So what can we do? We can't just let him get away with this."

"Trust me, I have no intention of letting him get away with anything."

Annja borrowed Henry's satellite phone and stepped out onto the deck for some privacy. She dialed a number from memory and waited for it to be picked up.

One…two…three…

"Yes, Annja?"

Garin Braden's voice was deep, sexy, with just a hint of the devilish attitude that constantly had her second-guessing how she felt about him. There was no denying he was a handsome man—tall, broad shouldered, with an immaculately trimmed goatee and long dark hair—but all Garin seemed to care about was himself. His selfish focus on his own wants and desires drove her crazy.

"Hello, Garin," she said coolly. How in heaven's name had he known it was her?

"Have you finally decided to give up the sword and live a life of luxury with me?"

Annja laughed. "Fat chance."

Garin was one of two people, not counting herself, who knew about the sword. As well he should, since he had been there on the day Joan of Arc had died, had seen the sword shattered into dozens of pieces by an English soldier, the same sword that Annja now carried whole. Somehow Garin and his mentor, Roux, the man charged with protecting Joan, had been transformed by the sundering of the blade. They had lived and quarreled off and on for the better of five hundred years since, only coming to an uneasy truce when the blade had been mystically re-formed in Annja's presence.

Garin and Roux believed the sword was responsible for their extended life spans and they kept tabs on Annja at every opportunity.

Garin grunted at her reply. "Well, then, I guess we don't have anything further to discuss. Good day, Annja."

"Wait! Please."

There was a pause on the other end. "You are being polite, Annja. Is something wrong?"

You don't know me that well.

"I need your help."

"I am always happy to be at your service."

She explained what she needed and why.

"And what do I get out of it?" he asked.

Same old Garin.

"You may have the pleasure of taking me out for dinner."

She regretted the use of the word *pleasure* the second it left her mouth. Garin was a true sybarite, with a love for luxury and women that apparently knew no bounds.

"Last time I took you out we nearly got killed."

"What's life without a little adventure?" she asked.

"Adventure indeed," he growled with a laugh. "We'll see how much adventure you can take. Give me a few hours to arrange what you need."

With that, he hung up.

She could handle dinner with Garin if it meant she'd have the resources she needed to recover the Heart-stone from Porter.

THREE HOURS LATER, as dusk was settling over the old mission, Annja and Henry were finishing up a meal in the kitchen when the sound of an approaching helicopter reached their ears. Henry looked worried, but Annja laid a hand on his arm reassuringly.

"It's okay," she said. "They're friendlies."

She went outside to greet their visitors.

The chopper circled the property once and then set down inside the fence line. It was black, which might have made it hard to pick out in this light if it wasn't for the bright gold logo of a dragon in flight painted on the side. That was the corporate logo for DragonTech Security, one of the high-tech defense and protection companies Garin owned and ran. She knew from experience that her backup would be well trained and well armed, which was just what she needed for the expedition she had in mind for later that evening.

Before the rotors had stopped spinning the passenger door opened and a medium-size black man with a shaved head and wraparound sunglasses climbed out. He was dressed in a set of dark fatigues and combat boots. He ducked beneath the rotors and hurried over to her side.

Annja nodded at him. "Mr. Griggs."

He nodded back, all nice and civilized. "Ms. Creed."

"Shall we go inside where we can talk?"

The hint of a smile crossed Griggs's smooth-shaven face. "As my employer is wont to say, I am at your service."

The planning didn't take long. Griggs had arrived with detailed layouts of Porter's compound, including real-time satellite photos from less than an hour earlier, courtesy of Garin's connections in the aerospace industry. They used those to map out general scenarios that they would follow once on-site.

They spent some time discussing what they would do if problems arose, knowing that no plan ever fully survives contact with the enemy. Porter would not be expecting them and that would certainly play well in their favor, but there was no doubt that something would go sideways at some point in the mission—Murphy's

Law and all that—so they wanted to have a few fall-back ideas.

When they felt they had exhausted all the obvious possibilities, they moved to get the mission under way.

Annja pulled Henry aside. "If something goes wrong, I want you to call this man," she said, handing him Doug Morrell's card. "Tell him everything that's happened. He's the producer of the cable television show I work for and will have the connections to expose Porter and make him pay for what he's done."

Henry looked confused. "Why aren't we just taking the information to him now, then? Why the rest of this nonsense?" he asked, pointing at the Griggs and the helicopter waiting outside.

"If we bring in the media, the Sho will never be the same. They'll be invaded by every jackass with a camera. Is that what you want for them?"

Henry shook his head.

She patted him on the shoulder. "I'll be back soon. You probably won't even need the card. It's just in case. Understood?"

The older man nodded. "Understood."

"Excellent. I'll see you in a few hours."

45

The flight from the old Dutch mission to Maun didn't take long. Griggs kept at a steady altitude and speed—just another corporate chopper ferrying suits from a business meeting somewhere—and only seemed to wake up when they drew closer to their destination.

Porter's compound was on the outskirts of Maun—a sprawling three-story home, a swimming pool and several outbuildings surrounded by a six-foot wall of solid concrete. There was a guard gate at the entrance to the drive and, according to the information they'd been given, foot patrols that covered the grounds at regular intervals. Annja didn't care if Porter had brought in the entire French Foreign Legion to guard his place, she was going in and not coming out again until she had the diamond.

"Coming up on nine-thirty at my mark…five, four, three, two, one, mark," Griggs said, and Annja synchronized her watch to match his.

Griggs took the chopper in a wide arc around the compound and then brought it down to hover a few feet above the ground in a clearing they had previously picked out. Annja stood by the rear door, waiting for his signal.

"Once you're in you've got ten minutes," he reminded her.

She nodded. If she was inside any longer, something
had gone wrong. At that point she was on her own.

She gave Griggs the thumbs-up, then slid the door
open and jumped out.

Even though it was only a few feet she rolled with
the impact, not wanting to end up with a twisted ankle
at this stage of the game. She climbed to her feet, noting as she did that Griggs was already on the move, the
helicopter climbing into the sky above her. It was lost
in the darkness moments later.

Annja looked for and found the lights to Porter's
compound in the distance and then headed out at a
brisk pace.

MALCOLM PORTER SAT in his study and stared at the diamond on his desk.

After leaving the city behind, he and his men had
made their way back through the maze of canyons to
where they'd left the vehicles. They'd dumped extra
gear to make room for Hawser's men and then gone
straight back to the compound in Maun. Bryant had
paid the mercenaries what was owed them and then
sent them on their way, while Porter had the wound
on his face properly dressed by his staff doctor. When
his injuries had been cleaned, stitched and bandaged,
Porter had retired to his study to sit and stare in fasci-
nated wonder at the massive gemstone in front of him.

Over all, the expedition had been a stunning success.
Not only had they managed to locate the Lost City, but
they'd come home with one hell of a prize. Even better,

he'd finally had the chance to put that bumbling excuse for a father in his place.

Remembering the look on his father's face when he realized he'd been shot brought a burst of laughter from Porter's lips, and he held up his glass of Scotch in salute. "Here's to you, Dad," he said. "I hope you rot in hell."

Yes, it had indeed been a successful expedition.

Except for that Creed woman.

Porter grimaced. Who would have thought one woman could cause so many problems? She was a cable TV host, for God's sake.

He should have killed her when he had the chance. Just gunned her down in that hotel of hers and taken the map. Would have saved him considerable frustration. Never mind this gaping knife wound in his face.

Where had that sword come from, anyway? One minute she was empty-handed, the next she'd been swinging a freaking five-foot piece of steel at his face.

He shook his head. If Creed showed her face again he'd kill her.

Porter got up to refill his glass and that's when the first explosion shook the house.

ANNJA WAS CROUCHED in the shadow of the compound's security wall, waiting for Griggs's signal. She took a pair of thick leather gloves and a set of nylon knee pads out of the backpack she was wearing and put them on.

A glance at her watch showed her she had thirty seconds left.

Stepping out of the shadows, she moved back ten feet from the wall and got into position, counting down in her head.

Six…

Five…

Four…

Three…

Two…

She started running as the final second ticked down.
One…

The missile Griggs fired at the guardhouse in front
of Porter's estate struck with a thunderous roar, light-
ing up the sky with flames of red and orange.

Annja ran for the wall, put one foot against it and
pushed up in a single smooth motion. Her hands easily
cleared the top and she grabbed hold, the thick gloves
protecting her from the broken glass seeded along the
top. She boosted herself up and over, landing gently on
her feet on the other side.

She stopped. Waited.

The guards were most likely responding to Griggs's
decoy attack out front, but she wanted to be sure. When
she didn't hear or see anyone, she crossed the yard to the
back of the house. According to the plans, she should
be standing beneath the third-floor balcony, and when
she looked up it was right where it was supposed to be.

So far, so good.

There was another explosion from somewhere out
front—Griggs's second, and last, rocket.

That should keep them busy for a bit, Annja thought.

She reached into her pack and pulled out a device
that looked like a sawed-off shotgun with a three-
pronged hook stuck down the barrel. Annja pointed the
weapon at the balcony above her and pulled the trigger.

There was a small hiss and the hook shot out of the

barrel of the grapple gun, trailing a thin nylon climbing rope behind it. It shot up and over the balcony's railing. When she heard a dull thunk, Annja tapped a button on the weapon's grip that caused it to release the line, leaving her with a rope secured to the balcony above.

She grabbed the rope and swarmed up it, hand over hand.

As she climbed over the balcony railing less than two minutes later, Annja could hear gunfire coming from the front of the house. Porter's security team had finally gotten into the act, it seemed.

Annja didn't waste any time, just stepped to the sliding glass door and tried the handle.

It slid open.

She gave her eyes a moment to adjust. She had expected to enter the house through Porter's bedroom and she took a second to verify that as soon as she could see clearly.

Unfortunately, the room was empty.

His study, she told herself, naming the next likely place she'd find him.

She crossed the room, slowly opened the door and then slipped out into the hallway, looking for her target.

PORTER NEARLY DUMPED his drink in his lap at the sound of the explosion. He stalked over to the intercom on his desk and hit the button.

"What's going on out there?" he barked.

He didn't get an answer.

"Bryant! What's going on?"

Still no reply, but he could hear small-arms fire

coming over the circuit now in addition to another explosion.

"Answer me!" he yelled, and then, when no one did, he threw his glass of Scotch across the room.

"Tsk, tsk. Someone's got a temper."

Porter spun around, his eyes wide as he spotted Annja Creed standing in the doorway, dressed in black.

"You!" he said.

She smiled but it wasn't a pleasant smile. "Yes, me. Were you expecting someone else?"

"What do you want?"

Creed laughed. "Only a buffoon like you would ask a question like that. What do you think I want?"

Porter didn't answer, but his gaze drifted to the diamond.

Creed didn't even glance in that direction. "Is that what you think? That I want the diamond?"

"Why else would you come here?"

She looked at him, her expression unreadable, and all of a sudden Porter felt like a bug under a microscope.

"Did you think you'd get away with it, Porter?" she asked. "Did you think I wouldn't come for you?"

Annja watched him carefully. If he was going to try something, now would be the moment. She wasn't sure if he was stupid enough, but…

As it turned out, he was.

His gaze flicked to his desk for the second time and Annja realized he wasn't looking at the diamond at all. Must have a gun in the drawer.

But for all his faults, Porter was a clever bastard and when he made his move he didn't go for the desk. The looks in that direction had been a diversion, cover for his real target, which was the drawer of the liquor cabinet directly in front of him.

He was fast, too. He had his hand in the drawer and the gun out before Annja had realized the true extent of the threat.

As he spun back toward her she did the only thing she could think of to stop him.

Her hand came up past her ear, as if she were winding up to throw a pitch, her sword materializing in her grip at the top of the arc, and then flying straight and true when she released it as her hand came hurling forward again.

The sword flashed across the space separating them at the same moment Porter pulled the trigger, the bullet whipping past Annja as she dove to the floor.

She rolled to the side and came up in a crouch, but her caution was unnecessary. Porter stared across the room with unseeing eyes, the blade of her sword buried hilt-deep in his chest.

That had been closer than she liked.

Annja released her sword back to the otherwhere, letting Porter's body slump to the floor in the process, and then stepped over to the desk for the Heartstone. A pile of wrappings lay nearby, and Annja appropriated them for her own use. She wrapped the stone and then stashed it inside her backpack.

A check of the watch told her she'd been inside for six and a half minutes.

Time to go.

She gave one last glance to the body on the floor and then slipped out of the room, retracing her steps to the balcony and then back across the lawn to the wall without being seen.

Ten minutes later she was in the clearing, climbing into the helicopter next to Griggs.

"Any problems?" he asked once she had her headset on.

She shook her head. "Nothing I couldn't handle," she replied, and left it at that.

46

Early the next morning, they returned to the Lost City.

At any other time Annja would have gone alone. Maintaining the Sho way of life meant keeping the location hidden from the public eye, just as it had been for the past several hundred years. Given the size and value of the Heartstone, it was particularly important to keep it a secret.

But Annja was worried. The elder's prophecy, if you could call it that, had set her teeth on edge and she was growing increasingly more nervous that something would go wrong if she didn't return the Heartstone fast.

She had therefore planned ahead, requiring Garin to swear on his honor that he would not personally attempt to recover the diamond from !Ksanna, send another individual on his behalf to do it for him or disturb the Sho people in any way.

Annja knew Garin would rather die than break a sworn oath like the one she made him give, so she felt safe in asking Griggs to take her back.

Because of the height of the crater, which blocked the sun in the early part of the morning, most of the city was still in shadow when Griggs brought the chopper over the walls and down into the valley. Annja was looking out the window as they descended, searching for survivors. She couldn't see anyone.

The streets were empty.

Deserted.

Maybe the sound of the helicopter has scared them into hiding?

She didn't think so. Griggs's chopper was much quieter than Porter's had been and they wouldn't have been able to get everyone undercover that quickly.

Annja felt a deep sense of unease. Something was wrong; she could feel it in her bones.

"Circle the palace once, will you?"

"The palace?"

"Yeah, that building over there," she said, pointing.

"Got it."

He did as she asked, taking them in low and slow. The wreckage of Porter's helicopters lay right where they'd been abandoned, though the bodies of the dead had been removed from in front of the palace steps.

That, at least, was a good sign.

And yet no one came outdoors to see what the noise was about.

"There's another clearing on the other side of the palace. Why don't you set it down there?"

"Roger that."

Griggs brought the chopper over the roof, giving Annja a view of the riverbank where she'd seen the elephants bathing in the shallows. There was no sign of them now.

That, more than anything else, convinced her that something was wrong.

The garden was their home; the elephants should be there.

Griggs set the chopper down without so much as a bump. They waited until the rotors were silent and had stopped moving before disembarking. Annja was carrying the Heartstone in a small backpack slung over one shoulder, leaving her hands free for her sword if she needed it. Griggs held an automatic rifle, scanning the building before them.

"Hello?" Annja shouted. "Nagamush? Hello?"

No answer.

"Now that you've let everyone from here to South Africa know that we've arrived, why don't we see if anyone is home?"

Annja glanced at Griggs.

"Did I tell you about the poisoned arrows?"

The smart-ass smile on Griggs's face died. "Poisoned arrows?"

"Nah, didn't think I had," Annja said with a grin of her own. Then she walked away from the chopper, headed for the door at the back of the palace she'd used last time she was here.

"Just a moment, Ms. Creed," Griggs said, hurrying to catch up. "What's this about poisoned arrows?"

Annja glanced back over her shoulder. "Just don't get hit with one and you won't have anything to worry about, all right?"

Griggs went back to scowling at her, not knowing if she was serious or not.

Teach him to smart-mouth me.

They reached the door and stopped, listening.

Nothing but the whisper of the wind.

"Where did they all go?" Griggs asked, looking around as if at any moment said tribe was going to jump out of the woodwork.

"I wish I knew."

They entered the building and cautiously made their way through the halls to the audience chamber. That was where she was supposed to return the diamond and that, more than any other place, was where she expected to find someone who could tell her what was going on.

But the audience chamber was as empty and silent as the rest of the city.

The elder's voice seemed to echo through her mind.

I saw you standing alone in the ruins of !Ksanna, a look of sorrow and dismay on your face....

Annja shook herself, trying to get rid of the chills that swept over her as she stared at the empty throne room.

Could the legends have been true? Could the Heartstone have been responsible in some strange and unusual way for the Sho's well-being and safety?

If so, what would happen if she put it back?

Only one way to find out.

She crossed the dais, stepped around the throne and stopped in front of the empty socket on the wall where the diamond had rested for centuries. She slipped the pack off her shoulder and laid it on the floor. Kneeling next to it, she unzipped it and slid the diamond out.

"Give me a hand with this, will you?" she said over her shoulder.

Griggs grumbled but did as he was asked. Together they carefully lifted the diamond and held it up to the socket, then rotated it until it slid into place with a distinct click.

"We good?" Griggs asked.

"I think so."

Annja kept her hands close as they let go, just in case the diamond wasn't secured properly, but it stayed where they had put it.

She let out a breath she didn't know she'd been holding. She had expected to feel better at this point, to feel some sense of relief now that she'd fulfilled her promise and returned the Heartstone to its rightful place, but all she felt was empty.

She suspected she was too late.

"This place is giving me the creeps," Griggs said. "How about we get out of here?"

She had to admit she felt the same way.

She turned, saying, "All right, let me just…"

Her voice trailed off in midsentence as her gaze fell on the images painted on the dais to the right of the throne.

Painted where they would only be seen by someone standing where she stood.

As if in a trance, she stepped forward so she could see them better.

Just as in the canyon temple, there were several different frames, all telling a sequential story. They appeared to have been drawn with a stick of charcoal. In some places, the image was already starting to smear or fade.

The first panels detailed the attack on the city by Porter's men. Oval shapes with lines above them represented the helicopters and they could be seen swooping over the buildings that made up the city. The stick figures lying in front of the palace steps represented the last stand made by the elder's guards, and the two stick figures on the elephant had to represent her and Nagamush.

But, as before, it was the last image that made her eyes widen.

The picture was larger than the others, as if the artist wanted to draw her attention to it immediately. It showed a long line of people, stick figures again, passing through the rush of the waterfall and disappearing from view.

Beside her, Griggs cleared his throat. "You don't think…"

He didn't finish the question.

But Annja didn't need him to. She knew what he was going to ask.

"Only one way to find out, really."

They searched the area around and behind the waterfall for more than two hours, but they didn't find any cave mouths or other locations where the city's inhabitants could have gone.

They wound up sitting on the riverbank, wet, tired and wondering just what the artist had been trying to tell them.

Once before, the Sho had disappeared from history's notice, slipping through the "hole in the world," as they called it, to find a new home here in the Lost City. Now it seemed they had done it again.

Annja didn't know how it was possible, but then again, she'd encountered more than her fair share of unexplained events over the past several years and decided that, maybe just this once, she didn't need to understand.

It seemed that the Sho were safe, wherever they might be, and for now, that was good enough for her.

She and Griggs returned to the chopper and were soon airborne over the city once more. As they lifted out of the crater and turned the nose of the aircraft toward home, Annja looked back down at the city below her and wondered if she'd ever see the Sho again.

Somehow, she thought she might.

* * * * *

TAKE 'EM FREE

2 action-packed novels plus a mystery bonus

NO RISK

NO OBLIGATION TO BUY

JAMES AXLER

DEATH LANDS®

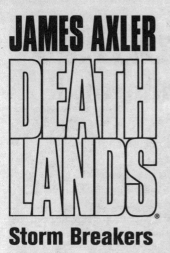

Storm Breakers

Staying alive is the best revenge....
The *only* revenge.

Staying alive is the best revenge.... The only revenge.

On the coast of what used to be Maine, the group's armorer, J.B. Dix, lies dying from a gunshot wound. Having no other choice, Ryan makes a deal with a local baron and his strangely beautiful wife. J.B. will get the surgery he needs when Ryan and crew rescue the couple's daughter, abducted by slavers. But the cold, deep Atlantic waters harbor pre-dark secrets, including the terrifying specter of a U.S.S.R. nuclear submarine...and its descendants.

Available in July wherever books are sold.

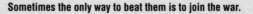

Don Pendleton
COUNTER FORCE

A marine unit's withdrawal from Iraq becomes a death trap.

What begins with marines being detained by Iraqi insurgents during an attempt to withdraw from Iraq escalates into retribution killings in Montana by a militia of former veterans of the same marine company. For Stony Man Farm's Phoenix Force, it's a race against the clock to rescue the marines in Iraq as Able Force struggles to quell the combat-hardened militia in the U.S.—with as little loss of American life as possible— before the terrorists kill every single hostage.

Available June wherever books are sold.

31901052011378

GSM125